THE FOUR TASKS OF PROTEUS

Jack Leathem is a retired civil servant. Formerly employed by HM Customs and Excise, he worked in many parts of the UK. He was born in Lurgan, Co Armagh and educated at the local grammar school, Stranmillis College, Belfast, and Queen's University, Belfast, where he took a degree in Economics. With his wife, Maureen, he still lives close to his roots in the village of Waringstown, about three miles away.

He has been active in a local rugby and football club for many years and counts reading, golf and gardening among his other hobbies. He also writes poetry and short stories, mostly for his own pleasure.

THE FOUR TASKS OF PROTEUS

To Hilda & Ronnie

Hope you enjoy!

Jackie
13/11/12

Jack Leathem

THE FOUR TASKS OF PROTEUS

Olympia Publishers
London

www.olympiapublishers.com
OLYMPIA PAPERBACK EDITION

A CIP catalogue record for this title is
available from the British Library.

ISBN: 978-1-84897-181-3

This is a work of fiction.
Names, characters, places and incidents originate from the writer's
imagination. Any resemblance to actual persons, living or dead, is
purely coincidental.

First Published in 2012

Olympia Publishers
60 Cannon Street
London
EC4N 6NP

Printed in Great Britain

To my parents for giving me a love of reading

PROLOGUE

It started shortly after he got up. It ended with a most peculiar incident in the middle of the night, though, as it turned out, he did not remember anything about this afterwards.

The first indication that it was going to be an unsettling sort of time began with his mother. He was just about to leave for school when she amusedly pointed out that he wasn't wearing any socks. The fact startled him. He didn't do silly things like that. Absentmindedness and he were not companions, not brothers, not cousins, not even distant relatives, twice removed. He was always careful, meticulous, in fact, to the point of being fussy. It was the way his father had him; which was why he could not understand the oversight. By the time he had rectified this, having raced up to his bedroom and hastily donned a woollen pair more suited to winter than summer, he had missed his bus into town. Consequently, he was late for class and got a roasting from the physics teacher for turning up halfway through the first period.

Things got no better after that. For some reason he could not concentrate on what was being taught. It was as if some force was subverting his will, diverting his mind from present matters and leaving him powerless to resist. More than once he found himself gazing abstractedly through the window and being reprimanded for his inattention. He could not remember anything like this happening to him before.

When morning classes ended, he discovered he had forgotten his lunch and only then remembered that he had left it on the kitchen table earlier. With his weekly pocket-money already spent, a snack in the canteen was not an option. As a result he went hungry.

By mid-afternoon a feeling was growing in him that something strange was about to happen. There was no logic to the premonition, but as the day went on, the more he became convinced that he was on the cusp of an unusual situation.

He could not say why. He only knew that the world seemed to be out of kilter. Nothing was running smoothly, which was a state of affairs totally foreign to him. His life was always well-ordered, and the unsettled nature of the recent, strange occurrences was beginning to disturb his normally calm outlook.

When he got home his mother sensed an oddness in him, and fearing he was coming down with something, sent him to bed early. Strangely, he could not raise the effort to protest.

Once there, he lay and listened to the breeze ruffling the leaves in the tree outside. It was close to the house – too close. He feared that some day a storm would bring it crashing down on top of him. The image gave birth to the rueful thought that the way things had been going of late it could well happen at any moment.

He could hear the birds singing in the orchard. A thrush, in particular, was in fine voice, giving expression to the joy of being alive on a summer's evening, a warbled paean to freedom and a full crop. He envied the bird. Freedom was a rare commodity for him. School and the farmhouse were prisons. Parole was occasional and generally only under the supervision of his parents.

He sighed and picked up a book – *The Woodlanders* by *Thomas Hardy*. His dad had instructed him to read it, and read it he must. Questions about it would be put at the next mealtime they were together, and, if satisfactory answers were not forthcoming, privileges might be withdrawn. He liked reading, but not under duress. Hardy was all right, but he was hardly a laugh a minute. The author wouldn't have been his choice, but then he rarely had a say about anything. His dad selected his reading material and anything that smacked of the frivolous was eschewed.

He read for a few minutes, but he couldn't concentrate. Hardy's turgid prose and the peculiar mood he was in saw to that. He put the book down on a chair beside his bed. He snuggled down and watched the deepening shades of twilight invade the room. He lay for a few minutes before realising that something wasn't quite right. At first he could not think what it might be. Then it hit him. The sounds of evening were gone. No birdsong, no breeze, no creaking of the branches in the tree. All should still have been evident. It was too early for the birds to settle for the night and, according to the forecast, the breeze should have been strengthening, not diminishing. A corncrake suddenly broke the silence, its harsh dirge carrying clearly to him across the quiet air. That too was strange. Apart from a small area up in County Fermanagh, the bird had disappeared from the Province.

Somehow he found the sound comforting. And more, he felt privileged. He was lucky to have heard the bird. In a few years' time there might be none left. Five minutes later the song ceased and all was quiet again.

He turned on his side and closed his eyes. He lay like that for some time, his mind still occupied with the events of the day. He was just drifting towards sleep when a tremendous gust of wind shocked him fully awake. The windows shook, the branches of the tree crashed against the roof of the bedroom and every door in the house either rattled or banged shut. Seconds later he heard his mother's footsteps hurrying on the stair. By the time she entered his room to enquire if he was all right, the wind had died and it was completely calm again.

When she left, a look of bafflement on her face and muttering about the need for *that* tree to be cut down, he rose and went to the window. It was now almost dark outside. He stared down, not sure why he was bothering, for all he could make out were the shadowy shapes of the trees in the orchard. Just as he was about to turn away he thought he saw the gleam of two eyes in the twilight, but he couldn't be sure, as they seemed to disappear almost instantly. *Probably a fox,* he thought, *in search of a kill.*

He went back to bed. Drowsiness soon overtook him, and just before he fell asleep he thought he heard a cough-like bark. That seemed to confirm it was a fox he had seen.

He opened his eyes.

A blue light filled the room, a bit like a night light in a hospital.

He sensed a presence.

He sat up.

His twin sister, Lucy, was sitting at the foot of the bed, legs crossed, dressed in the white frock in which she had been buried. The light emanated from her, a soft glowing aureole round her head.

For some reason he didn't think this peculiar.

She was pale, as always, delicate looking, the blue veins in her almost translucent skin still evident. Her expression, usually animated, was more sober than usual, her generally mischievous demeanour absent.

She spoke. "You were snoring."

On opening his mouth to reply he found he had lost the power of speech. But his thoughts carried to her, the old telepathy between them still extant.

"I was not."

"Yes, you were. Your mouth was puckered up and you were making puffing sounds like Thomas the Tank engine."

"Who?"

"You remember; the character in that children's programme on TV."

"What happened to your memory? We don't have TV."

"We saw it at Maxie's – at least I did. You were probably arguing about the academies."

"What academies?"

"Best Ham, Brummyham, Tottyham, Farcenal, and that one from Manchester – Ham United." Lucy used to like cutting pictures from the sports pages of the Belfast Telegraph. She ticked off each name on her fingers.

He looked disgusted. "You see, your memory has definitely gone."

"Don't think so. My names are much more appropriate. You only have to read about the silly dramatics of their players to know that. You'd think they'd been to RADA."

He tried a snort, but, being soundless, it was totally ineffective. "You're the one who's being silly. And why are you disturbing my sleep?"

"Perhaps I'm not disturbing it. Perhaps you *are* still asleep."

"If I am, maybe I'll concentrate on waking up and that will get rid of you."

"Do you want to get rid of me?"

"You bet; you're being your usual nuisance."

"All right – cheerio." The light faded and she vanished.

"Don't go," he shouted ineffectually. "I didn't mean it."

"Of course you didn't," she replied, reappearing. "I was only teasing."

Her words seemed at odds with her manner, which seemed a bit strained, making him think she was trying too hard to be natural.

"You didn't answer my question."

"What question was that?"

He sighed inwardly. "You know very well. Why are you here?"

She considered his words, a subtle change in her demeanour. A delicate hand rose to stroke her neck, a habit she used to display when considering something worrying.

"I'm here to warn you," she said simply.

"What about? Is sneaky Sam about to report me for doing Maxie's homework?" Maxie was his friend and schoolmate. Sneaky Sam was the Headmaster's son. Envious of Michael's ability, he took every opportunity to undermine him with the teachers.' To their credit, none of them gave his endeavours much credence.

"I'm serious."

"So am I. Sneaky Sam's worth the watching."

"Stop it," she scolded. "This is important."

Having got his revenge for her earlier mockery, he dropped his attempts to frustrate her. "All right, I'm listening. Go on, frighten the life out of me."

"That's the last thing I'd want to do. In case *your* memory's going, I'm the expert on that situation."

He was immediately contrite. "Sorry," he mimed. "I was forgetting."

"I forgive you. Now, pay attention."

"Yes, ma'am."

Again her hand rose to her neck, fingers tracing an erratic path from just below the lobe of her right ear down to her collarbone. She hesitated momentarily before she spoke, her forehead creasing in concentration. "You're going on a journey," she announced.

"Anywhere interesting?"

Stifling her irritation at his flippancy, she answered sombrely, "I believe so."

"You don't know?"

"Your destination is beyond my knowledge. All I can say is that you will be contacted and whisked away from here."

"On my own?"

"Stop interrupting," she said crossly. Then she considered his question, her eyes narrowing. After a bit, she said slowly, "Perhaps, perhaps not; that information is a bit hazy. My feeling is you'll have a companion."

"That's a lot of help."

Lucy's lips tightened. "What did I say?"

"Okay, okay; I won't utter another word until you've finished."

"You're not uttering one now, but no matter." She paused again, collecting her thoughts. "Where you are going I cannot say, so, once you arrive, I will be unable to help you. When you get there, you will be faced with danger. Rely on your brainpower and you should be all right. And, above all, never panic. Be calm and let logic guide your actions."

Michael broke his promise. "And if I can't?"

"Then I fear for you."

His sister looked so concerned that, at last, the boy began to take her seriously, and he wondered if he were really dreaming.

"Will I remember this when I wake up in the morning?"

"No."

"Not much point in telling me, then."

"What I've said will be lodged in your subconscious. When you have need of my advice it will surface without you having to think about it. Use your intelligence well. It could be all that lies between you and disaster."

"Now you *are* beginning to frighten me."

Lucy smiled grimly. That's why I'm here. If I increase your awareness of danger, without knowing it you will raise your ability to combat whatever hazards you encounter. It's all I can do for you."

"Thanks very much," he said, somewhat sarcastically.

She didn't react. "Don't mention it. How's mum?"

Thrown by the abrupt change of direction, and still thinking about what she had said, he answered automatically. "Seems to be all right. Has her moments, but they're getting fewer."

"Poor, mum. Still hasn't got over me?"

"Never will. How do you know I'm going somewhere that's dangerous?"

"Does she still get depressed?"

"Occasionally. Can you see into the future?"

"And, dad – is he missing me as well?"

"If he is, he doesn't show it much. Just makes life miserable for me."

"I'm sure he has a reason for his actions."

"There's a reason, all right – I just don't agree with it. Now, will you forget him and answer my questions."

She ignored his entreaty. A dreamy expression softened her features. "Goodbye, grumpyhead; remember what I said. Trust in yourself and you should make it through."

"Through what?"

The light began to wane and the girl with it.

"Wait," he cried desperately. "I need to know more."

She wriggled her fingers at him, and then she was gone.

Hardly had she disappeared, when his head slumped down on the pillow. His eyes closed and darkness engulfed him.

The blue light returned momentarily. The girl was at the side of the bed. She leaned over and kissed the sleeping figure on the cheek.

"Good luck, lovely brother," she murmured. Then she gradually faded away, a look of anxiety on her face. The night filled the room again.

CHAPTER ONE

Michael was in a temper. At that moment he hated his dad. It was the hatred of a twelve year old, superficial and self-pitying. His dad was a tyrant, a disciplinarian, a killjoy. *And* he was odd. So odd that there was no television set in Michael's house; no opportunity to watch the programmes everyone at school talked about; programmes like *Top Of The Pops* or, *Who Wants To Be A Millionaire*, or *The X Factor*. His dad thought the 'box,' as he called it, was a distraction that could be done without. And as for boy and girl bands, screeching out their cacophony of awful dirges, he considered them to be purveyors of mind-rotting rubbish, whereas, the work of serious composers like Mozart and Bizet and Beethoven was uplifting and could be listened to on the small radio he had given Michael for Christmas. Radio 3 or Classic FM always broadcast *good* music, something which would instil in him an appreciation of quality.

He was even more scathing about game shows, with their over-the-top prizes, boring everyone with the oft-repeated contention that they only served to reinforce the base emotions of greed and envy in those who watched them. They pandered to the intellectually inadequate and were proof of the dumbing-down policy now being effected by what were no longer responsible institutions.

So Michael was given books to read; books with colour plates of fine art by the great painters; Turner, Constable, Van Gogh, Gaugin, Canaletto, Stubbs, the Impressionists, the Pre-Raphaelites, the abstract dabblers. The list was endless. He had books on Kings and Queens, Monarchs and Emperors, books on natural history and the universe, books on the great civilizations, books on myths and legends. For access to biographies and auto-biographies of great men and women, a membership card for the local library had been thrust upon him. He loathed great men and women, just as he loathed art and philosophy and mythology and anything else in which he was forced to take an interest.

His life was filled with books – and he had to read them. His dad quizzed him about their contents when he came home from work. When Michael wasn't doing his homework, he had to read and read and read and read and read.

His mother was no help. Any time he complained she simply said his father knew best and one day Michael would thank him for the guidance he was now being given. Then she added mysteriously that it was all a preparation for what lay ahead.

Occasionally he got a respite. When his dad had to go off on a business trip, his mother usually relaxed the strict regime and allowed him to visit his friend, Maxie. Maxie couldn't understand why Michael didn't have a computer. He nagged Michael to persuade his father to buy him one, then they could exchange E-Mails. Michael promised he would, but he didn't bother, for he knew the request would be futile. The only time he had broached the subject he had been told firmly that practice in the computer room at school was sufficient for his needs. A PC at home would only be an encouragement to play games and become a distraction that could be done without. When Michael said it would be educational – he could surf the net and use the information highway, his dad was unmoved. His reply was instant. "Books," the boy was informed pompously, "were the greatest font of understanding known to man."

Michael's only rebellion against this surfeit of learning was secretly to purchase ear phones for his radio, so he could listen to it under his bedclothes at night without it being heard. There, he would tune in to the popular stations and hear what he wanted to hear and not the heavy stuff insisted upon by his dad. This was his only relief from the constant burden of imbibing culture and knowledge. He would have bought an iPod if he could have afforded it, but his pocket money was so meagre that it would have taken him forever to save up the required amount.

Michael's only other respite was on a Saturday morning, when he was permitted to join a few classmates from school in the activities of a local youth club, vetted, of course, by his father. In the afternoon, when his companions of the morning were enjoying themselves at a soccer or cricket match, depending on the season, he was traipsing round a museum, or out on a nature walk being lectured to about fauna and flora or some arcane subject like the medicinal properties of plants.

From time to time his parents took him to the theatre in Belfast to see a play or an opera. He quite liked these outings, not so much for the performances of the players, but for the ice-cream his mum bought him at the interval, and then the rare treat of a meal on the way home. And not any old meal, but an Indian delectation, with its amazing variety of colours, tastes and smells. Seated in the exotic surroundings of the Taj Mahal restaurant, he could pretend he belonged to a normal family. Such moments were fleeting, however, for as soon as he was home, the tyrannical regime was back in place. This was amply illustrated by the way his dad reacted to the discovery of his earphones.

Usually Michael took them with him everywhere he went, but that morning, late for school, he had dashed from the house leaving the precious item behind him. His mum had discovered it while tidying his bedroom and passed the offending article over to his dad when the latter came home.

There were no lectures. The earphones were placed theatrically in the bin and the boy informed that, for his silliness, he had forfeited the next visit to the youth club. As a further punishment he was banished to his room.

It was then that Michael realised he hated his dad, even more than his Latin teacher, Beefy Taylor, who believed sarcasm was wit and who loved to ridicule his pupils. Michael had been the object of his attention on one occasion when, on being asked the Latin word for father, instead of answering *patris*, he had inexplicably blurted out *canis*. Beefy had never let him forget the slip, sometimes referring to him as a young hound, or son of Pluto, or our eager little terrier. The cheap gibes always brought gales of laughter from his schoolmates, eager to toady up to the teacher in the hope of escaping his vicious tongue. When he was picking on Michael he wasn't picking on them, and they didn't mind Michael being the butt of Beefy's wounding remarks. After all, he was the class swot and knew things that were beyond them, so he deserved all he got. He was too brainy, too different to fit in comfortably with them.

It was for that reason that Michael concealed his knowledge at times, deliberately giving a wrong answer in class, or messing up his homework to show he was human. But even that didn't improve his lot, for his errors were seized upon by his classmates and he was ridiculed for actually making a mistake. It seemed that no matter what he did he couldn't gain favour with his peers. After a while he didn't bother to try. Apart from Maxie, who was easy-going and had a generous nature, he had no close friends.

At the moment, Michael was in his bedroom surrounded by his books. To say he was currently dissatisfied with life would be to voice a gross understatement. His radio had been confiscated and would not be returned to him for a week. With no television, no computer, and no means of entertaining himself other than reading, his mood was foul. Morose and resentful at the unfairness of it all, he had no intention of complying with his dad's exhortation to study. Dickens and Thackeray would remain on the shelves; the plants and animals of the Amazon basin would not be pored over; the mysteries of the universe would be left unexplored.

He was ready to rebel. The callous disposal of his earphones had been the decisive factor. Enough was enough.

CHAPTER TWO

Michael lived with his parents in a house originally owned by his grandparents on his mother's side. Both had died before he was born.

It was situated at the end of a narrow lane about three miles from town. The nearest neighbours, his friend Maxie's family, lived two hundred metres away.

Michael's bedroom overlooked a small orchard. Close by was an overgrown apple tree. His dad was forever threatening to cut this down, but somehow it had survived. Its boughs, thick and gnarled, were high and wide-spreading, and often rapped sharply on the sloping roof of his bedroom in blustery weather.

The tree was his means of escape from the house without his parents being aware that he was gone. If he decided to come back, and at that moment he had no thoughts of doing so, he could return to his room the same way.

Throwing on his old windcheater with the Greenpeace logo on the back, chosen by his dad, of course – Michael would have preferred one proclaiming U2, he pushed up the old-fashioned sash. Ducking his head, he clambered through and manoeuvred his backside until he was sitting on the sill. The kitchen lay directly below his dangling feet. He sat there for some moments, just listening. Then, satisfied that he had aroused no-one's curiosity, he turned his attention to the apple tree. Immediately he noticed there was something different about it. It seemed to have swivelled round. The branch that constantly rapped the roof was now running parallel to the house. It was also thicker, and it was closer. Now only a metre away, it was much easier to reach. At another time he would have pondered on the peculiar fact, but at that moment he was concerned only that it looked solid enough to support his weight. He glanced down. The ground was farther away than he'd thought and, as he looked at it, it began to move, rising and falling in a rolling motion, just like waves on a sea. All of a sudden he felt dizzy. Forced to close his eyes, he gripped the sill so hard his knuckles turned white. Taking a deep breath he expelled it slowly. He did this three times. When he opened his eyes again, he did not glance down, but kept his gaze fixed firmly on the bole of the tree directly in front of him. The dizzy spell began to ease and, bit by bit it left him.

The moment of vertigo had passed.

Taking a firm grip on the branch, he eased himself out until his feet were swinging free, his arms taking the weight of his body. Closing his eyes again he lifted one hand clear and brought it beyond the other until he was able to grip the far side of the branch. His body turned naturally with the movement. He repeated the procedure until he had reached the main fork. Quickly making the descent to the ground, his trousers and windcheater green from the moss on the trunk, he set off in a crouching run. Making his way hurriedly to a gap in the bordering hedge, he was about to go through and into the narrow lane leading to the main road, when a sudden impulse made him stop. He turned and looked back at the tree. It was now some distance away and he couldn't be sure, but it appeared to be back to its original shape. Torn between the urge to investigate and the need to get away, he decided that he had been lucky so far and to take the first option would be too risky. His mind made up, he quickly scooted through the gap.

Once there he straightened up. His heart was pumping, not from his exertions, but from the knowledge that he had never consciously disobeyed his parents before. He hoped none of them checked his room before he returned.

He made off down the lane towards the road to town. He felt safer now. Because of the overgrown hedgerows on either side of him he couldn't be seen from the house. His dad was a conservationist and refused to cut these back. He was loath to interfere with any living thing, which was why he had probably never done anything about the apple tree. He was forever saying that there were too many species of plant and animal disappearing and he wasn't going to aid the process. Hedgerows were the habitat of small animals and shouldn't be disturbed. Michael agreed with him, but he wished the point wasn't laboured so much.

As he scurried down the lane, he found that he was automatically identifying the type of plant-life he passed; rowan tree and holly bush, the ubiquitous sycamore and ash, hazel and birch; the climbers, ivy and bindweed, and the nascent stems of beech and willow, all growing near to, or in the midst of a thick, hawthorn hedge invaded by tangled briars of wild roses and honeysuckle and the hawthorn's near relative, the blackthorn, its sloe fruit still green and immature.

In the sheugh[1] that ran along one side of the lane, and which

---

[1] Ulster Scots name for ditch

constantly filled with rainwater in winter, various types of toadstool flourished in the damp conditions, alongside ferns and the occasional deadly nightshade. On the opposite side to the sheugh, a steep bank stretched the length of the lane. Here, a great variety of grasses, some with heads like wheat, others with seeds tight and bushy, competed for space with outbreaks of violets, dandelions and buttercups. Also in evidence were wild foxgloves, from which, the boy knew, digitalis, a heart stimulant, could be obtained. When the grasses grew too long and were in danger of swamping the wildflowers, his dad would carefully cut them back using a sickle or an old-fashioned scythe. To justify his actions he would maintain that many of the old flowers were dying out and had to be protected, adding that grasses were hardy and would always grow back. In particular, he always made space for primroses, which were his favourite, and which Michael, on pain of death, was ordered not to pick.

When he reached the road, Michael turned in the direction of town. Telegraph poles, spaced at one hundred metre intervals, lined one side of the route. He walked briskly to the first pole, then jogged to the second. He kept up the sequence of alternately walking and jogging to shorten the time his journey would take.

At the tenth pole a dog suddenly appeared beside him. He hadn't seen it before and couldn't imagine where it had materialized from. It was black and white and shaggy, and a bit like an English sheepdog, but about half the size. Hair curled unkempt over inquisitive brown eyes that were fixed on his face. As he jogged along it matched his pace. He stopped and tried to shoo it away, exhorting it to go home. Ignoring his instruction it sat down, still gazing up at him, tongue lolling. He started off again and the dog continued to accompany him. Again he stopped and entreated it to go away. It paid no attention. He spotted a stick, which he picked up and threw over a gate into a nearby field, hoping it would chase after it. The dog didn't budge. It simply wagged its tail. Giving up, he decided to ignore the animal, hoping it would eventually get tired of his company and wander off.

A few cars passed him on the way, none of their drivers stopping to offer him a lift. One of the vehicles contained boys from school who knew him. They were twins and they were bullies who made a point of trying to make his life miserable. When they saw him, they filled the back window, hands jerking up and down in V-signs, their mouths working grotesquely in silent obscenities, venom in every gesture and every silent epithet. In the front seat, their parents, oblivious to what was happening behind them, conversed serenely.

Michael pretended not to see them. Things like that were commonplace and he had learned to conceal his feelings.

Beside him, the dog rubbed up against his leg. For some reason he felt the animal was conveying sympathy, and when he glanced down, he could have sworn its expression was like that of his friend Maxie's when he sometimes said consolingly, *never mind*. He shook his head as if to get rid of the absurd notion. Melancholy suddenly invading him, he walked on.

The evening was heavy with warmth and, close to town, the sun, now low in the sky, took on a peculiar orange tinge as light cloud began to dim its rays. A great anvil of cumulonimbus began to form on the horizon and move slowly eastwards. The atmosphere became very still, and at the far reaches of his consciousness, he could hear birds singing and chattering in trees a hundred metres away, the mellifluous thrush and blackbird competing for territory with the harsh-throated magpie. Normally he would have been happy to listen to them, play his usual game of determining how many he could recognize unseen: but not this evening. This evening he was in no mood for frivolity.

As he passed by, swallows performed miracles of aerodynamics in neighbouring fields, swooping ever closer to earth as the deepening air pressure forced midges and other insects downwards. Michael saw none of this, his mind turned inwards, still brooding on the unfairness of his world.

He couldn't understand why his father was so obsessive, so hard on him. In other ways he was not unkind. He didn't beat Michael; he was good to Michael's mother, and he even had a sense of humour, though he didn't smile a lot. He knew Michael resented the constant pressure to learn, yet this was seldom relaxed. And it wasn't as if the things he imbibed were any use to him. His schoolwork took different directions altogether, and it was this that would eventually provide him with a chance to be successful in life, not the eclectic range of knowledge his dad insisted on stuffing into him.

Still consumed by the unkindness of it all he reached town, where he considered what he should do next. His elation at breaking out had been fleeting. Gloom had soon taken its place and, morosely, he headed for the park, not sure why his feet were taking him there. The dog still padded alongside him.

The park was the playground of the town, and had once been part of the land settled on an English aristocrat in the 17th century, a gift from the 2nd King Charles for favours done. More caring than most of his ilk, and unlike the more prevalent absentee landlord, the aristocrat had lived in a castle on his estate and found work for people living nearby. During the potato famine of the 1840s, to provide employment for starving tenants, a descendant of the original settler had ordered the enlargement of a river, which flowed through his land to Lough Neagh. The result was a lake with an area of some 50 acres, the level of which was regulated by an overflow system at one end.

During the 1st world war, both sons of the last direct descendent had been killed in battle, one at Ypres, the other at the Somme. Having no other offspring the line died out. As a final act of family generosity, this last owner of the estate bequeathed both the castle and much of the surrounding land to the council for upkeep and development. As a result of his altruism the park was created, with the lake within its confines.

As he entered it through ornate, iron gates, the dog bounded away from him and began to chase, and be chased in turn by, a springer spaniel that had escaped its owner. The entrance to the park was on a slight hill and Michael had a panoramic view of water, trees, shrubs and walkways. Much of the flora had been imported by the previous owners, some of it quite rare. The grounds boasted, among other things, great oaks and monkey-puzzle trees and Scots pines, one of which was reputed to be the tallest in Ireland. A double row of lime trees, planted over a hundred years ago, formed an avenue along the main path, stretching for half-a-kilometre and ending at an exit adjacent to the Belfast Road on the other side of town. Due to what his father called their *field trips*, Michael could recite the Latin names of many of the species of plant life there and the wildlife they attracted.

The centre of the park was developed for leisure activities. At the end nearest to him there was a play-area, with swings and roundabouts for the very young. Beyond it, soccer and rugby pitches adjoined a rail-enclosed square of greenery, where a local cricket team played. Men in light clothes were practising in the nets and a myriad of small boys and youths were engaged in impromptu soccer matches on other grassy areas close by. Michael knew some of them. If they noted his presence, they didn't acknowledge it. He was neither surprised nor offended, being accustomed to snubs and indifference.

To his left the lake sparkled in the evening sun. Ducks and coots and moorhens gathered at a little pier. Young couples and their offspring were feeding them. Seagulls circled noisily overhead waiting to pounce on any scraps overlooked. A number of greylag geese waddled and pecked, unconcerned by the close proximity of their benefactors.

He stood for a while taking in the scene before him. There was noise and laughter, children yelling and dashing around, adults calling out to them or chatting to people they knew. He was uncomfortable with their gaiety. It made him feel out of place. Perhaps his proper environment *was* the confines of his home, his natural occupations that of reading and studying. The walk to the town had induced a calming effect in him, his burning anger now only a fraction of what it had been. As he lingered there, uncertainty made him hesitate. Should he return home, accept his small rebellion had been a mistake and born out of emotion, not rational thought, or should he continue and see where the ill-considered impulse led? As he pondered the matter, a commotion nearby intruded on his thoughts.

On a grassy patch near the bowling green, two rottweilers had broken their leads and were racing towards the shaggy dog and its companion. Their owner, a shaven-headed man with tattooed arms and a large belly, was lumbering after them. He was vainly exhorting the brutes to come to heel, his commands liberally laced with threats and curses.

Pandemonium ensued.

Grown-ups in the vicinity grabbed those children they could, while screaming at others to run. Everyone scattered. Shouts of alarm rent the air. The rottweilers hurtled on, teeth bared and clearly out of control. The shaggy dog's companion fled.

Then a strange thing happened.

The little dog turned to face the threat. Bravely it stood its ground. Head erect and not a hackle raised, it stared fixedly at the onrushing animals, body motionless. On the massive rottweilers came, closing the gap with every long stride, heavy muscles straining on heavy torsos, mouths agape and slavering in anticipation, their intentions to savage the other dog obvious.

Michael watched, powerless to prevent the impending savagery. And as he watched, horror fixing him to the spot, something flashed between the little dog and its attackers. Too fast for the human eye to pick up, the boy failed see this, but he did witness the extraordinary effect it had on the rottweilers.

About ten metres from their prey, and just when it seemed the little dog would be torn asunder, they skidded to a halt. Their heads went down; their massive bodies seemed to deflate; their vicious intent dissolved. Seconds later they turned away, whining, unable to meet the gaze of their intended victim. Bellies close to the ground, they began to slink back towards their master, who, by now had given up the chase and was watching the scene with utter disbelief. In an instant he had them back on their leashes and, shamefaced, was leading them from the park as quickly as he could walk. At one point he stopped to kick them, cursing the animals for their docility, their recent display of cowardice an obvious affront to his manhood. The disturbance over, children and adults in the vicinity tentatively resumed their previous activities, some huddling in groups to discuss what had just occurred.

As if nothing untoward had taken place, the little dog took off, nose to ground. It began to explore a nearby coppice, stopping now and then to raise a hind leg and make its mark. Only then did Michael realize he was holding his breath. Letting it out in a long whoosh, he breathed deeply in an attempt to slow his heartbeat. And in that moment, as he marvelled at what had happened, somehow he was uplifted by the show of courage just displayed, and decided to extend his defiance a little longer.

Without having to think about which route he should take, he found himself heading away from the populated area and following a quiet path round the side of the lake. He was soon hidden from all view by a rash of rhododendron bushes of different types. Pink, white and red blooms hung heavy on stems clustered between shiny, green leaves. Other varieties, later flowering, were sticky with bud.

He glanced back to see if the dog had followed him. There was no sign of the animal. Strangely, he experienced a sense of loss. He was used to being on his own, the company of his peers being a rarity for him, but, unlike earlier, he would now have welcomed the dog's presence.

The path circled the lake. Reeds and bulrushes grew thickly at the edge. The odd tree, felled by winter winds, and with branches still protruding, poked out into the water, forming a playground for more adventurous youths.

Dragonflies flitted daintily above the foliage, while, out on the lake, two adult swans sailed serenely past with four cygnets in tow, the young yet to gain their full plumage, their brown feathers dowdy in comparison with the pristine whiteness of their parents. Two months hence and the offspring would be gone, chased from the breeding area by the older swans. In due course the banished birds would find their own stretches of water, breed, and become as territorial as their progenitors.

Michael's pace slowed. He was aimless now, simply following

the route he had unthinkingly taken. Above him clouds began to form. The sun was now casting a peculiar light over his secluded world. The air grew more humid and dense as if the vital oxygen was being sucked from it. He wasn't aware of the fact, but young people were abandoning their games, adults collecting coats and children, putting pets on leads and making their way hurriedly to the park exits. They sensed something odd was about to happen.

Michael was oblivious to both weather and their concerns.

Fifty metres on something caught his eye. In a narrow break in the bulrushes, a rowing boat lay tethered to a tree stump. He had walked this path many times and was sure he hadn't seen it before. Curious, he approached the object and noted the two oars nestling in the bottom.

His dad had once taken him out on the lake to see the wildfowl at close hand, but he hadn't been allowed to row. He could see the calm water through the channel in the greenery and, on impulse, he untied the little vessel and pushed it from its mooring. Jumping in, he settled on the cross-seat and fitted the oars into the rowlocks. As he pulled away from the bank, his recent companion, the dog, burst from a clump of shrubbery and leapt over the widening gap of water to land at his feet. The boat rocked violently with the impact and for a frightening moment he thought it was going to capsize. Then the craft steadied, and with the animal, tail thumping on the wooden boards, seemingly at ease with the situation, he pulled raggedly out into clear water.

Inexpert at first, either dipping the oars in too much or too little, he eventually got the depth right and, as his coordination improved, progressed steadily into the middle of the lake.

He found rowing hard work and soon stopped for a rest. His problems forgotten for the moment, he took the chance to relax and look round him. From out on the water everything had a different perspective. The trees on the bank seemed smaller, the buildings lining the avenue to the park much grimier, the dark edifice that was the castle somehow more foreboding. For some reason he shivered. And in that moment he became aware that he couldn't see anyone. Usually there was an abundance of figures on the golf course on the far side of the lake, and there were always walkers with their dogs on the path beside it. No longer were the duck-feeders in evidence, and even the football pitches, which he could just make out through some trees, were deserted. Something was wrong.

His eyes were drawn to the sun. Almost covered in cloud, a hazy, pink aureole had formed an orb, creating the most peculiar light he had ever seen. It streamed from the sky in slanting beams of orange and violet, striping the lake and making it look like a gigantic work of modern art. Even as he noticed the strange phenomenon, a gust of wind rocked the boat and the sky darkened. The sun's rays were instantly blotted out and the amazing display vanished.

The wind died as suddenly as it had risen. For breathless seconds everything was calm, the water around him so still that it was like an immense, grey paving stone.

Then there was a howl like a demented animal. The dog sank to the well of the boat, ears flattened and eyes tightly shut. Behind him, the trees at the edge of the lake bent like grasses in a field as a tremendous current of air roared through their branches and whipped up waves in the shallows. The storm moved with fearsome intensity towards him, and hardly had he time to grip the sides of the boat before it was seized by a mighty force and tossed into the air. The oars flew from the rowlocks and disappeared into the foaming waters of the lake.

Down came the boat with a great splash. Water poured over the sides, threatening to sink it. Miraculously it stayed afloat, and Michael, drenched and terrified, and now flat on his back beside the dog, felt himself being rushed towards the far side of the lake, powerless to halt the frantic momentum being generated by the tumult.

Out of control, the vessel raced in the direction of the golf course, which was now almost hidden in a blinding rain that had begun to hammer down from the dreadful sky. He struggled upright. Grabbing hold of the sides again, he hung on for fear of death and, just when he hoped that they might be beached on the bank below the clubhouse and he could escape into the shelter of fringing trees, the wind changed direction and the boat swung round ninety degrees and began to hurtle towards the overflow system.

Normally this was closed, with iron bars across the outlet used to channel the excess water under the ground along the old river route to Lough Neagh. The bars were there to prevent boats or wildfowl being sucked through. Today, for some unknown reason, the outlet was were open and the safety bars no longer there. A black hole, through which white-flecked waves were pouring, beckoned the unstoppable craft. Michael opened his mouth to yell for help, but his words were torn from his lips by the gale and lost in the maelstrom.

The boat careered forward, with the boy still desperately clinging on to the sides, his knuckles white with effort, body soaked and buffeted, his mind no longer functioning. At his feet, the dog lay motionless, paws pressed against its eyes. On and on they sped towards the black orifice – fifty metres – thirty metres – ten metres, the distance to it diminishing rapidly by the second, the prow of the boat heading inexorably for the outlet and the underground channel to the great Lough.

And just before that climactic moment came, amazingly, the rain ceased and the wind dropped. Lightning flashed and was followed almost immediately by a frightening explosion of thunder. Simultaneously the sun broke through the lowering clouds. For a nanosecond Michael witnessed the transformation. Then he was through the beckoning gap and being hurled into darkness. But in that instant before he was swallowed up, the sun turned to crimson, and the sky, the land and the water seemed to blend into one, and everything he could see turned to the colour of blood.

CHAPTER THREE

Once over the threshold of the outlet, Michael found himself in complete darkness. He could hear water rushing all around him. The channel he was in was narrow. The boat careered along, occasionally scraping the sides and causing the wood to screech in protest at the contact, making him fear it would spring its planks. He threw himself flat, knowing that the height of the roof might dip at any moment and a sudden impact could throw him overboard or knock his brains out. Surprisingly, he now felt calm. Closing his eyes he reached for the dog seeking to comfort it. It wasn't there. He hadn't heard the animal jump overboard, so he had no idea where it could be.

Before he could ponder on the fact he sensed something had happened. Opening his eyes he raised his head and found he could make out the shape of his companion. The dog was sitting at the front of the boat staring straight ahead. Two yellow beams streamed out in front of them illuminating the way ahead. To his amazement he saw that his companion was the source of the light. The dog's eyes had become two glowing beacons like the headlamps of a car.

On either side of them the water gushed and frothed, the constricted space forcing the torrent through a channel no more than three metres wide. The walls consisted of blue clay, wet and waxy and pitted with rocks, the roof high enough to enable Michael to sit up and look around him.

He didn't have long to take stock of his surroundings. Up ahead the river had vanished and the fierce gushing around the boat was now drowned out by a rumble that grew louder by the instant. Michael recognised what he was hearing, having experienced the same sound when his father took him walking in the Mournes. It was the din of a torrent crashing over a waterfall. His moment of calm disappeared and, suddenly terrified, he grasped the protruding rowlocks and hung on with all the power he could muster. The dog scuttled back and lay down between his legs. Everything was dark again and he could feel jaws clamp on his trouser leg for support.

Within seconds the boat gave a lurch and then tipped forward. A moment later it was sliding downwards at breakneck speed, almost vertical, and in danger of turning over. Despite his desperate grip on the rowlocks Michael felt himself begin to slide about, banging and jostling the dog beside him. Instinctively, he knew that once his hold was broken he would be toppled over the side. Fear lent him greater strength and for a few moments he was able to regain his equilibrium by jamming his feet against the sides of the boat. But a sudden collision with something beneath them broke his hold and he tumbled towards the prow, unable to control his movements.

Just as he thought he would be thrown into the torrent and swept away, the vessel slammed into flatter water and swung crazily about, the erratic motion making him feel dizzy. Fortunately the frantic gyrations didn't last long and he soon found himself being carried along at a more moderate pace. He felt the dog stir and move away from him. Once more two beams of light shot out and illuminated the area ahead.

They were on a wider stretch of water moving towards its centre. As they got closer he could make out darker patches, circular in shape. He wasn't sure what these might be, but something told him they were the harbinger of something worse than he had experienced so far. The dog remained at the same spot until Michael felt the current quicken, then the light went out and he knew instinctively that it was time to take refuge in the well of the boat once more. The dog quickly joined him.

As he felt it grip his trouser leg again the vessel swung sideways. It began to spin, slowly at first, then quicker and quicker in ever decreasing circles, moving in a controlled fashion towards the middle of the black patches he had seen. With mounting dread Michael realized what was happening. They were caught in a whirlpool and being drawn gradually towards its core. Once there, they would be sucked downwards and their fate sealed.

He was powerless to halt their progress, so fast now that his head was spinning. Still they continued to gyrate until his ability to think diminished and strange shapes began to appear behind his tightly closed eyes, a kaleidoscope of light and movement. This odd activity in his head didn't last long. In a very short time the flickering lights began to fade and somehow he knew they had reached the centre of the vortex. The little craft began to sink into the centrifuge of the whirling waters. As it plummeted, still being spun at a tremendous rate, he began to lose awareness of what was happening. Just before he lost consciousness, he sensed rather than felt the dog land on his chest. A wet nose snuggled against his ear and he closed his arms round its warm body for solace. After that, everything went black.

CHAPTER FOUR

He wakened slowly, feeling at peace. Everything was silent. He thought he was at home in bed enjoying the lovely, drowsy sensation that precedes waking. He was sure he had been dreaming and smiled to himself as he remembered his daft idea about running away. The memory was so vivid it could almost have happened – the trek to town with the dog, rowing on the park lake, the funny looking sky, the storm and —. At that point he suddenly came fully awake. He opened his eyes and sat up. And as he looked about him he realised that he hadn't been dreaming at all.

He was on a beach. The sand was almost white and felt hot to the touch. Another stretch of water lay before him about one hundred metres wide. Waves lapped gently on the shore making him think that this was a narrow sea and not a lake. The sky above him was orange. Reflected in the water the sea looked like a giant pool of lucozade. "What a strange place," he murmured.

He got up to investigate, and soon spotted the rowing boat. It was lying on its side, close by, with the oars a few metres further away. There was no sign of the dog. Remembrance of the animal made him consider how he had got here. The vessel, with him in it, must have been carried down into the sea and washed ashore, the oars following on separately. Perhaps the dog had survived also. He decided to look for her.

He started out along the beach, his wet clothes beginning to steam in the heat. There was no sign of a sun in the sky and he wondered where the warmth was coming from. His socks squelched in his trainers as he walked.

The landscape was barren, not a tree, not a bush, not a blade of grass anywhere. There was just white sand and an orange coloured sky. Stopping, he did a 360-degree turn. He found he was quite alone, not another living thing to be seen.

He gazed at the narrow water. It stretched away, left and right, as far as the eye could see, its surface calm, and apart from the ripples at the edge, not a movement anywhere. A great sense of desolation enveloped him and he wondered what he should do.

"You feel lost, I think," a deep voice said behind him.

He started in surprise and turned to discover the source of the comment.

A man stood there; the dog was beside him. She wagged her tail and gave one sharp bark of welcome.

"Quiet, Canis," the man said. "Sit down." The dog immediately obeyed the command.

Michael was beginning to get used to these sudden appearances. He stared at the figure before him. The man was dressed like some of the characters he had seen pictured in his Dickens novels. He wore breeches, a waistcoat and a top hat, the latter most incongruous seeing it was such a warm day.

The man noticed Michael's surprised stare. "You feel my attire is unusual, young man."

Michael wasn't sure how to reply. To agree with his new companion might give offence.

"Your own raiment is just as strange to me, but then the last time someone arrived from your world he had long hair, sideburns and trousers so wide at the bottom he could have been a sailor." Michael had a vision of someone from the nineteen seventies when everyone dressed like that, or, at least, the photographs of the period he had seen suggested they did.

"I d-don't understand," he stammered.

"I know you don't, the man said kindly. "I am here to explain."

"What is this place?" Michael enquired.

"You are in an underworld," came the reply. "Where you are precisely is the starting point for the selected ones."

"Selected ones," Michael echoed in bafflement.

"Every so often, usually a quarter of a century or so, one of your age is chosen to attempt four tasks. On this occasion it is you. If you succeed you set everyone here free. If you fail, you join us and wait a number of years until the next attempt is made."

Michael was bewildered. "Who makes this choice, what are these tasks, what age are you, why me?"

The man held up a hand. "Patience, my young friend: you are in too much of a hurry. Pause for breath and I will attempt to enlighten you. Firstly, to satisfy your curiosity about my age, in your calculation of time I have been here 170 years. I was the first person chosen in this cycle."

"But you've hardly aged," Michael interrupted, more confused than ever.

"Ah, but I have. Life is much slower in this world. Like you, I was twelve years old when I made the journey here. And also, like you, I had Canis as my companion. I age one year for every twenty-four seasons that pass. In your time I am now over 40 years old. As for the dog, I have no idea how long she has lived or the length of her year in your terms. All I know is that her expected life span is different from mine. I could be older than her, I could be younger than her."

By now Michael's mind was reeling. "Why were you chosen?" he asked, feeling unnerved.

"A good question, about which I have had much time to ponder. Perhaps it was because I was a child prodigy, skilled in music, verse and the mathematics. Perhaps it was because I was an orphan with no relatives to be concerned about me. You see, my father, who was in business as a bookbinder, went bankrupt and hanged himself. Then my mother died soon after and my life was changed utterly." He said this all quite matter-of-factly as if the tragedy had not affected him. "But that is another story," he went on, "and I do not wish to burden you with it. However, whatever the reason, it must have been decided that I was suitable."

"For what? And who's behind all this?"

"You go too fast again. I will answer one question at a time. Which is it to be?"

Michael hardly heard him, so eager was he for explanations. "Who chose you, and me, and all the others? Was it the same person?"

"It was indeed. He is the ruler of the Underworld – a malign individual from a time long gone. It amuses him to keep us here. It is a sport to him. He watches with great delight when a new contestant arrives to take up the challenge."

"What is he like?

"That, I am unable to tell you for I have never met him. My knowledge of his existence comes whispered in the wind or in the babblings of rippling water or from the songs of birds in the air. When he speaks only the wind and the wildlife and the bubbling brook can hear him. It is believed he is very old, the only survivor from an island that sank beneath the Atlantic Ocean many centuries ago. It is said he was in a state of banishment, living alone in the wilderness, a punishment for offending the rulers of his Kingdom."

"You mean, Atlantis."

"Perhaps, perhaps not. No one knows."

"Why did he alone survive?"

"He knew of ancient ways. Today he would be called a sorcerer or a magician or a warlock or a wizard. Take your pick. He had the secret of life, but only in his own land. He can never leave here in human form. To do so would mean instant death. So time hangs heavy on him and he needs amusement. We are the means to alleviate his boredom."

"And he chose me?"

"No. He only made the rule that after a suitable period, usually twenty-five years, but not always, an attempt can be made to set free the people who are kept here. I see you are bemused. Allow me to explain.

"The dog is the only inhabitant of this place allowed to leave. She spends much time in many lands searching for the right person. Canis decides who that is to be and when to make the choice. Now she has decided it is your turn to attempt the four tasks stipulated by the wizard."

"Why me?" Michael asked, his mouth dry and unconsciously acknowledging the fact that the dog was a female.

"Because your range of knowledge is great, probably greater than any other twelve year old boy in the land above. Canis always makes the selection most appropriate to the tasks set. She knows what these are before she begins her quest."

"And each appropriate selection has never succeeded, otherwise I wouldn't be here," Michael said bitterly. "So what chance have I?"

"We live in hope," his companion replied quietly. "Others have succeeded in previous cycles. Someday, someone will be triumphant. There is no reason why it shouldn't be you. Now," he said briskly, "it is time for you to begin your journey."

"Journey," Michael echoed blankly.

The man continued as if he hadn't been interrupted. "First you must cross the *sea of cruelty*. Beyond that there is a path. You will follow this until you come to a gate. The gate will be impassable unless you are able to complete a small test correctly. This is to see if you are fit for the four tasks ahead. If you are successful in this the gate will open and the real challenges will begin. If you fail, your journey is over and you will be confined here like the rest of us. Along the way there may be traps, so be wary. There may be other tests. These too must be tackled and overcome. Canis will accompany you. She will always be close at hand and will help you in small matters, but when it comes to the important challenges, she is forbidden to help. You will also have guides who will explain what has to be done. They too may give you aid in some small way, but, sometimes, things are not what they seem so always watch out for trickery.

"Now go. The *sea of cruelty* awaits you."

"Why is the sea cruel?"

"You must discover that for yourself. One more thing I will tell you. You cannot wish for things yourself, but others may do that for you. Sometimes they will know your mind and will act on your behalf without being bidden and your requirements will materialize. That is all I have to say. Good luck, and remember, all here are depending upon your abilities. I hope to see you again in happier circumstances."

Michael felt something rub against his leg, causing him to glance down. It was Canis. The dog had now moved to his side. When he looked up again he found that, apart from the animal and him, the beach was empty. The man in Victorian dress had vanished.

Michael felt very alone and daunted by the responsibility that had been placed upon him. The thought entered his head that if his dad hadn't insisted on him learning so much he wouldn't have been in this position. More than ever he wished he were like other boys living a normal life. More than ever he hated his dad. But he had one small piece of satisfaction. If he never returned to their world his parents would never know what had happened to him. They would be devastated. *And serve them right*, he thought viciously, *for the life they've forced me to lead and the predicament their teachings have landed me in.* Hardly had the words formed in his mind than he knew they were unworthy of him. He should have felt guilty for thinking this way, but an innate stubbornness would not allow him to do so. *It's the way they've made me*, he said to himself, but the argument was not convincing. Feeling uneasy with his reasoning, and not wishing to dwell on the matter, he pushed it hastily from his mind Sighing, he accepted his fate. He decided that the thing to do was concentrate on his situation, ignore negative thoughts and get on with the problems that lay ahead. He hoped he was capable of solving them, for that seemed the only means for him to escape.

At that point his stomach rumbled and he realised he felt hungry. That could be his first problem. If he had nothing to eat or drink, lack of food might weaken him and it was a well known fact that a person's mental processes operated better on a full stomach.

Hardly had the thought entered his head when Canis barked twice. With each bark a tree materialised close by. Bananas, some green some yellow, were clustered tightly on one, cocoanuts on the other. Some of the fruit from both trees had fallen to the sand beneath. Amazed at their appearance, he recalled the words of the Victorian gentleman. Michael had been sceptical about what he had been told, but now that the food was here, all doubts about the man's veracity disappeared. Canis must have read his mind and summoned up the fruit.

He peeled and ate a couple of bananas and, hammering a cocoanut against the bark of a tree, managed to put a crack in its hairy shell. Widening the gap with his fingers he drank some of the milky liquid within. Nothing had ever tasted so delicious.

Canis whined up at him so he peeled and tossed her pieces of a banana, which she caught adroitly before swallowing them. After subjecting another cocoanut to the same rough treatment he gave her a drink of the nectar also.

His hunger gone he put his mind to crossing the narrow water. He was about to step into the shallows to test their depth when Canis jumped in front of him and barked. When he tried to go round her she did the same thing, blocking his way. It was then he remembered the description of the water used by his recently vanished companion; the *sea of cruelty*. There must be a reason why it was so named. Obviously the dog knew and was warning him not to enter.

Thoughtfully he picked up another banana and tossed it into the orange liquid before him. As it hit the calm surface the water seemed to boil for a few moments, then it became placid again. Soon only spreading ripples indicated the violent disturbance that had occurred.

He had thrown the fruit about twenty metres, which was too far for him to ascertain the cause of the turbulence. He repeated the procedure, only this time the second banana entered the water only a short distance away. Immediately the area where it had made contact became a seething broth of fury. Small fish, in their dozens, tore the banana to pieces, skin and all, their razor-like teeth dissecting it in seconds. Shocked at their ferocity, and even though he was on dry land and in no danger, he stumbled backwards putting more distance between himself and the gentle tide. If he had walked into the sea the fish would have stripped the flesh from his feet and legs. "Piranha," he exclaimed a bit too loudly. "The water's full of piranha."

Shaken, and thankful the dog had dissuaded him from his intended course of action, he realised at once that the way ahead might be dangerous and he would have to consider his decisions more carefully in future.

Now he noticed something else. He hadn't thought about it before, but he realised there was no sign of wildlife on the sea, no waterfowl, no moorhens, no ducks, no swans. And he knew the reason why. Any birds landing there would only have been a quick meal for the voracious little predators; a *sea of cruelty* indeed. He shuddered at the thought of what might have happened to him.

The dog bounded towards the boat as if to say, we've got to get across, so get on with it.

He collected the oars and threw them into the vessel before hauling it to the edge of the water. A good shove saw it afloat, and as he hopped in, the animal followed safely after him.

A dipping of the oars saw the piranha rise to the surface, but even their sharp teeth could make little impact on the paddle ends of the wood. Occasionally, on the way across, fish would leap into the boat, but Canis deftly caught them by their tails and quickly flipped them back over the side. It was like a game to her and each time she caught one her body quivered with excitement. Others tore at the bottom of the boat trying to shred it, and despite the fact that the vicious little predators had no chance of succeeding, he was extremely relieved to reach the other side.

Beaching the boat on another strip of white sand, he headed for a path he had spotted while on the water. It had to be the one mentioned by the Victorian gentleman. It led to a wooded area. With the dog trotting a few paces ahead of him, ears pricked and eyes alert, he was soon surrounded by dense foliage and trees so high that he caught only occasional glimpses of the sky. This was no longer orange but a dark green. Indeed, everything around him was green, and as less and less light filtered through from above, the environment grew increasingly dark in colour and faintly threatening.

The greenery held the heat in and soon Michael was sticky with sweat. He removed his windcheater, but it made little difference. Underneath this he was wearing a woollen sweater, knitted by his mum, and this was soon clinging to him. He didn't know why he had put it on. He didn't like it and normally he didn't wear it. Now he was sorry he had.

The path grew narrower and narrower until the dog and he were walking in single file. The trees and undergrowth were so closely entwined, and so profuse along the edge of their route, that there was no way to deviate from the thin track. Their only recourse was to follow the path where it led.

Soon there was hardly any light at all and, at times, they found their way blocked by fallen trees and encroaching plants, many exotic and foreign to him. Even if he had recognised some of the species, he would have not been interested in them, his whole time now being taken up with the effort to make progress.

Finally, they broke free from the obstacles hindering them and found themselves in a clearing. The clearing led to another larger opening in the forest. Sweaty and tired and in need of a drink, Michael wanted to rest, but when he stopped and sat down on a tree stump, Canis nudged him from behind, forcing him up, and, reluctantly, he moved on again.

The new path, although still narrow and gloomy, was thankfully free from encumbrance and their pace quickened. About one hundred metres further on they came to a door. It was made of heavy metal and had neither key-hole nor handle. It couldn't be opened. Six metres high, its surface was completely smooth; it couldn't be climbed. Two giant redwoods acted as sentinels to it, one growing close against it on either side. The forest adjoining them was impenetrable; the door couldn't be by-passed. As he stared at it, a giant python suddenly emerged from the forest and slithered sinuously along the top and into the foliage at the other side.

For a few moments he stood transfixed, then he pushed the door using all his strength. It didn't move. He charged at the thing and rammed it with his shoulder, causing not a tremor in it. All he achieved was a sore shoulder. An elephant couldn't have budged it. The way forward was comprehensively blocked. He sat down and contemplated the problem, aware of a growing thirst. The dog lay beside him and closed her eyes. She seemed to go asleep.

Michael thought for some time, trying to work out how to negotiate the obstacle. At one stage he got up and carefully ran his hands over all parts of the obstruction he could reach, hoping to find a panel or a secret catch. He discovered nothing that would help him. When he had exhausted all ideas on how to get to the other side, the dog sat up and cocked her head. Then she gave two barks and jumped to her feet, tail wagging. The door suddenly swung wide, and framed in the opening was a large, black man, about two metres in height and with bulging muscles. The animal leapt forward and straight into the newcomer's arms. As she did so the man stepped through and the door slammed shut behind him.

"Canis, you old ruffian, here you are again." The stranger ruffled the dog's coat affectionately, a great grin exposing ultra-white teeth. "Hope you're successful this time, dog."

He turned his attention to Michael. "Hiya, Bud," he said in a distinct American accent.

"My name's not Bud," Michael replied primly.

The man laughed. "A culture clash, I see. What am I to call you, then?"

"I was christened Michael," he responded, a tad petulantly.

"Michael," the man mused. "A bit formal for me. How about, Mikey, will that suit?"

Michael was about to object, but the American looked so big he thought it better not to offend him. "I suppose that will be all right," he replied grudgingly.

"So, Mikey, you're the new challenger." He placed Canis back on the ground where she promptly lay down, her intelligent eyes switching from one human to the other as they conversed. "Think you can do it?"

"I don't know. I hope so."

"Sure you can. Think positive, that's the secret."

Just like my dad, Michael thought. He was always saying that too. All grown-ups must think the same. "I'll try. Can we go on now?"

"Hold your horses, old buddy – sorry, Mikey. To pass through the door you must demonstrate your fitness to continue. If you fail I'll have to leave it shut, then you'll just be like all the rest of us here; a prisoner here until some smart kid, smarter than us, comes along to release you."

"What do I have to do?"

"A small test, that's all."

"Let's get on with it then," Michael replied tetchily.

"Eager to proceed, are we. Okay, let's see what you're made of. Think food."

"Pardon?"

"Think food. Anything will do."

Michael thought of a nice, cool drink of orange, with cold beads bubbled on a frosted glass.

A small table instantly appeared with food on it, but it wasn't what he had wished for. Three identical items, each the size of his fist, sat on a plate. They were almost round, light brown, and embedded on top with little, diamond shaped bits of granulated sugar. They were buns, Paris buns.

"That's not what I wanted."

The man grinned again. "That's life for you, Mikey. "We don't always get what we desire."

"What are they for?"

"To eat. That's your test."

"Is that all?"

"That's it. You have to swallow every last bit."

"That doesn't seem too difficult."

"You think so; well, we'll see. The man's grin had died and he sounded serious. "You have seven minutes to get them down. If you haven't managed it by then..." He didn't finish the sentence. But then there was no need to. Michael knew what his fate would be.

"Are you ready?"

Michael nodded.

"Then off you go."

As he picked up the first bun and took a bite, the man began to count out loud, "one, two, three, four." The time between each spoken number was a second. The dog watched Michael intently.

The confection was sweet and crumbly. He was half-way through it when he realised he had a problem. His mouth had been dry to start with and the consistency of the bun was such that it was sucking up the remaining moisture in his mouth at an alarming rate. As he chewed, the food became gooey and began to stick to his palate, making it hard to swallow. He wished he had a drink to wash it down, but none was forthcoming.

Now he knew why the test had been set. The trek here, peppered with obstacles and carried out in hot and humid conditions, had been devised to drain his body of fluid and create a thirst. He chewed ever slower, trying to conserve the scarce moisture in his mouth. By the time he had finished the first bun, two minutes had elapsed.

The next bite left him spluttering when he tried to swallow. Then a crumb went down the wrong way and he began to choke and cough and make funny, braying sounds as he struggled to imbibe air. Just when he thought he was going to pass out for lack of oxygen, the coughing dislodged the offending bit of food and the spasm ceased. After a few deep breaths, and with his face red and his eyes and nose streaming, he resumed his task.

Up until then he had refrained from activating the saliva glands under his tongue, but he now realized he could hold off no longer. When he did so, he discovered that they had almost run dry. With their aid he just about managed to finish the second confection. But this precious reserve of liquid had now been exhausted. And still the count went on relentlessly, the counter beginning to look grim.

Time seemed to race by. Five minutes had now elapsed and Michael knew that at this rate the clock would beat him. His challenge would be over almost before it had started.

He stopped to think, using up precious seconds. The dog was on her feet as if willing him to continue. If ever an animal could have looked anxious, Canis did. The count continued, drawing ever closer to the end of the allotted seven minute time-span.

Suddenly coming to a decision, he sat down and removed his trainers and then his socks. They had been saturated during the watery journey from the park. There was bound to be moisture left in them. Quickly he screwed a sock between his hands and a few drops of a dirty, brown liquid dripped into the heel of a trainer. Repeating the procedure with the other sock, he managed to squeeze out another small amount. He took a sip. The liquid tasted gritty and horrible and the smell of it almost turned his stomach but, at least, the concoction wet his mouth. He started on the final confection. He was now able to chew and swallow quicker, although he still had difficulty in getting the food down.

With thirty seconds remaining, the water in the trainer had been drunk and he still had two bites to masticate and swallow. There was only one other thing he could try. He bent and picked up the socks from the ground. Thankfully they were the woollen pair he had put on by mistake and were able to retain moisture better than the nylon variety. Putting one to his mouth, he sucked the toe. It had picked up sand along the way and grains as well as moisture entered his mouth. Frantic now, he didn't care what was in the mixture. He took a chew, sucked again, chewed again, and, miraculously, sand and portion of food went down. Then he was on to the last piece of bun. Sucking and chewing the other sock in similar fashion, draining it of as much moisture as he could, he managed to get one final swallow in, almost choking over it before the food disappeared. The taste in his mouth was awful.

The big man was still counting. "Finished," Michael croaked.

The counting stopped. There were three seconds left. Somehow he had done it.

The dog barked and cavorted round him. The black man hit him on the back, the congratulatory slap making him stumble forward and almost causing the hard ingested food to come up again. He gagged and then his stomach settled.

Beaming, the former said delightedly, "Well done, Mikey, well done. Now, wish for food. Have another go." The boy didn't need a second bidding. This time a large glass of orange squash, frosted and inviting, materialised on the table. A dish filled with cold water appeared beneath it for the dog. Both of them drank long and thankfully, he making a mental vow never to eat another Paris bun as long as he lived.

When he set the glass down, mysteriously it filled up again, this time with lime juice. He drank once more, but now at a slower pace, sipping it, savouring it, appreciating the sharpness of its flavour. When finished, his throat was no longer parched and he had eradicated the foul taste of the potation he had sucked from his socks. His mouth was nicely damp again.

Canis continued to drink. When she'd had her fill, she gave a bark and wagged her tail as if trying to tell him something. He looked around and saw that the great door was ajar. So preoccupied had he been with slaking his thirst he had failed to notice it swing open.

"Feeling better?" the black man asked.

Michael nodded.

"Then, Mikey, it is time to proceed, he announced solemnly. "Time to go on to the first task."

CHAPTER FIVE

Once through the massive door, it slammed shut behind them with a great boom. Feeling relaxed, now that he had passed the test, Michael took an interest in his surroundings.

The forest had gone to be replaced by a plain with open pasture and only the occasional tree. It crossed his mind that if there had been a few hedges to break up its flatness, it would have looked much like the countryside at home. Daisies and buttercups abounded, birds swooped and sang, butterflies and bees searched for nectar on the flowers of thistles and ragwort. It all looked very peaceful.

The sky was now like cream.

In the distance a great house with tall chimneys gave definition to the landscape. What looked like an extensive garden surrounded it. As the crow flies, the building was about five kilometres away. The path had petered out and they set out in that direction over meadows thick with poppies and cornflowers.

The temperature had moderated. With a slight breeze to refresh them and the grass soft beneath their feet, walking became pleasant again. Canis took off and began to chase the bees and butterflies, jumping into the air and snapping at them. She was spectacularly unsuccessful in making contact.

Michael broke the silence that had grown between him and his companion. "You seem to know who I am but I don't know anything about you." Normally he wouldn't have been so bold with someone he had just met, but this man no longer seemed like a stranger to him.

"I'm a loser, like everyone else here," came the reply. "That's probably all you need to know."

Michael refused to be put off, as ever his inquisitive mind refusing to be denied. "I take it you tried and failed. How long ago was that?"

"You really want to know?"

"Of course. I might learn something to help me with what lies ahead."

"I doubt that."

"I think I'll be the judge of that," Michael replied shortly.

"Kinda pompous, aren't you."

No one had ever accused him of that before and it angered him. "No, I'm not. I just say what I know is right."

The black man looked at him pensively. "It's not what you say, I think. It's how you say it; your tone, that is. Have you ever had problems with your pals back home?"

Michael shook his head, knowing he was being misleading.

"Has no one ever accused you of being a know-all or a big-head?"

The probe struck home. Michael knew he wasn't popular and was aware he was called names behind his back. But he wasn't going to admit to the fact.

"People accept me as they find me."

"Hmm, they do, do they. Well, I suppose I'll just have to do the same, then. What did you ask me?"

Somewhat mollified, Michael repeated the question.

His inquisitor took a moment to consider his reply. Then he asked, "Do you want my whole story, or just how I came to fail?"

"I suppose the whole story. Then if I hear anything that's useful I can memorize it for the future."

"Okay, Mikey, I'm allowed to help up to a point, and if that's what you want, here we go."

He was silent for a moment, collecting his thoughts, his face sombre, then he began his tale.

I was born in Louisiana in 1853. My mamma and pappy were slaves. They lived on a plantation owned by a man called Silas Barnstaple. Life was hard. My mamma had six childer, of which I was the eldest. Four of the others died, either in childbirth or shortly after. My sister, Hester was only six when I saw her last.

"My pappy worked on the plantation from first light till after darkness fell, sowing or picking cotton, tilling the soil, anything that had to be done. When my mamma wasn't bearing childer she laboured alongside him. The slaves on the plantation numbered eighty-seven at the last count. The Master, as he was called, encouraged them to breed to keep up their numbers. I guess my mamma didn't do a very good job. She died giving birth to Hester.

"I started work when I was five years old, at first just a few hours a day and then, as I grew older and stronger, longer and longer periods till I was doing the same time and the same work as the older slaves.

"The Master was a God-fearing man. Each Sunday we were all herded into a barn to listen to a preacher and give thanks to the Lord for our existence. I enjoyed the hymn singing. That was the only break from toil that we got.

"I was big for my age, which was surprising, for my mamma was smaller than me when she died and pappy wasn't a tall man, though he was very strong. Sometimes he got into fights with the other bucks and he was never beaten.

"By the time I was seven I was as big as him. When I was eight I was a head taller, and by my tenth birthday my muscles had started to develop. By then I was as strong as a man. I suppose I was unusual, but then the hard labour might have affected my development. As it was, I never grew much more after that. I've often thought that being so strong so young was the reason I was chosen to take on the four tasks."

Michael broke into the narrative. "Why do you think you failed?"

"That's easy. I had no education. I was just a young buck with muscles. You need more than that to succeed here. The challenges change. I suppose mine were mostly based on strength and endurance, and I've seen since that they tend to suit the skills and abilities of those chosen to tackle them. In my case that only went so far and I discovered that to succeed I needed to be cerebral as well as physical.

"You don't speak like a man with no learning. How can that be?"

The big man's visage relaxed a bit. "That's because of the dreams."

Michael looked perplexed and his companion laughed. "It's a very strange place I live in, as you've probably noticed. The wizard is a cruel man. He gives you glimpses of what your life might have been and he doesn't limit them to your own time. I've been blessed with a good brain and a good memory, and I've had a long time in which to learn."

"You're talking in riddles."

"You might think so, but it's really very simple. Each night we're allowed one dream, which we can remember in the morning. When I wake I memorise everything in it. Sometimes it takes me hours before I'm satisfied I won't forget its contents.

"My dreams have covered nearly a century and a quarter in your time and more than twenty-one years in the time here. I have seen the evolution of the United States of America to the greatest nation on earth. I have witnessed the dropping of the atomic bombs on Hiroshima and Nagasaki; beheld the first man in space, the assassinations of the Kennedys and Luther King; lived to see at last the great yoke being removed from black people everywhere. I could go on and on, but I'm sure it would bore you. If I'd had the knowledge I have now when I was a boy of twelve, this place would never have contained me. I would have been John Wayne, Mohammed Ali, Michael Jordan and Albert Einstein all rolled into one. I would have been invincible."

Michael stared at him open-mouthed. Up until then, without actually being patronising, he had considered the black man to be his intellectual inferior. Now, he realised he was in the presence of someone with probably a greater knowledge than anyone he had ever known, even his dad. He felt suitably humble and didn't know how to make amends.

"Don't apologise," the man said, reading his thoughts. "You weren't to know."

Michael's old self was immediately reasserted. "I wasn't going to," he snapped. Then there was an awkward pause. "Sorry," he mumbled, realising his tone had again been acerbic.

"Don't worry," his companion replied charitably. "It's your nature. Sometimes that's hard to change. Maybe by the time you leave here you'll come to understand that there will always be people cleverer than you are, though I'm not saying I fall into that category."

Chastened, and making a mental note not to rise so quickly in future to other people's remarks, he asked in a contrite manner, "Would you continue with your story now, if you want to, that is."

The man smiled. "See, you're learning already. "Of course, I'll continue. After all, there might be something in it which could prove useful to you."

Michael knew he was being gently mocked, but this was done with such good humour that he felt no resentment. Now that his companion was more than his equal, he began to like him.

"Now, where was I?" The man paused before resuming his extraordinary history.

"When I was growing up on the plantation, the Civil War began; 1861 that was, and I was eight years of age then.

"It didn't touch us at first, but as time went on and the Northern States began to gain the upper hand, word filtered through to us that all over the south slaves were deserting the plantations and joining the Federal army in the hope of gaining their freedom. We also heard that many were caught, and when they were returned to their owners, they were beaten so badly most of them never attempted to leave again.

"Silas Barnstaple tried to ensure there was no unrest at Oakleigh, that was the name of our plantation, by threatening to hang any buck who was caught absconding. At first no one did, because everybody knew he would carry out his threat.

"Then, in Washington in 1863, Abraham Lincoln drew up the legislation for the emancipation of slavery. By law we were all free men. Only, in Louisiana that didn't mean a thing. The southern states didn't recognise any Washington decree, or for that matter, any law enacted by the Yankees. We were still slaves until someone freed us physically as well as legally.

"That was when my pappy got some of the younger bucks together one night in the slave sheds to discuss what they should do. A few were for making a break for freedom, most were too frightened to go along with the bolder spirits."

"But surely this was their chance to escape their bondage," Michael interrupted. "Why didn't they all act together?"

"It wasn't as simple as that. You must remember that these men had always been subservient to the Master. They had taken orders from the moment they were born. They'd been treated as chattels, as non-persons, and they'd never had to think for themselves all their lives. It wasn't in their natures to rebel. And they were afraid, not only of the retribution promised by the Master, but of leaving the only place they knew. They had food, and a shelter to sleep in. Some had women and children to consider. What would the Master do to them if they left? And if they were to abscond, they would be on their own, hiding and being hunted, without food and with no one to make decisions for them. They might have to go hundreds of miles north before meeting up with the Federal forces. And then there was no guarantee that life would be any better there than the one they'd left behind. They might even get killed in the fighting.

"And if they did make it safely away from Confederate territory, and if the war was won by the northern forces, and if they got their freedom, what would they do with it? They would be in what was a foreign land to them, with few or no friends, no home and no means of earning a living. They were ignorant black men with only basic labouring skills. Were the politicians in Washington going to find work for them? I think not. So you see it wasn't an easy decision for them to make."

"What did they do?"

"Some went, most stayed."

"And you?"

"I was only ten years of age, and there was my sister, Hester, to look out for. If my pappy went, I had to stay. If I went, he had to stay."

"So, did any of you go?"

"Six young bucks, hotter headed and more adventurous than the others, took their chances one moonless night and broke out of the slave sheds. My pappy went with them. Next morning I saw the dogs being brought in to hunt them down and I had a great fear in my heart. Less than a week later, all of them except my pappy, had been brought back in chains. Then one morning the six recaptured bucks were brought out one by one and tied to a tree. Everyone on the plantation was assembled to watch the punishment. In his turn the shirt was ripped from each man's back and one of the other slaves was ordered to whip him. Each rebel was whipped by a different slave until he was senseless. But at least they were still alive. I suppose the Master valued their labour enough not to kill them.

"Two days later, my pappy, also in chains, was dragged into the enclosure in front of the slave sheds. He was covered in blood and dirt and had been badly beaten. His legs and arms had great open wounds were the dogs had savaged him. He was kept in isolation overnight and in the morning Silas Barnstaple hanged him. He was judged to be the ringleader and received no mercy. He was hanged naked, the ultimate indignity.

"As his body twitched on the rope, I made a vow I would be kept a slave no longer. And even as the breath was leaving his body I was making my plans to escape. That night I rescued my pappy's clothes, his scant garments having been tossed on a dump where refuse was burnt."

The black man stopped speaking, pain deadening his eyes as he relived the memory of his father's awful death. Michael, engrossed by the tale, and a bit shocked by the brutality of the plantation owner, considered how fortunate he was to be living in less repressive times. Then he dismissed the thought. His dad was hardly that enlightened. Michael was forced to live his life to another's dictates and was little more than a slave himself.

"Go on," he said quickly, unwilling to dwell on the comparison, knowing instantly it was simplistic.

Roused from his reverie, the face of the black man became more animated. "Forgive me," he said. "Sometimes the hurt fades, at other times it is as if the event occurred yesterday." He thought for a moment and then he continued.

"I waited a few days for things to settle. During that time I washed my pappy's old cotton shirt. When it was dry I ripped off the sleeves and tied an end of each one, making them into pouches. Each day I held back a little of my food ration and put it in one of the pouches. When they were full, I was ready to go. Before I left, I arranged for Hester to be cared for by another woman, who was childless. I did not tell my sister what I was about to do for fear of her letting it slip. She was the only thing I regretted leaving.

Eight days after my pappy died I sneaked out of the enclosure at dead of night. The lights in the big house were out and I knew all there were asleep. I had about six hours before my absence was discovered and another two before the hunting dogs were brought in to track me down.

"Most runaway slaves headed north in an attempt to reach friendly forces. Most were caught within a couple of days.

"I headed south, further into Confederate territory and towards the Louisiana swampland. Once there, I could lose my trackers and in the wetlands the dogs would be unable to follow my scent.

"I travelled by night, holing up during the day in old outhouses or woodland, anywhere I could find cover. For two days I saw no one, then a group of Confederate soldiers breasted a rise close to where I had taken cover in an overgrown ditch. They camped within fifty metres of where I was hiding and I thought they were bound to discover me. But after they had eaten, and a couple of them had relieved themselves within touching distance of where I lay, they broke camp and headed off again.

"That night I heard dogs in the distance and knew I had to reach my objective before morning.

"I ran the whole night, never stopping, the sounds of the dogs getting closer with each hour that passed. I knew the men with them would be on horseback and would make greater speed than I would.

"As I reached the swamps, the baying of the hounds took on a higher note, more excited, and I realised they had found my scent. By then I was almost exhausted. The animals were no more than half a mile behind me. They would be off the leash by now and becoming more and more frenzied by the chase. If they caught me before the huntsmen did I could be torn to pieces.

"I stumbled towards the mangroves that were growing thickly in the midst of the steamy shallows, my legs trembling with the effort to keep going. I kept to any shallows I could find, but more often than not, having to tread on the thick islands of coarse grass surviving above the waterline.

"As I reached the trees, the air grew dark and fetid, with strange smells bubbling up from the rank morass. Insects buzzed and mosquitoes stung and evil things lurked beneath the stagnant pools. It was a place no man in his right senses would come. But I had no choice. It was only here that I had a chance to evade my pursuers.

"At last, with little strength left, I was forced to stop and take refuge in the split roots of a mangrove tree rearing up out of the water. Wriggling inside, body aching and lungs seared by the effort to escape, I prayed that I had done enough to throw the dogs off my scent.

"They were close now, no more than a hundred yards away from my refuge, but they seemed to have stopped, their muted yelps suggesting they were milling around and no longer on my trail. That state of confusion lasted for a few minutes, then I heard a voice ordering them in another direction.

"At that moment I thought I had a chance. But the hope was short-lived. One dog, cleverer than the rest, suddenly appeared from a direction at right angles to the main pack. It stopped at the edge of a scum-covered pool, nose twitching, sniffing the air. A man on horseback arrived a few seconds later and stopped behind it.

"The dog, as large a hound as I'd ever seen, caught my scent and growled. Then it leapt straight into the water and began to swim towards me. It was then I thought my time had came. But fate took a hand.

"Halfway to my lair, a long object which, in the gloom I had taken to be a thick log, suddenly came to life, and large, teeth-filled jaws snatched the unsuspecting dog as it tried to pass. One moment it was in full stroke, the next it was cut in half, only its head and long-tailed rump remaining. The horse reared, almost throwing its rider, and the alligator, for that's what it was, crunched and swallowed the middle section of its prey in a flurry of blood.

"The rider swore violently and controlled his horse. Wheeling the animal round, he rode away as quickly as he could. Less than a minute later I heard him yelling at his companions to get the dogs out of there. The swamps were alive with 'gators.

"I'd been lucky in more ways than one. I hadn't been discovered, and if I'd taken the same route as the dog, I'd have suffered a similar fate to the unfortunate animal.

"As the 'gator finished its meal I wriggled out of the roots of the mangrove tree and climbed up until I was hidden in its branches. And there I stayed for two days, before I made my way cautiously out of the swamps to head north towards more friendly territory.

"My pursuers must have considered me dead for I neither heard nor saw a hunting pack from that time on. Six days later, hungry and weak, I stumbled upon a troop of Yankee soldiers out on patrol. I had done what my pappy had hoped to do; escape the harsh regime of Silas Barnstaple and join the fight to make Abraham Lincoln's hope for the emancipation of slaves become a reality."

Almost in awe, Michael asked, "Did you ever get back to the plantation?"

"Never did. Either fate or our friend the magician saw to that. The speaker gave a wry grin. "But I haven't given up hope yet. You might make that possible."

Michael didn't like to disillusion the man, but, if by some miracle he did succeed in getting the former slave out, then logic dictated that the latter would return to the twenty-first century and not to 1863. That would mean the black man would never return to his roots.

"I guess you want to hear the rest of my tale."

"I guess I do," Michael replied, unconsciously mimicking him.

"Well, there isn't much more to tell. As I said before, I was big for my age, and when the troopers questioned me, I told them I was sixteen and run-away from my plantation. They took me at my word and brought me back to their main encampment. There, I was given a uniform, a gun, and taught how to shoot.

"For the next two years I fought the Confederates. I killed my foes, some of which, I'm sorry to say, were black men like myself, and I saw many of my comrades killed in return.

"I learned many things during those two years. I always tried to attach myself to men who seemed more capable than others – soldiers who could think for themselves, who always seemed to make the right decisions and who were calm under fire. I studied them, copied their ways, even tried to improve upon them, and in a short time I considered myself to be as able, if not more so, than them.

"By the time the war was nearing its end I was the best-educated black man in the *university of life* in all America. I was clever, I was crafty, I was strong; and I never really got to put those attributes to their full use."

"Why was that?"

"I thought it was fate, but now I know better. As the conflict drew to its conclusion, I was with a band of foot soldiers mopping up the remnants of the enemy troops who had not surrendered, and I found myself in Louisiana near my old plantation. A number of renegades had holed up in the very swampland where I had fled after my escape.

"We caught up with them after a couple of days hard trekking. Originally, twenty of them had taken refuge there, but drownings and 'gators had reduced their numbers to thirteen by the time we got to them. Short of food, exhausted, and utterly lost, they gave up without a fight.

"We spent the night there, and after I had done my spell of guard duty on our prisoners, I got to sleep about two in the morning. It was the deepest sleep I ever remember, no dreams, no restless twitching or turning, just black unconsciousness.

"When I wakened in the morning I was alone. Somehow my comrades had broken camp and, along with the captured men, had moved on. Such was the intensity of my sleep I hadn't heard a thing. To this day I can only assume they didn't waken me because they weren't meant to.

"I said I was alone, but that isn't quite the truth. I had a companion. You've guessed it. There was a dog curled up beside me. Our friend Canis had appeared from nowhere.

"I gathered up my pack and my rifle and set off in pursuit of my comrades. Hardly had I gone a hundred yards when the sky darkened and it began to rain. And it rained and rained, so hard that the waters of the swamp began to rise and flood the firmer ground. Mist swirled up from the mire and obscured my landmarks. Soon I began to lose my bearings and in no time at all I realised I was lost.

"It was then the dog became my guide. Stepping out ahead of me she began to lead me to what I presumed was safe ground. I relied on her instincts, and eventually we came to an old wooden jetty, rotten in parts and obviously abandoned. Moored to the jetty was a small skiff, probably used at some time by a swamper to catch catfish. The dog jumped into it.

"Something seemed to be influencing my actions and I untied the boat and followed her in. Immediately it drifted off and was taken by a strong current away from its mooring. Still it rained, torrential now, and harder than I had ever seen before.

"Then the wind got up and the water was whipped to a frenzy of white, scudding waves. The skiff was taken as if by a giant hand and propelled towards a dark circle on the surface of the pool some fifty yards ahead of me. The dark patch turned out to be a whirlpool, created by the wind. Straight into it I was driven, and once caught in its unbreakable grip, all I could do was hold on to the sides of the craft and pray for deliverance. It whirled me round at an ever-increasing pace until my head began to spin and I felt the dog grip hold of my clothing to prevent being thrown over the side.

"I tried to retain my senses, but it became impossible and

eventually I backed out. I should have perished in that swamp. Instead, I came awake some time later and found myself here. And here I am still, a long time later, and each day I wonder how my life would have turned out if some other unfortunate soul had been chosen as one of the wizard's playthings."

There was no hint of self-pity in the black man's words. He had accepted his fate with equanimity and was prepared to make the best of it. And he had not given up hope of being released. His attitude made Michael feel glad to know him.

Struck by the similarity in the circumstances of their arrival, the boy was silent for a few seconds. Then, curiosity getting the better of him, he enquired, "And your name, you haven't told me your name."

His companion considered the question for a moment before answering. When he did, his tone was measured. "I could give you the one bestowed on me by my mamma and pappy, but I won't. That was special and will not be used by me until the day I'm free."

"But you're free now."

"I beg to differ. This is not an unpleasant life, but it's not freedom. Freedom is choice, the liberty to go where you want, when you want; to eat too much, to drink too much, to make decisions about your own welfare and not be told what you can or cannot do by any other man. I'm still a prisoner here, still a slave, only my master is different."

"So what shall I call you?"

The big man thought for a moment, his brow furrowed. "Jim Crow," he said softly, at last. "Jim Crow. That will be my name until I return to the world above and live as a free man." His face cleared and he smiled.

Michael nodded in understanding. The term, Jim Crow had more than one meaning. It was the term used for the practice of segregating African-Americans and it was also a derogatory name for a black man.

"Is there segregation here?" he asked, a bit embarrassed at raising such a sensitive matter, but driven by the need to know, and excusing his inquisitiveness by the fact that the big man had broached the subject.

"Not as such. But in some people's minds there is. Because of that I tend to keep largely to myself."

"And has anyone called you, Jim Crow?"

The question elicited a grin. "They wouldn't dare. I can use it in an insulting way, but that doesn't mean anyone else can."

The boy smiled. "I'd better watch what I say, then," and they both laughed.

They walked on, Michael not the least disconcerted by the unusual nature of his companions, the mighty black man with the great age, an age that belied his youthful appearance, and the dog with the Latin name whose eyes could light up in the dark. Long regarded a bit of a freak by his peers at school, to him, they felt like kindred souls.

CHAPTER SIX

As Jim Crow's tale was unfolding, they had made good progress in their walk to the big house. As they got near, two figures emerged from its extensive grounds and started up a long, sloping meadow towards them. Michael was conscious of a lark singing somewhere above them in the firmament, and in the buttercup covered grass of the pasture surrounding them, a corncrake suddenly shattered the peaceful atmosphere, reminding him that it was the second one he had heard recently. He wondered if this had a hidden significance and its raucous interruption symbolic of a darker period to come.

"Oh, no, not them," he heard Jim Crow mutter beside him.

"Who are they?" Michael enquired.

"The siblings Grimm, Trixie and Pixie, Tweedledum and Tweedledee. Take your pick."

"You don't like them."

"You guessed, did you? No, I don't like them. They're identical twins, and they're alike in more ways than looks. They're childish and spiteful and think they're better than everyone else here. Watch them. They might just take pleasure in seeing you fail."

"But that would mean they wouldn't get out of here."

"They might consider that an acceptable sacrifice. They're a peculiar pair and contrariness is second nature to them. They don't like others to succeed when they didn't."

Michael said nothing. Jim Crow put a hand on his shoulder to halt him and they stood watching the two approaching siblings. Their gait was lively, something between a skip and a fast walk. Arms waved as they talked, hands moving rapidly to emphasise a point or express an opinion. They were animated to the point of being hyperactive.

As they got closer, Michael saw two slim figures about the same age and size as himself.

Dressed identically in white tee-shirts and blue, denim trousers, belted low at the hips and flared at the bottoms, they reminded him of photographs he had seen of his parents when they were younger. Immediately he recalled the Victorian gentleman's words. *These are the arrivals from the nineteen seventies*, he thought. Their hair was fair, the boy's as long as the girl's, and each had pale, delicate features with deep, blue eyes. They were the epitome of unisex fashion and the only word Michael could think of to describe them was pretty.

"Well, Mikey, I guess this is where you and I part company." Jim Crow sounded regretful.

"You're not coming to see me tackle the tasks."

"Afraid not; my role ends by delivering you to this point. The twins are in charge from here."

At that moment a high pitched voice said, "On your way, boy; let your betters take over." The comment was accompanied by a fit of giggling from the newcomers.

Michael sensed Jim Crow stiffen.

"Only joking, only joking." a second voice of almost identical falsetto went on. "Don't be so defensive."

Michael felt embarrassed, but was saved from further discomfort by Canis, who arrived on the scene and began to prance around the black man's tormentors.

The boy aimed a kick at her.

Jim Crow erupted. "Yo harm that dog, boy and I kick yo ass." In his fury he had reverted to the dialect and vernacular of his youth.

The twins pretended astonishment. Throwing their arms in the air they chorused, "Glory be, we meant no harm. Please accept our sincere apologies."

Jim Crow glowered, knowing they were mocking him. Michael placed a hand on his arm. "Go now, Jim," he urged softly. "They're not worth your attention."

Jim Crow's anger diminished. "I guess you're right, Mikey. What's the expression about empty vessels?"

"They make the most sound."

"Well, I think that fits them nicely." He took hold of Michael's right hand in both his own large hands. "Don't be like me. Don't let those two rile you. Anger clouds your judgement and you need to be clear-headed at all times. If it's any succour to you, I think our hopes are in good care. Remember, be confident, always think positively, and good luck. I know I'll see you again."

With those parting words, he turned and set off up the incline and back the way he had come.

Michael experienced a sense of loss at his departure. In a very short time he had developed an affinity with the large, black man. He got no time to dwell on the fact.

"So you're the new champion."

Michael swivelled to see the twins appraising him. He felt

uncertain. They began to circle him, sizing him up. It was the girl who spoke next, wrinkling her nose up as she did so. "You're not very big, you're not very broad, you don't look very strong – ARE YOU VERY SMART?"

Michael wasn't drawn. Fighting off a feeling of inadequacy, he said, "You're very pass-remarkable."

"Pass-remarkable. That's a funny expression. What does it mean?"

"It means, you're cheeky, you're insensitive and you're insulting."

"Oooh, we've got feelings, have we?"

Michael caught a hint of a transatlantic twang. "Where I come from it's customary to be polite on first meeting someone. Don't they teach you that in America?"

The twins erupted in laughter, doing high fives. When they'd calmed down, the boy said, "We're not from America. We were born in Billericay. We only live in America."

"And you haven't answered my question," the girl insisted. "ARE YOU VERY SMART?"

Michael hesitated, deliberately delaying his answer, while trying not to be overwhelmed by their exuberance. A saying of his dad's came to mind. "Never be rushed into anything; try to control each situation, and stay cool."

"I'm not sure," he replied slowly. "Some people think I am, but maybe I just know a lot of things."

"Anyone can know things," the boy said dismissively. "You have to be smart to succeed here." He looked at his sister. "Shall we try him?"

"Let's."

"Yes, let's."

"What shall we do?"

They thought for a moment and then the boy said, "I know. We'll give him a conundrum."

"What a fab idea."

They both giggled and then became serious. Turning to face each other they touched foreheads. Closing their eyes they went very still. After a few seconds of concentration they leapt apart, and with legs akimbo, pointed at him. Fingers wagging like schoolteachers, they shouted in unison, "What is the connection between a dragon and the Scottish play?"

Dancing round him they gleefully repeated the question. Then they began to chant in their high-pitched voices, "Quickly, quickly, what is the solution, what is the solution, quickly, quickly?"

Michael refused to be rushed or intimidated. Taking his time before replying, he asked, "Is it essential for me to answer the question? Does it really matter if I do or not?"

They hesitated for a microsecond and then, like a musical exercise they chanted in counterpoint, one voice bouncing off the other.

"Does it matter?"

"Oh, it matters."

"Course it matters."

"Yes, indeed."

They stared at him expectantly.

Methinks they doth insist too much, Michael parodied mentally. "Are you absolutely sure?" he fenced.

"Of course, of course. Not to answer means failure. Failure means you're not qualified to take on the first task."

Michael remembered the Victorian gentleman's comment regarding distractions and, latterly, Jim Crow's words about trust. The twins might merely be acting mischievously, intent on diverting his mind from his real purpose. On the other hand, their actions might have more serious intent and they might be trying to make him fail at something frivolous in order to undermine his confidence. He wondered if he should refuse to cooperate. After a moment's consideration he decided he had to answer. He couldn't afford to take the chance they might only be trying to make a fool of him. "Then I suppose I'd better try," he replied.

Thinking they looked too pleased at his acquiescence, he began to concentrate on the problem.

"What is the connection between a dragon and the Scottish play?" he mused aloud. His mind moved smoothly into action, and like a computer, began to produce alternative propositions for him to consider. He had never been posed a conundrum before and he found himself beginning to enjoy the challenge. In an amazingly short time he thought he had worked out the answer. Double checking his bank of knowledge to ensure there was nothing he had missed which might lead him in another direction, he decided he had ruled out every other possible solution.

"It's a date," he announced. "April 23rd."

Poker faced, the girl said, "It might be and it might not be. You could just say the answer was anything."

Her brother interjected. "You could say it was Mount Everest, or the Dalai Lama, or a cat or a mouse or an elephant's bum."

"You want me to explain how I arrived at my answer," Michael replied mildly.

"That would be nice," they rejoined sarcastically.

"Okay, here it is." Michael paused deliberately, making them wait, for he could see they were eager to hear what he had to say.

"Go on, go on," the girl demanded impatiently.

He smiled, enjoying the moment and was rewarded by seeing his tormentors stamping their feet in exasperation. Only then did he begin his explanation.

"The Scottish play is another title for Macbeth. Actors never refer to the play by its proper name. This is a superstition, which stretches back to the 19th century. Macbeth, as everyone knows, was written by William Shakespeare.

"A dragon is a fire-breathing monster of myth and legend. Some are benign like Puff, from the children's song by Peter, Paul and Mary, while others are fierce and people eating. Your dragon is of the latter variety and was slain by St. George, who is the patron saint of England.

"Shakespeare and St. George have one thing in common. Shakespeare was born on April 23rd and St George's day is celebrated on the same date. That is the connection you wanted, I think."

The twins looked disappointed. They didn't congratulate him on his reasoning. They couldn't even bring themselves to say he was right.

"That was an easy one," the girl cried spitefully. The next test will be much harder. Come on," she said to her brother. "Let's see how he does with the real thing."

They wheeled away, and momentarily the sky was reflected in their faces, turning them even paler. Michael thought that appropriate, given the blow he had just delivered them.

As they set off down the slope towards the big house he felt elated. He had passed their test easily, illegitimate or not, and was now feeling much more confident about tackling whatever was to come.

The twins hurried on ahead of him, their movements agitated, as if they were in the grip of St Vitus's Dance. He strolled leisurely behind them, refusing to be hurried, enjoying his victory over them. Canis trotted along contentedly by his side.

As he walked, the feeling of euphoria began to dissipate as thoughts of his predicament began to sink in. Up until now so much had been happening he hadn't had much chance to reflect upon his situation. Now he began to realise how much trouble he was in. Failure to surmount the challenges that lay ahead meant incarceration in this strange Kingdom for a long time, maybe twenty-five years, or more. By the time he got out, if he ever got out, his parents could be dead, and the world as he knew it, changed irrevocably. Suddenly the happy feeling of a moment ago was gone and replaced by one of anxiety. Was he good enough to succeed where everyone before him had failed? And if he failed would he be able to cope with the new situation that would obtain? Doubts began to assail him and his mood darkened.

How quickly happiness can disappear, he thought.

As if sensing his concern Canis took hold of his trouser leg. Tugging at the cloth, she forced him to pay her some attention. At the same time he noticed the twins had stopped and were waiting for him to catch them up.

When he was almost at their heels, the girl, in exasperated tones, told him he was a slowcoach and must hurry up. Then they were bustling on again, animated as ever, and his *Black Dog* mood began to slip away. *Be positive*, his dad was always saying, *be positive*, Jim Crow had said the same thing. So strong was the thought that both might have been standing there with him. Along with Canis, he felt as if there were now others giving him encouragement and, unconsciously, he raised his head and squared his shoulders. He would give it his best attempt, and if he failed, he failed knowing he had done everything in his power to succeed. With a new-found determination, he continued on his way and in a much better frame of mind.

Soon he reached a gate set into a hedge of trimmed Leylandi. Following the twins through the opening he found himself in a garden of paths and flowers and perfectly manicured lawns. The paths were winding lanes of crazy paving, which somehow seemed appropriate, for the garden was the most peculiar one he had ever seen.

The seasons seemed to have no meaning here. Snowdrops and crocuses, daffodils and tulips, mixed happily with beds of busy Lizzies and double begonias, while pansies and dahlias were clustered alongside bluebells and mayflowers. Lupin and foxglove looked down in a lordly way on masses of primroses and alyssum. Roses, both standard and floribunda, cast their petals among drills of hollyhock and sweet pea, and everywhere he looked, bees and butterflies and ladybirds hunted in swarms among the glorious confection in the scented air.

"It's all so silly," the girl said, seeing Michael's look of incredulity. Everything's mixed up and makes no sense. Things should make sense," she ended petulantly, sounding a bit like Alice straight out of Wonderland.

"The world is out of joint, oh cursed spite. That ever I was born to put it right," quoted Michael softly.

"What was that?" the girl asked sharply.

"Oh, nothing," Michael replied. "I agree. Nothing in this whole place makes sense. But I still like the garden. It's bizarre, but it's beautiful."

"Flower gazing is not what you're here for," the boy said abruptly. "A more serious pursuit is at hand. Follow on," he ordered.

They started off again, wending their way past a row of red-berried holly bushes interspersed evenly with wisteria. Round the back of the house they went. Here they were confronted by a large fountain spouting water into an ornamental pool set in the centre of another lawn. Beyond the fountain was a smaller pool, and beyond it again Michael saw a maze, planted in laurel, through which the heads of white flowers peeped at irregular intervals. They looked like convolvulus.

The second pool was shaped like an arrow and pointed towards the maze, which struck Michael as somewhat odd. Halting beside it he noticed blue carp sliding ponderously through its depths, appearing from and disappearing under wide leafed, exotic looking flowers. They looked like water lilies, but he knew they weren't. Something clicked in his brain and he was instantly wary of them. Moving quickly away he had a momentary feeling of foreboding and all his senses came alive. *Keep your wits about you*, he admonished himself. *Everything you see here might be significant.*

The girl broke into his thoughts. "Now for your first task," she announced importantly, her chin lifting imperiously as she spoke "If you fail, you join the rest of us here until the next challenge is mounted."

Michael's fears began to flood in on him again, but the words of Jim Crow and his dad came to him, quickly dispelling his misgivings. Nevertheless, he felt he was not quite ready to proceed and, thinking they were trying to rush him, he decided to try and slow things up.

"Before we go ahead, perhaps you could tell me who you are and why you were chosen for your role in this."

"Don't procrastinate," the boy said.

"And don't be presumptuous," added the girl. "We never divulge anything about ourselves to people like you. Succeed in the first task and we might consider you worthy of our confidence. Fail and you will learn nothing about us."

"Now, listen carefully," her brother continued, "for I will only say this once. The door to the big house can only be opened by a special key. That key can be found in the centre of the maze fixed to a block of stone. If you manage to get that far you will have to find a way to detach the key from its holder. You will then be able to unlock the door to the big house. The second task awaits you inside.

"You will have sixty minutes in which to find and secure the key and escape from the maze. Failure to do so within the allotted time span means your challenge is over. I would warn you that whenever this task has been set before, no one has achieved the feat within the hour. *And*, I don't expect your attempt to be any different.

"One other thing I am instructed to tell you." He said this with obvious reluctance. "Solving the riddle of the maze will not be straightforward, so be wary of obstacles and be prepared to take action to overcome them. Do you understand that?"

Michael nodded.

"Very well. You have five minutes to prepare and then the clock starts to run down. Do you wish to ask me anything before you begin?"

"Where's the clock?" Michael asked, looking round him.

"I was speaking metaphorically," the boy answered. Because time passes so slowly here, normal timepieces are useless. We will be using an older method of time measurement."

"And that is?"

"You will discover that in due course. Trust me: it is just as accurate as any watch or any clock."

Michael wasn't sure he *could* trust him, but he had no choice in the matter. He felt there should be something else he should be asking. Again he had the feeling that everything was happening too fast. It seemed as if he were being rushed into something before he had time to consider his options. But then he decided that he was only trying to buy time again. There were no other options.

Accepting the situation, he said, "Thanks for the advice. If there's nothing more I need to know, I might as well begin."

"As you wish. Remember, five minutes and then the countdown begins." And with those parting words he went off to find his sister, who, pretending disinterest, had departed a few minutes before, leaving her twin to impart the final instructions.

With him gone, Michael was left to consider how to tackle what lay before him.

CHAPTER SEVEN

Michael didn't proceed to the entrance of the maze immediately. Instead, he hurried round to the front of the house to where he had spotted a bed of lavender. Plucking a number of shoots, he broke these up into small pieces and rubbed them between his fingers. A strong aroma was instantly released from the crushed herbs. Placing them in his handkerchief he moved to the fallen rose petals he had noticed earlier, and then to a trellis festooned with honeysuckle. At each stop he repeated the procedure, plucking and squeezing just a few bits of each flower before placing them along with the lavender in his handkerchief. When he had finished, he made the square of cotton into a ball by tying the four ends together. Sniffing the rich odours a couple of times, he satisfied himself that he had made an efficient nosegay.

Canis, who had accompanied him round the garden, barked twice as if she approved of his actions. When he placed the strong smelling bundle in a pocket, she darted away and returned a few seconds later with something in her mouth.

With his five minutes almost expired Michael set off for the maze. The dog trotted ahead of him and momentarily he thought she was going to accompany him inside. But at the entrance, she stopped and deposited the thing she was holding on the ground before him. It was a tiny wren, still alive and clearly none the worse for its experience, for the moment it was released it took flight and, chattering furiously, quickly disappeared into the leylandi.

Canis looked up at him and Michael patted her head in understanding, causing the animal to wag her tail furiously. The twins watched all this and said nothing and Michael knew he had been given a warning. About what, he wasn't sure, but he knew he would find out in due course.

There was no good luck chorus from the silent pair. They sat cross-legged on the grass watching him, a large hourglass about a foot high placed between them. Once Michael was through the entrance they would turn this over and the sand inside would begin to spill slowly from top to bottom. When the last grain had fallen, one hour would have elapsed and his time was up. His heart beating rapidly,

Michael stepped into the maze. As he did so the sky darkened in colour, causing him to hope it wasn't a bad omen.

With a finely cut carpet of grass beneath his feet, he set off down the first path. The hedges on either side of him were about three metres apart, room enough for two people to walk comfortably abreast. Their laurel leaves were dark green and very shiny, in contrast to the convolvulus clinging to them. The laurels must have been sturdy for, normally, convolvulus, or bindweed, as it is better known, choked many of the plants it wrapped itself round. Michael eyed the bindweed closely, especially its white flower, which seemed a particularly fine specimen, being larger than any he had seen before. He saw no reason for concern.

There was no variation in the maze walls for about twenty metres, then the path split in two. Michael hesitated for a second before deciding which way to go.

He thought he had read somewhere that in the Hampton Court maze if you took nothing but left hand turns this led you to the centre. He didn't know if this were true but it was a modus operandi and he thought he would use it until it proved to be false. On the basis that this maze would hardly be modelled exactly on the English one he changed the format and took the right hand lane. If this hypothesis turned out to be incorrect, he could easily return and start again at the other fork.

Three right hand turns later he came to a dead-end. Retracing his steps he took the left hand turn. In an even shorter time he was at an impasse and knew that the method required to reach the centre was utterly different to that of the alleged solution to the Hampton Court model. Once again he went back to where he had started. This time he decided he would go right, left, right, left and if that proved ineffective, he would reverse the order.

Five minutes later he was no further on. He began to use other permutations such as, one left and two right turns, and vice versa, all the while conscious that time was moving on.

None was successful.

He realised then that by sticking to a set pattern he would not solve the riddle. From now on he would have to proceed at random, taking turns or forks as the fancy took him. However, the problem with this trial-and-error approach was the danger that he might become confused and forget which turns he had already taken. He might even get lost and be unable to find his way back to his starting point.

He considered the problem. But not for long. Into his mind flashed the mythical tale of Ariadne and how she had helped her lover, Theseus escape the labyrinth built by Daedalus for King Minos. After Theseus had slain the Minotaur, a fabulous beast, half man, half bull, she had laid him a trail of glittering gems to show him the way out. This gave Michael an idea.

He removed first his windcheater, followed by the woolly sweater his mum had knitted him. Donning the windcheater again, he proceeded to loosen the stitches of the woollen garment at the end of one sleeve. Unravelling this to the shoulder, he then did the same thing with the other sleeve. Tying the two lengths of wool together, he quickly wound them into a ball. Next he fastened the loose end to a stem of laurel. Satisfied with his handiwork, he set off again, playing the wool out behind him. Now he couldn't get lost. Anytime his way was blocked all he had to do was backtrack using the trail he had laid to guide him. Then he could go off in a direction which he had not previously investigated. This worked very well, and by marking the entrance to each dead-end he came to with a plucked flower, he was able to eliminate routes he knew were not worth taking. Soon he was deeper into the maze than he had been before and was hopeful of reaching the centre in good time.

His spirits rising, he came to a straight path where, once again, a few metres on he saw a fork in the route. He had been on many sections like this, most of which had proved a hindrance to his progress, but this time he felt he was close to the end of his quest.

He was about to proceed as before when something fluttered in the grass ahead of him. It was a thrush. The bird was lying on its side, with one wing splayed at a peculiar angle, its speckled breast turned towards him. He was used to birds crashing into the front window of his house at home. Some broke a neck, some were just stunned and, on revival, flew away none the worse for their collision. The thrush must have flown into the laurel hedge and injured itself. He moved towards it, intent on lifting the hapless bird, but at the last second, some inner sense made him hesitate. It was then he remembered Canis and the wren.

He stopped. His warning antenna fully activated, he began to scan the area round the spot where the thrush was lying. The first thing he noticed was the grass. It wasn't cut quite as close at this point as anywhere else. The longer patch was about three metres square, with the bird located in the centre of it.

Wondering about this, he got down on his hands and knees and crawled cautiously forward, testing the ground with one hand as he went. At the edge of the longer area, he gently parted the grass with his fingers and discovered a thin line of soil stretching across the patch from hedge to hedge. Further exploration exposed other lines of earth at regular intervals and running at right angles to the first. These were about one third of a metre apart and it was clear what they signified. The grass here had been lifted in rectangular sods and then replaced. Whoever had done this had allowed the grass to grow a bit longer in order to conceal the fact.

Michael thought he knew why.

Snapping off a stem of laurel he quickly scraped out part of the soil round one sod. Inserting his fingers into the gap he had made he prised out a chunk of earth and grass. The first sod removed, he lifted a few others until he had cleared an area about a metre square. A hole in the ground was exposed.

As he was doing this, the thrush made a miraculous recovery. It skipped to its feet, its wing swung back into place, and it took off at speed up and over the top of the maze and out of his sight.

Michael removed a couple more sods to give himself a clear view of what lay beneath. By now he had exposed a fretwork of bamboo rods, ends sharpened and embedded in the earth about twenty centimetres down and attached to every side of the hole. The rods were there to support the sods.

Parting the bamboos, he peered down into the cavity. It was about four metres deep, its sides sheer. If he had stepped forward to aid the bird his weight would have taken him through the flimsy structure and down into the pit. The bird had been a decoy, and but for the warning given by Canis, it would have succeeded in luring him into a trap.

The pit would not have held him for long. It was not overly deep and, unless he had been injured in the fall, he would have been able to make foot and handholds in its side using the sharpened end of a bamboo rod. Climbing out would then have been a relatively simple operation.

For that reason he felt certain the purpose of the trap was not to incapacitate, but to delay him, and use up precious time. Ten or fifteen minutes lost trying to escape might be the difference between reaching or not reaching the core of the maze and then getting out with the key within the allotted hour.

One obstacle down, he thought. *How many more to come?*

Freeing the ends of the bamboo rods he could see, he pulled one out and prodded the remaining sods until they collapsed inwards bringing the remaining lengths of bamboo with them. He could now see the extent of the trap, which was no more than three metres long. Unwinding the wool to a length greater than the hole in the path, he tossed the ball over to the other side. Going back a few paces, he ran forward and leapt easily over the excavated patch to the firm ground beyond.

Picking up the ball of wool he moved on, all senses alert, looking for anything odd, while continuing to play out the wool as he went. He took the left hand fork on the path and soon came to a gap in the hedge to his right. He entered this, but it went nowhere.

Back he moved to the fork, rolling up the wool again, and took the right hand lane. A few metres along another gap opened up, this time on his left. Through he went and within ten paces he came to a spot where the path split three ways. Tiring of making deviations he went straight on. He turned a corner and there, no more than a dozen metres away, was the centre of the maze.

Wary now, after his previous experience with the concealed hole in the ground, he stopped and took stock of his surroundings.

He found he was looking at a perfect circle of ground, beautifully grassed and mown. The four hedges forming the circle were still of laurel, but their green leaves could hardly be seen, being covered almost completely by a mass of white flowers. In the centre of this stood a stone plinth about one metre high. Protruding from the top of this was a silver key.

He eyed the scene carefully, looking for danger. The first part of his task was at an end, but he knew there might be other obstacles to trip him up. If there were he wanted to be prepared for them.

He stood for a while longer, unwilling to proceed, scanning the whole area around the plinth, caution prevailing, loath to believe he could just walk across to it and lift out the key.

But hard as he tried, he could see nothing to cause him alarm. Being bullied at school had heightened his senses to danger, but no warning bell rang in his head and the only thing he thought slightly odd was the shape and size of the flowers. As he had noted before, they were bigger and more bell-shaped than any other convolvulus he had seen. Apart from that, the area within the circle was like any other patch of ground within the maze.

He went forward gingerly, pausing at the edge of the circle. One last look round and he moved hesitantly towards the key.

He had taken but three steps when he smelt the most wonderful aroma. The air within the circle was heavily perfumed. Immediately he felt drowsy and languid, and a sensation of utmost contentment began to envelop him.

The flowers, he thought, his head reeling. They're the same as those in the lily pond. But those weren't lilies, and these aren't convolvulus. He knew now what they were. Stepping back, he reached urgently for the nosegay is his pocket.

They were lotus flowers.

He remembered his Greek mythology – Odysseus and the Lotus eaters. The fruit of the lotus flower induced forgetfulness and a dreamy languor in those that consumed it, making them indifferent to their surroundings and purpose in life. Here there was no fruit, but the scent from their blooms was producing the same effect. A couple more inhalations and he would not have known where he was and in all likelihood would have fallen into a drugged sleep. The pond shaped like an arrow, pointing towards the maze, had been a sign indicating a connection between the two. The connection had been the lotus flowers. He had sensed there was something evil about them and had made his preparations on that basis.

He inhaled the scent given off by the nosegay, once, twice and then again. After breathing in the third time his head cleared.

Placing the little bag of scented petals over his mouth and nose, he once more stepped cautiously into the area polluted by the lotus flowers. Breathing gently, he found, as he had hoped, that the mixture of smells from his makeshift pot-pourri, cloaked the scent of the mind numbing plants. He walked slowly towards the plinth, ready to take flight at the first hint of drowsiness.

Reaching the centre, he inspected the structure before trying to remove the key, aware that there might be more traps in store. It was shaped like a pyramid. It had three sides, and was of a metal that looked like bronze. At its base there were three small feet, spread outward to give the structure support. Their shape looked familiar. Above one of the feet he could see some writing which he couldn't make out. The key was embedded in the apex of the pyramid.

When he was satisfied that there was no overt sign of danger, he reached forward and took hold of the key with his right hand. He tugged at it, trying to pull it out. It didn't budge.

He tried again.

Still he couldn't move it.

He placed the nosegay on the ground. Holding his breath and using both hands he tried once more. It resisted all his attempts to free it.

Retrieving the nosegay, he pressed it to his face once more. Stepping back he gave the problem some thought. Nothing came to mind. He inspected the top of the plinth. The key was held in a narrow slit like the jaws of a vice. There had to be some way to open them. The trouble was he couldn't think of one.

He walked round the structure. Kneeling, he felt every part of its surface, searching for a switch or something that seemed incongruous. He found nothing.

While he was bent down he was able to make out the tiny lettering on the sides. It read, *HE WHO DARES WINS*. It was the motto of the Special Air Service.

That puzzled him. He knew it must mean something, but he didn't know what. It seemed to make no sense.

He wracked his brains, trying to make a connection between the motto and his problem. Words of his dad's filtered through to him again. When something is couched in elliptical terms, think laterally.

All very wise, he thought, *but not much use if lateral thoughts fail to materialise.*

He tried again. Eyeing the plinth, he studied it bit by bit. Perhaps there was a hidden panel in it. He inspected the surface again, searching for the slightest groove, mark or indentation.

Nothing.

He tried twisting the top where the key was embedded; pushed at it to see if it would move sideways; pulled at it to see if it would slide out.

No success.

In despair he turned his attention to the feet – the oddly shaped feet – the only things he hadn't really examined. He studied them more closely, and a zephyr of understanding flitted through his brain. Then it was gone,

He tried to recall what it was. He couldn't.

It had to do with something he had seen – something normally barred to him. The frisson had undertones of guilt, which was probably why he couldn't remember it.

What could it be? His mind was a fever of frustration. What could it be?

And then he had it.

It was a television programme – seen on an occasion when his dad was away from home. His mum had permitted him to visit his friend Maxie. Maxie's family had been watching something called, *Only Fools And Horses*. The main character had been someone called

Delboy. Delboy had used as his catchphrase the SAS motto inscribed on the plinth.

Now he knew what the peculiar-looking supports were. They were in the shape of pig's feet, or trotters. The surname of Delboy and his family was Trotter.

That was the connection.

Quickly dropping to his knees he ran his hand round each one. They seemed set solidly on the ground – immoveable. He did the same again, looking for a switch.

No switch.

As he had done with the key, he pushed at each one, he pulled at each one.

Nothing happened.

"The answer lies with them," he muttered. "It has to. But what is it?"

Almost as an afterthought he tried to raise the nearest foot. It didn't move. He tried the next one. It was solid on the ground. In despair he put a finger behind the last one and tugged upwards. And it moved. Just a centimeter, and not enough to unsettle or tilt the plinth. He looked closer and noticed something different about it. Unlike the others, it was hinged, the workmanship so fine that it was hardly noticeable. With this foot, all the weight was being taken by the heel and there was a slight gap between the toes and the grass. He inserted two fingers in the gap and prised upwards. The foot moved again, more than the first time, and, almost at the same moment, something hit him on the head.

He stood up and looked at the vice. It was open and the key was gone. Glancing down, he spotted it at his feet. A great wave of elation engulfed him, and he punched the air, while at the same time, emitting a muffled shout of triumph and relief through the nosegay.

The moment of euphoria quickly passed and he almost felt ashamed at his outpouring of emotion and the accompanying loss of control. It was too soon to be celebrating. He still had to get free of the maze within the time limit. More pragmatic considerations were the order of the day.

As he picked up the key there was an abatement of the light. He looked up to see an immense cloud moving swiftly across the sky. It was falling at an astonishing rate, a dark grey mass, and it was aimed directly at the maze. It would be upon him in seconds.

Thrusting the key into a pocket, he rushed from the ring. Once clear, he returned the nosegay to his pocket and just had time to grasp the, by now diminished ball of wool, which he had left lodged in the hedge, before the cloud was all around him, cold and clammy and reducing visibility to only a couple of paces. It was worse than a London smog.

A few steps on and he was utterly blind and completely disoriented. Keeping close to the laurels and feeling his way along, he knew that if he hadn't thought of using the wool as a means of guiding himself out, he would soon have been completely lost,

Carefully keeping the string taut by rolling it into a ball as he proceeded, he soon arrived at the strait where he knew the pit to be. He snailed his way forward, crawling the last few metres on hands and knees until he came to the edge. So dense was the fog that he could not see the pit, never mind the far side of it, and only his groping hands told him that it was there. Standing again, he threw the ball of wool well in front of him. Then he took a few careful steps back, counting out the number of paces as he did so. Pausing only to crouch slightly, he raced forward and, one stride short of the number he had counted, he hurled himself into space as far as he could. Unable to see where he was going, he landed in an ungainly heap on the other side, winding himself in the process. But that was the least of his worries and, at least, he was clear of the last obstacle.

When he got his breath back, he groped around until he retrieved the wool. It had become a bit tangled during its flight and fall, so he straightened it out and, taking up the slack, regained his feet. Still keeping it taut, and continuing to roll it up as he went along, he moved cautiously through the gaps and forks, the twists and turns of the maze, working his way steadily towards the exit.

When he came to the point where he had tied the end of the wool to the laurel hedge, he knew he was in the final stretch. And miraculously, as if the final card had been dealt in a losing hand, the mist lifted and the way ahead was clear.

Speed was now of the essence and he sprinted the remaining distance, the big house now partly visible in the gap through which he had taken the first cautious steps to commence his search for the key.

Only one thing now concerned him. During his time in the maze, he had been so consumed with finding a route to the centre and overcoming the various obstacles to his progress, that he had put the time factor to the back of his mind. Now that those were behind him, the period he had spent inside became all-important. Any delight in his achievement would be completely nullified if the sixty minutes had elapsed. And so preoccupied had he been with the problems he had faced, that he had no idea how long he had spent trying to solve them.

Bursting into the open, the gardens and the big house materialized before him, all bathed in a purple light. Frantically he scanned the area where he had last seen the twins. They weren't there. Canis hadn't moved. She lay prone, eyes fixed on the spot where he had gone from her view. At his appearance she sat up and pricked her ears.

And then he spotted them. They were in the shade of a large, copper beech tree about fifty metres away. The hourglass sat on the grass between them. At that distance he could not make out if it was empty. He ran towards them, fervently hoping he was in time, the dog racing at his heels. He got closer. Soon he was at the point where he could see the timepiece perfectly. His heart leapt.

The sand was still flowing.

The twins sat up. Like Canis, they looked at him expectantly.

Slowing almost to a halt, he lowered his head and allowed his shoulders to droop. Putting on his most woebegone expression, he dragged his way disconsolately towards them.

Canis lay down. Placing her head between her front feet, and with ears drooping, she emitted a low, doleful whine.

The twins were up in an instant, their faces animated and lacking concern. Their doubts about him had obviously been realised.

He stopped. Allowing them to get within a few paces of him, he drew the key from his pocket and tossed it into the air.

Before he could catch it, Canis was on her feet and hurtling towards him. Jumping into his arms she bowled him over and he fell to the grass laughing, her tongue licking any exposed bit of flesh she could find.

When he finally managed to sit up, the girl had the key. She handed it to him solemnly. Not a word was spoken by her or her brother; not a congratulatory comment, not an expression of satisfaction at a job well done. For once, they had nothing to say.

As he looked at the silent pair, Michael felt his energy begin to drain away. He hadn't realised how much stress he had been under since arriving in this strange world, and now that the first task was complete, the adrenaline that had sustained him until now was exhausted; and so was he. It had been a long day for him and it seemed it might not yet be over. The key to the big house had been secured and the next task loomed.

He knew he was in no state to tackle it. He needed to rest, to recoup his energies. If the problems posed by the maze were any pointer, then he would have to be at his best, both mentally and physically. The shady patch where the twins had been resting looked inviting.

He turned away. "See you later," he said tiredly, and trudged across to it.

Finding a comfortable spot, he lay down and closed his eyes. Canis, who had accompanied him, settled down by his side and laid her head on his chest. He put an arm round her and, almost instantly, fell asleep. The twins watched him for a time; then they walked away, still silent, their manner subdued, their expressions inscrutable. They looked as if they had much to think about.

As the boy slept, the colour of the sky softened to twilight.

CHAPTER EIGHT

When Michael wakened he felt completely refreshed. His sleep had been dreamless, or, at least, he had no recollection of having dreamed.

Canis was nowhere to be seen.

The twins were a few feet away from him sitting cross-legged. They appeared thoughtful, almost subdued, as if something was troubling them.

"How long have I been asleep?" he asked.

"Ten minutes."

"Two hours."

"Ten minutes in our time."

"Two hours in yours."

Their rat-a-tat method of delivery hadn't changed. "What now?" he enquired.

"Indeed, what now," the girl said. "We've had a discussion. We've made a decision. We think you should know a little more about us."

"Do you think I'm worthy?" Michael replied with heavy irony.

"We consider you have earned the right," she continued, missing entirely the pointed nature of Michael's reply. "I'm Paula and my brother's name is Paul. Jim Crow, if that's his name, called you Mikey, but I'm sure you feel that's being familiar and would rather not be addressed as some form of abbreviation. We'll refer to you as, Michael."

The boy took over from her, neither of them asking if the method of address was all right with him. Michael thought their sense of self-importance was staggering. Nevertheless, he was interested in what they had to say, so he didn't make an issue of the matter.

"We were child prodigies," the boy announced immodestly, "born in 1963. At the age of three we could read and write; at four we were learning to play the violin and piano. As a result of our precocity, one year later, we were sent to a private academy dealing specifically with children of exceptional intellect and talents.

Our father was an expert in electronics, our mother a mathematics teacher. Each evening, when they returned home from work, and we were back from school, they inculcated us into the mysteries of their

77

chosen fields.

"On our eighth birthday, mother removed us from school and began to teach us at home. She felt we were not being stretched enough at the private academy and were becoming bored.

"The same year we were earmarked for Oxford, the entrance examination to be taken by us when we were ten. But that didn't happen. One year later father was headhunted by Hewlett-Packard in California. You *have* heard of them?"

Michael nodded, and decided to unsettle them a bit. "William Hewlett and David Packard set up an electronics company in Palo Alto, California in 1938. Their success led ultimately to the creation of Silicon Valley. Hewlett Packard have developed many of the technological innovations of the last sixty years – audio oscillators, electronic pocket calculators, desk-top calculators, and some of the first personal computers. It is one of the most successful companies ever formed. Is that enough for you, or do you want more?"

The boy looked miffed at Michael's knowledge. Momentarily silenced, his sister saw her chance and quickly took over the narrative.

"Our father was a highly thought of innovator, and the salary offered to him was far in excess of anything he could have expected to receive in Britain, but, more importantly, the research facilities were the most advanced anywhere in the world and that's what really attracted him. So the family moved to America and settled in Woodside. Do you know about Woodside?"

Reluctantly, Michael shook his head.

The girl smirked. "You should do. It's just the wealthiest town in America. Of course, it hadn't that status when we moved there in the 1970's, but the high-tech revolution has made a lot of people in Silicon Valley very rich, and father is one of them." She almost seemed to swell as she boasted about this, taking pride in her good fortune. Looking overly pleased with herself, she continued. "He introduced us to the world of computers and even got the Company to install one in our home just for our use. He bought us electronic components and gave us a selection of manuals. Within a year we had built one for ourselves. And we were only *twelve* years old.

"That same year we began to write software codes. Unknown to our parents we even went into business and, under a pseudonym, made $20,000 on a computer program to regulate traffic in and around Woodside."

"Why did you keep it a secret?" Michael asked innocently.

"Because if our parents had known, they would have insisted on it going towards our university fees. We'd been accepted by Princeton and were due to start there in the fall. We couldn't have that because we needed the money as capital for further research. We were able to buy parts and materials, and with further experimentation, we created the kernel of a new computer operating system, in effect, the brains of a computer which could control the hardware and organise the programs. This would have revolutionised the whole hi-tech industry and, with it, created the prototype of today's PC.

Michael, his mind reeling, listened to this in growing amazement "Well, why didn't it?" he enquired tetchily, his voice rising.

"It did," the boy interrupted his sister. "But we'll come to that in a minute." He paused, collecting his thoughts. "We did all this in our rooms without telling our parents. Oh, they knew we were up to something, but they weren't aware we were developing something so advanced. They knew we would tell them in due course. That's the way things worked in our house. We could consult them about things and they would give us pointers, but we were expected to work our problems out by ourselves and, only when that was done, present the solution or, finished project, to them. This wasn't always possible and sometimes they had to help us. Their hands-off role was to teach us intellectual independence. In this case we knew we could complete it without their aid, and the piece of work had such major ramifications that we wanted to surprise them with the finished product. Only we never got the chance."

"Why not?"

"The completion of our enterprise coincided with the school holidays. Mother, who had begun teaching again, was free for the summer, so she whisked us away to Florida for a couple of months. She thought it would be good for us to take a break before starting university. Father was in Washington advising a Senate committee on new developments in the electronic industry and would join us in a month's time.

"While he was there he met a young man who was up from Seattle for the summer working as a Senate messenger. When he heard about my father's presence, he introduced himself, saying he was interested in computers and information technology. Father must have been impressed by his knowledge for he brought the youth back with him to Hewlett-Packard to give him some work experience and see how things were done there.

"We learned about this after father phoned mother to tell her the young man was staying in Woodside with him for a few days and would be sleeping in my bedroom. Naturally, when mother relayed the news to us we were furious. All our research was filed in our two rooms and there was a lot of information we needed to keep private. But because we didn't want mother to know about our invention, having decided to unveil it the next time the whole family was at home together, we made no objections to the interloper invading our territory. We were sure, anyhow, that if he looked at what we had done he would be baffled by its complexity."

The girl, who had been fidgeting on the sidelines, took over again.

"That same day something occurred that made our concerns about the young man seeing our work irrelevant.

"Within a week of arriving in Florida we'd mastered the technique of windsurfing; most things come naturally to us, and that afternoon we were out on the bay about a hundred yards from shore using the wind to take us round a buoy, one of a number utilised as exercise markers for more accomplished surfers. As we reached this we noticed the sky was beginning to cloud over. Although it hadn't been forecast, it was obvious a storm was brewing.

"We rounded the marker and headed for the beach, only to discover it was deserted and all the other windsurfers had disappeared. At that point we thought they must have noticed the impending storm clouds before us and taken evasive action.

"We were no more than ten yards from the buoy when a gust of wind at our backs hit us with tremendous force. It drove us forward at frightening speed and then, inexplicably, turned completely round and almost capsized us. Fortunately we managed to stay upright, but to remain afloat we had to run with the elements, with the result we were being swept out to sea.

"All this time we'd been no more than twenty yards apart, but as the tempest turned us, we drifted closer together. And, would you believe it, at that instant something appeared in the water swimming beside us. At first, we thought it was a dolphin, but then we saw it was a dog."

Michael sensed what was coming.

"We didn't have time to take this amazing event in, for on the horizon and bearing down on us at an enormous rate was a waterspout.

"As we rushed towards the spout our surfboards drew even closer together until we were no more than a couple of yards apart, with the dog still sandwiched between them.

"By now we were powerless to influence the direction of our

craft. All we could do was run with the storm and try to stay afloat. But by doing that we were heading straight for the waterspout.

"And, of course, the inevitable happened.

"As we got closer and closer, the sky turned purple and the sea whipped up into a frenzy. Then the spout was upon us and we were grabbed by the wind, which was howling like a dervish, and sucked into the swirling mass of water – up and up to its zenith, Paul, the dog and I, all fighting to breathe in an inner tube of spume saturated air. And, just as we thought we would be shot out of the top, we halted, and began to descend. In a dizzying spiral we were swept downwards at mind-boggling speed. Both Paul and I thought the end of our lives had come. But it was not to be. Just as we reached the bottom of the twisting spout, we blacked out.

"When we came to we found ourselves in this stupid place and in the same predicament as you."

"And the dog was, Canis," Michael said, "and she was here too."

"Exactly," the boy confirmed. "And we now know she was responsible for bringing us here. If I could get hold of her I'd give her a good kicking."

"If you did, you might find yourself in a worse spot than you are now. As you said, that dog brought you here. It might just have the power to transport you elsewhere, and to a less salubrious place."

"I still think I'd risk it," he rejoined petulantly."

Michael shrugged, irritated by the boy's childishness. He decided to change the subject. "And your new technology, what happened to it?"

"Haven't you worked that out, you being so clever?"

"I couldn't even begin to."

"Well, I'll tell you."

"No, let me," the girl said impatiently.

"No, I want to do it."

"Compromise, then?"

"All right, compromise."

"Together."

"Together."

"Okay."

Once again they began to speak in unison, their piping voices blending into one.

"You're probably aware that it's possible for us to keep up-to-date with what's happening in the real world through our dreams. Well, three months after we arrived here, we learned that our computer system with its attendant software was launched on the world, and the person who did this was the young man who came to our house and slept in one of our rooms. Unknown to father he must either have taken all our papers away with him or copied the relevant parts onto floppy disks."

"And what was the name of this system? Surely I must know it."

"Of course you do; everyone does. We were going to call ours Microtech. He called his Microsoft. Coincidence, do you think?"

Astonished, Michael stammered, "You d'don't mean———?

"Yes, we do. Bill Gates was the person who came home with father. He stole our ideas, our research, everything, and launched our blueprint for the world-wide web. All the credit he got should have been ours."

Recovering his equilibrium, Michael said, "I suppose you'll say the money he's made should be yours as well."

"Certainly. By right we should be worth billions by now."

So, all the time you've been here you've been watching him get richer and richer, more and more famous, and you haven't been able to do a thing about it."

"Galling, it's been, utterly galling."

"If it had been me I'd have gone crazy," Michael said. "What did you do to stop thinking about it?"

"Occupied our time as best we could."

"You weren't bored?" Michael enquired, genuinely interested, knowing he might soon be in the same position.

"Of course we were, of course we are, of course we will be, every day of our lives. Time hangs so heavy here."

"But it's so lovely – all the flowers and shrubs, and so many unusual species. Surely you could find something to do with them – paint them or catalogue them, there must be many that are extinct at home."

"Boredom, ennui, tedium," they shrilled.

"But you must do something to pass the time?"

"We exercise the mind. We play chess; we work out mathematical formulae and theorems; we calculate capacities; we could tell you the cubic capacity of the big house. We work out prime numbers – we know every prime number between one and a trillion. If we were at home that would put us in the Guinness book of records. We've become experts in statistical analysis and probability theory; we understand Einstein's Theory of Relativity. We read the books in the big house, especially those that deal with arcane scientific subjects.

We study the works of the Greek scholars, Pythagoras, Euclid, Archimedes and reconstruct their experiments. We debate the respective merits of the great astronomers and mathematicians; and we argue and argue and argue. In our proper time we would be among the most famous people on earth, known world-wide and advising presidents and governments and kings. We would be recognized as scientific giants and the greatest inventors of our age. Now, does that satisfy you?" they ended stridently.

Michael studied them for a moment, noting their faces, which were etched with distaste. He marvelled at their arrogance. They had just assumed he would want to hear about them, whether he wanted to or not. Their vanity and capacity for self-promotion were astounding. Like Mohammed Ali, in their own minds they were the greatest. Well, they were about to discover that wasn't the case.

Suddenly tired of their bombast, he got to his feet. "Do you know something," he said. "You two remind me of Jedediah Buxton. You've heard of him, I expect."

They looked at him blankly.

"Obviously not. Well, Jedediah Buxton was an eighteenth century prodigy, a bit like yourselves. On being taken to the theatre for the first time to see a performance of Richard the Third, he was asked afterwards if he had enjoyed it. For over two hours he had been treated to a masterpiece of drama by the greatest playwright the world has known – and do you know how he replied?"

Again they looked baffled.

"He said that there were 5,202 steps during the dances, and 12,445 words spoken by the actors. As I say, he was like the pair of you. He didn't have a soul either."

Michael walked away from them. After a few paces he stopped. Looking back, he said as if in afterthought, "Oh, by the way, I didn't believe a word of that yarn you spun about your invention being stolen by Bill Gates. According to you, you were twelve years old when Canis brought you here. As you were born in 1963, that made it 1975 when you arrived and just before you were about to make your great work public. I hate to tell you this, but Bill Gates formed Microsoft in 1974, a year before you claim to have put together Microtech.

"And one other thing. In 1970, when he was only fifteen, he sold a computer program for $20,000. It related to traffic congestion in Seattle. Sounds familiar doesn't it? Or is that just coincidence?"

He strolled on towards the big house. Glancing back once, he saw that they were dumbstruck. They stared after him, shoulders slumped, the picture of dejection.

Their lies had been exposed. He almost felt sorry for them.

CHAPTER NINE

The facade of the big house was impressive. There was an eye-catching portico with four, white columns which seemed to have been built of Portland stone, or something akin to it. The columns were Doric, heavily fluted, with each one lacking a normal square base. The mighty door giving entrance to the building was made of black oak.

As Michael approached it, the door swung open to reveal a stocky man with a flat, Slav face. To Michael's eyes he was in his late twenties and a few years younger than Jim Crow.

He was dressed in a peculiar fashion. He wore a tight-fitting vest and white tights, with what looked like pink underpants over them. He was muscular and fit.

"No need for key, Michael. I have spoken with twins. I know you solved riddle of maze." The man spoke with a strange accent, which Michael thought might be East European. "You give it me now."

Michael passed the key over to him, almost reluctant to let it go, seeing it had been so hard to obtain.

"How you like our friends, Paul and Paula?" the man asked, his eyes twinkling.

Not sure how to respond, Michael shrugged his shoulders and raised his eyebrows.

The man laughed. "Left you without speech, eh?"

Encouraged, Michael smiled. "Almost. I just don't know what to make of them. They hate this place yet they seem to want me to fail. If I fail they don't get out. Their attitude doesn't make sense. Where I come from there is a saying for it – cutting one's nose off to spite one's face."

"Where I come from we have explanation for it too. They like scorpion in fable of scorpion and frog. You know that olden fable?"

Michael wasn't sure.

Seeing the boy's hesitancy, the strangely garbed man said, "I tell you then. Scorpion was at bank of river it wished to cross, but could not swim. It asked nearby frog to take it over on frog's back. Frog said it would if scorpion not sting it to death. Scorpion promised not to sting frog. Half-way across scorpion sting frog. Dying frog start to sink, but before both go under water, it asks Scorpion why it did this knowing both would die. It's in my nature, Scorpion replies."

The man gazed at Michael, his face serious. "You take point?"

"I take point. It's in their nature to be contrary," he replied.

The man laughed again. Then he clapped his hands and looked business-like. "Now, Michael, I Yuri Gorbachev. I from circus family. I chosen to come here because I good at many things."

Now Michael understood why his new companion was in vest and tights. He noted again the Slav eyes and square shaped head. "Are you Russian?" he asked.

"I Russian," came the proud reply. "I from St. Petersburg. Later it called Petrograd, then Leningrad after Vladimir Ilyich Ulyanov. Long name; he later change to Lenin. You know that?"

Michael nodded.

"You boy who knows history – that very good."

"What did you do in the circus?"

"I do all sorts, but mostly I tumbler; you call it acrobat. I taught very young by parents. I very good. Today I win gold medal in Olympic Games as gymnast; become famous as Olga Korbut. But in circus you not just one thing. I also minature clown; I ride horses bareback and jump through balloon, now called paper hoop. Also animal trainer, flyer on trapeze and bender."

"What's a bender?"

"Contortionist. I not so good now, not so supple."

"Did you perform in a big tent?" Michael enquired, eyes shining.

Yuri laughed. "No, that modern way. Russian circus take place in special building with big arena. Circus performers highly thought of in Russia, like ballet, so have permanent site. But I perform in other places too, other countries – Germany, France, Great Britain, and once in United States of America. I meet Buffalo Bill and Annie Oakley," he finished proudly.

"And when did you arrive here – in my time?" Michael added hastily.

"Since more than one hundred years. Canis bring me after I drive troika on to ice."

Michael looked baffled.

I explain. I use circus horses without permission to pull troika. Very naughty. I drive beside river Neva. It frozen. Big wind get up and startle horses. They break traces and wind blow me on to ice. It springtime and ice thin. Canis jumps in troika and we fall through into very cold water. I cannot get out. I think I drown. Next thing I know we both in this place."

"You seem happy enough about it."

"Very happy. Dreams show me things I never know if I stay in Russia. Learn many things since I come. Live in three centuries, see many strangenesses, see how world change. Very nice place to be."

"You don't blame the wizard for taking you from your home?"

"Circus people have no home: home where we give next performance."

"But surely there are things you miss."

Yuri looked thoughtful. "Yes," he said slowly, "I miss things. I miss sky; here it just change colour and there are few colours. In Russia, sky different every day. I miss clouds, I miss sun, I miss stars – Cassiopeia, Orion, Milky Way. I miss full moon on frosty night. But that small sacrifice to make for dreams."

"Have you ever seen the wizard?"

"No one sees wizard, except, perhaps the gentleman from England. And then, only once, I think. Wizard only communicate with him. He tell us wizard's desires. That all we need to know."

"Will you be happy to leave if I'm successful with the other tasks?"

"Happy to stay, happy to go, happy anywhere. I am good circus performer. I make good living no matter where I am. I happy man."

Michael thought so too. There was something childlike about him, an innocence that was in complete contrast to the devious twins.

"Now, Michael, I show you house, and then I tell you about next task."

They were in a reception area, adorned with expensive looking furniture. Persian rugs lay on a black and white tiled floor. The Russian walked Michael towards a set of stairs in the centre of the large room. Black, wrought-iron railings, with ornate twists and curlicues, swept upwards to a landing which branched right and left at the top. The stairs were covered in a plush and very heavy carpet with a purple and red design.

On the wall of the landing, facing directly down the staircase, was an oil painting of a lion. It was accompanied on either side by a long Canaletto, each painting encased in a broad gold frame. Both scenes were of St. Mark's Square, which was appropriate, the lion being the symbol of Venice. Dark brown panelling covered the walls.

At the foot of the stairs Yuri did something surprising. He put his hands on the first step and proceeded to execute a perfect handstand. Then he began to walk up the staircase, feet waving in the air for balance.

A bemused Michael followed along behind him.

At the top, the Russian did a flip-flop on to his feet and, hardly out of breath, grinned at the incredulous expression on Michael's face. "Fine way to keep fit," he said.

Turning left, he led Michael along a few metres and then up another stairway of ten steps to a point where the iron railing ended. A number of doors, all made of the same dark oak as the front one, confronted them on the upper landing.

He proceeded to tour the house, introducing the boy to each room. Some were bedrooms, one was a library, well stocked, another a bathroom on the first floor, with shower and Jacuzzi. On going downstairs, he discovered a twin of this adjacent to an indoor swimming pool. There was also a very large dining room, an equally large drawing room and a music room containing two pianos, placed back to back, each with an attendant music stand, which suggested cello or violin accompaniment to the pianists. Each room was exquisitely furnished.

On the ground floor there was also a fully equipped gymnasium, and in an annexe off this, a weights room. All the equipment was modern. "I work body here every day," Yuri informed Michael.

Finally, they came to a kitchen, fitted out in mahogany, and with every conceivable appliance. Here, Yuri stopped. "Small test for you, Michael," he announced, walking towards a table on which sat a crock of eggs. "Twelve in crock, six rotten. Find rotten eggs without breaking any. That, first part. Second, I tell you if you successful with first."

"If I fail, can I still tackle the next task?"

"Sad to say, no. Little tests all part of qualification for big tests."

Michael knew what to do, having read about this in a Physics book at his local library.

He carried the crock of eggs over to the sink unit and set them on the draining board. Yuri watched him with interest, saying nothing.

Michael put the plug in the sink and began to fill it with water. When it was half full, he turned off the tap and, one by one, carefully placed the eggs in the water. When he had finished, six eggs lay on the bottom and six were bobbing on the surface. He removed the floating eggs and put them back in the crock. "These are the rotten ones," he said.

"How I know you right?" Yuri asked.

"Stale eggs float, fresh eggs sink," Michael replied. "Do you want me to crack one open to prove it?"

"No, no," Yuri said hastily. "You right, of course."

"And the second part of the test?" Michael enquired.

"I use your words. "Why stale eggs float, why fresh eggs sink?""

"It's quite simple. If you look at an egg you'll see one end is rounder than the other. Inside the egg at this end there is a tiny air bubble. As the egg gets older it loses water to the atmosphere and more air is drawn in through the shell to replace it. This air gives the egg buoyancy. The older it is the more buoyant it becomes. All rotten eggs have a more than normal amount of air in them. Fresh eggs containing little air won't float."

Michael took one of the eggs from the crock and placed it back in the water where once again it floated. "Quod erat demonstrandum," he said.

Yuri clapped his hands. "Very good. Tests passed. Now for real thing. Come with me."

The kitchen was spacious and Yuri did two backward somersaults towards the door. Opening this, he again did a handstand and, upside down, proceeded ahead of Michael down a corridor to the reception area. Michael was beginning to get used to the Russian's eccentric behaviour and, amused by the man's peculiarity, followed on behind.

Michael's amusement didn't last long. When Yuri, upright once more and serious faced, started to outline the nature of the task, Michael grew tense, and the by now familiar anxieties began to manifest themselves. Anger at his dad for inadvertently placing him in this position began to flare up again.

The reception area was large, a purple light flooding in through the casement windows, making it seem even bigger. Yuri walked to a wall and flicked a switch. Immediately, shutters came down over each window and the light vanished, leaving them encased in gloom. Yuri hit another switch, and two chandeliers, one directly above their heads, the other suspended from the ceiling on the first landing, lit the place with brilliant intensity.

Edgy now, Michael waited to hear what was in store for him. It was like the minutes before sitting an examination; the not knowing what had been set and if he was capable of answering the questions. He waited, trying to control his nerves.

"Second task easy to explain, Michael," Yuri said. "House now like fortress. No egress through doors or windows. Only one way out. You to find it. Like first task, time set for completion. When shutters rise again to let in light, time up. If you not finished by then, you fail."

"How long will that be?" Michael blurted out, his voice higher than normal and betraying his anxiety.

"Not know exactly; only wizard knows. Few hours, perhaps; perhaps less. Only know task hard. I could not do it. But then, I only tumbler, clown, high wire artiste. I not good at books" As he uttered the last sentence he gave a huge wink.

"Where's Canis?" Michael asked, hoping the dog would be allowed to keep him company and maybe give him some guidance.

As if reading his thoughts, the Russian said, "Canis not allowed in. Might nose and sniff and discover something to help you. That not permitted. Will stay outside until task completed, or not completed, as case may be."

Michael experienced a sense of disappointment. Already he was beginning to feel isolated. With the dog around, willing him to succeed, at least he would have had a bit of moral support.

His mood darkened. As before, he felt he was being rushed. Again, everything seemed to be happening too quickly. He was being given no time to reflect on what had happened to him, no time to relax, savour his recent success. Two hours after the last task and here he was faced with another one. Doubts assailed him. He wondered if he was ready for it. Perhaps his mental powers were exhausted by his tussle with the maze and he would not be able to do himself justice. He felt a rising sense of panic.

Control yourself, a voice said in his head. It sounded familiar, just like Lucy's; but then that couldn't be.

He breathed deeply and the moment passed. And with it came a realisation that being rushed was probably not an accident and was done to make the task more difficult for him; just another test to see if he could operate under stress. And with that realisation, his nerves settled and he felt ready for what lay ahead.

"Is there nothing more you can tell me?" he asked and was pleased to hear his voice was steady.

Yuri was studying him. He nodded his head as if satisfied. "Know no more," he replied. "Rest up to you. Be cheerful. This not bad place if you not succeed. Think well. You solved riddle of maze. Have confidence you solve this. Have faith in brain. Is good."

And with that final word of encouragement he suddenly pulled Michael to his chest and gave the boy a bone-crunching hug. Then, turning abruptly, he hurried to the big door, the key appearing as if by magic in one hand. A few seconds later he was outside and Michael heard the sound of the key being turned in the lock.

CHAPTER TEN

Michael gazed round him helplessly. How was he to find a way out? The house was so big. Where would he start? What would he look for; a trap door, a way to the roof, a secret panel? And if there was one of these, where would he find it, and would he recognise it if he did? At least with the maze he had something to work with, the wool from his sweater, the warning from Canis, the SAS motto on the plinth. Here he was starting with nothing to help him. True, Yuri had closed one eye when he said he wasn't good with books, but Michael was not at all sure that meant anything. He might have been affected by a smut, or the wink was merely a mannerism. He hadn't known Yuri long enough to know.

But he had to start somewhere. Despite the previous conquering of his anxiety, alarm began to surge in him. He made a conscious effort to quell it. *Make panic your friend,* undercover soldiers were told. *Harness it; make it work for not against you. Panic means adrenaline. Put it to something purposeful, and don't let it become a negative factor. Negativity destroys clear thinking and positive action.*

He breathed deeply, once, twice and then again. He felt his nerves steady. *Try logic,* a voice inside him said. The same voice as before. *Be methodical; try not to think that time is important. You don't know how much you've got, so forget about it.*

With that advice drumming in his ears, he decided on a modus operandi. He would scan each room, just in case there was something obvious that would help with his problem. He didn't expect there to be, but sometimes solutions were under one's nose and he couldn't afford to ignore the fact.

So, starting on the ground floor, he went from room to room. All were shuttered, all were brightly lit.

In the room housing the swimming pool and jacuzzi, he found the controls operating the flow of water to each. He hit the switch that would empty them and moved on. In the drawing room he found pens, pencils and writing paper. In the music room he discovered the pianos were Steinways. In the kitchen, the many cupboards he opened yielded nothing more than the usual crockery and cooking utensils, while in a children's play-room, he saw a rocking horse, soft toys,

Mickey Mouse wallpaper and a selection of children's books. Nowhere did he see anything that looked like an escape route.

Upstairs, he tried the five bedrooms. Each was furnished in a different style of art; one contained works of the modern painters – Picasso, the Dadaists and the like, another was art deco, a third housed paintings by eminent Pre-Raphaelites – Millais, Rossetti, Holman Hunt. In the fourth he found Monet, Renoir and Pissaro to the fore, with the walls decorated with exquisite examples of impressionism. The last bedroom was given over to the works of Constable and Turner and these pleased his eye in a manner the others couldn't, especially the works of Constable. They struck a chord with his love of the outdoors.

Each painting he saw looked like the real thing, but his head told him they were probably forgeries, there being much about the strange world he was in that hinted at mystery and camouflage.

When his tour was over he was no closer to solving his problem.

Returning to the swimming pool and jacuzzi, which were now drained, he inspected the outlet systems hoping there was a way out by that means. There wasn't.

He had but one room left to search and that he left to the last, for his instincts told him that this was where the solution to the task was most likely to lie.

On the way there he stopped off in the drawing room and collected a writing pad and a couple of pens.

Armed with these he entered the library, the centrepiece of which was a long, oak table with six Queen Anne chairs placed around it. One book, unopened, lay on its polished surface. An hour had now passed since he'd begun his tour of the house and he felt as if he had made no progress whatsoever. In that time he had not seen a single thing to suggest a way forward. Again he thought of Yuri's wink. By now he was willing to believe it meant something and, if so, then the answer he was seeking was within the four walls now surrounding him.

The library was bulging with books, thousands of them, stacked floor to ceiling in elongated bookcases along two facing walls. A tall ladder, with split supports, gave a means of access to the tomes on the upper shelves. Like his public library at home, the books were categorised under headings – Biography, Autobiography, Science, Economics, Thrillers, Westerns, General Fiction, Poetry, and so on.

A feeling of helplessness came over him. There were so many titles they almost made him feel dizzy. Hitler's, Mein Kampf;

Churchill's, History Of The English Speaking Peoples; Gibbon's, History Of The Decline And Fall Of The Roman Empire; Adam Smith's, Wealth Of Nations; The Complete Works Of William Shakespeare; Canons by the great philosophers, scientists, astronomers, mathematicians; novels by Scott, by Thackeray, by Austen, by the Bronte sisters, by Rowling and by all the modern thriller writers; poetry by Shelley and Wordsworth and Longfellow and Keats and the moderns like Hughes and Heaney. The writings seemed endless. His task seemed impossible. "Where do I start?" he groaned aloud.

Immediately he admonished himself. "Stop it," he scolded aloud. "Thinking like that's not going to help. Use the mind you've been given and just get on with it."

Strangely, the fierce sound of his voice seemed to help and he settled to his task.

He still didn't know where to begin, so, to do something, he began to pick books at random from each section, hoping an idea would come to him. Nothing did, and not knowing what he was looking for, he soon began to feel frustrated as nothing moved in his brain to suggest an alternative course of action.

Breathing deeply, he stepped back and took a good, hard look at the book-filled shelves in front of him. Then, taking the headings of the sections, and using the first letter of each, he joined them up to see if they would form words and so constitute a message. They didn't, so he tried the same thing with the last letters of the same sections. The result was gobbledegook. Undeterred, he looked at first titles in each row from top to bottom, then side by side, then the last row using the same sequence as before, hoping that some connection would emerge. None did.

He began to use combinations; one title from the top middle row, one from the bottom left and then bottom right. He mixed and matched and varied, trying permutation after permutation until he had used so many that he found himself beginning to duplicate what he had already done. Still he continued, but despite the variations he made, the resultant grouping of letters made no sense. And always in the back of his mind, no matter how hard he tried to ignore it, he was conscious of the fact that time was moving on.

When he had exhausted the possibilities of hidden messages in the sequences of titles, he climbed the ladder and explored the areas between the books and the shelves above them. There was nothing there. Next, he felt along the gap between the bookcase and the ceiling from one end to the other. Again nothing. He repeated the procedure on the other side of the room. All he got for his trouble was a hand smeared with dust.

At that point he took a break, his bladder telling him he needed to go to the toilet. His mind was so much in turmoil that he hardly realised it when he got there. He relieved himself and was washing his hands when he thought of something.

In the bathroom of his friend Maxie's house there was a trapdoor in the ceiling giving access to the roof-space. When the trap door opened, a sectionalised ladder dropped down. Michael glanced up. There was a trapdoor above his head. He rebuked himself. He hadn't thought it worthwhile to look at the bathroom on this floor and he now knew that was a bad omission.

Jubilant, and, with hope, at last beginning to stir in him, he rushed back to the library and proceeded to manhandle the ladder back along the corridor. Moments later he had it set up in the bathroom and was mounting the steps. At the top he pushed at the trapdoor expecting it to open.

It wouldn't budge.

No matter how much force he applied he couldn't move it. And he understood. Like the shuttered windows and the locked doors, this too was not meant to yield him an exit.

Utterly deflated, he hauled the ladder back to the library, where he slumped down at the table and put his head in his hands. He didn't know what to do next. He had thought he'd made a breakthrough and his hopes had been dashed. Despair lay heavy on him. The task seemed impossible. Yet, hopeless as his position seemed, he did not yet feel he was ready to give up. All those hours of studying his dad had insisted he do had inculcated in him a durability, a stubbornness which would not allow him to accept defeat. Many a time in the past he had worried away at a problem that had seemed intractable, only for him to find a way of tackling it, which finally led to a successful conclusion. Obduracy was now an in-built trait.

He raised his head, and almost by reflex, stretched out a hand to the book lying on the table. So consumed had he been with attempting to find an answer in the stacks of books round the walls, he hadn't given it a thought.

It was a thriller. The author was someone called Ian Rankin. He hadn't heard of him. He turned to the flyleaf at the back, hardly conscious of doing so. The writer was a Scotsman who set his stories in Edinburgh. His principle character was an Inspector Rebus.

Michael sat bolt upright, completely energised. It was as if a charge of electricity had surged through him. How stupid he was, ignoring the one thing that had been under his nose. It had been placed there for a purpose. He was certain of that.

Non verbis sed rebus, he knew was the Latin phrase for, *not by words but by things*. Deriving from this was the meaning of the word rebus. It meant, picture book. But not just any picture book. A rebus consisted of pictures representing syllables and words. In such a book the word HEAR might be represented by the letter H followed by the drawing of an ear.

He should be looking for such a work.

It wouldn't be in the library; there was no children's section here. But he knew where there were children's books. Hurriedly pushing his chair back, he jumped up and ran downstairs to the playroom. Here, he found a small bookcase full of them. Others were scattered all round the place, on tables, on window-ledges, on chairs, even on the floor.

He started on the loose ones first. What he was looking for wasn't there.

Slightly disappointed, he began to go through those in the bookcase. There were about one hundred of them, of all sizes and types from simple stories to ones containing nothing but puzzles or plain drawings waiting to be filled in with paint or crayons. The fifty-ninth book he looked at was the one he wanted. But to make absolutely certain, he quickly scrutinised the remainder, and only when he was sure there were no others like it, did he turn his full attention to his original selection.

When he opened it, his mouth slightly dry, he found that the first page contained a picture of a hen with the letter T in front of it, and below this there was a drawing of a cycle prefixed with the letters BI. He had found a rebus.

Quickly, he flicked through it, not sure what he was looking for. It contained other pictures and symbols, with letters prefixing everyday things such as can and cat and log, along with picture puzzles and drawings. Nothing seemed unusual about it until he came to the last page. Here, he found something that was out of character with the rest of the book. He studied it for a moment, hoping for inspiration. When it didn't come, he picked the book up and returned to the library to inspect his find more thoroughly.

The incongruous section consisted of ten lines of writing, each line followed by a set of numbers. To give himself more space, he wrote it all out on one of the writing pads and tried to figure out what it meant.

ANOKNWLLEWSINONACENO 154253
HTIRSBIANOTUBARQEUSOTN 712363
NNIFAANMDOWOANOEWKNEDNA 4117343
SAWMEANOTOWTNDARAHESA 3423351
EBANEVYLEAHETHLUODCGISNRIDHT 2183545
HTTAARODIREPDHEASGHETMINOS 412559
DNIFLIWLHETYVOCERNUOYUPLEHMTEH 4447344
LROWDAOTYAWDSUTEIOHTE 512373
HENWTUBTAETHMEMREREBSTHITEIS 4323844
NADSIGHRITTEFLGTHIRSIATTHFETL 32545244

At first the jumble of letters and numbers made no sense to him. It looked like some sort of code to which he hadn't the key. And if it were a code, each line of letters was without a break so there were too many for them to represent just a single word.

Perhaps each line was a phrase or sentence. This idea seemed more probable, so he began to look for two of the most common words in the English language, A and THE. He found plenty of the former and none of the latter. But if a line was a phrase or sentence then there had to be the odd THE among the jumble.

Deciding to treat each line as a compound of anagrams, he tried again, this time looking for the appropriate letters in groups of three. Almost immediately he found one in each of lines six and seven. Heartened by this he began to search for other small words and soon he had exposed four more – AND, IS, TO and AT. He knew then he was on the right track. Now he had to think of a way to put the words into a meaningful order. His mind raced. At first nothing came. Then he thought of something. He began to count; and he found that there were twenty letters on the first line. He added up the adjacent numbers: they too came to twenty. Another thought quickly followed; the letter A was a single element in any sentence. Therefore, the A on the first line might correspond to the number one in the set of numbers. If so, the next number in the line, which was five, would mean the next five letters also constituted a word, and each of the other numbers after it would also correspond to words in the line consistent with the amount shown.

Deeply attuned to his task now, he quickly worked out that ANOKN could be KNOWN, the next four letters, LLEW, could be

WELL, and so on until he had the following.

A KNOWN WELL IS CANON ONE

Not waiting to arrange them in better order, he moved to the second line. Here the twenty-two letters were matched with a count of twenty-two numbers. He was on the right track. When he had that lot deciphered, he went on to the third line, then the fourth and so on until he had eight lines written out as follows.

A KNOWN WELL IS CANON ONE
BRITISH A ON BUT SQUARE NOT
FINN A A WOODMAN ONE KNEW AND
WAS NAME TO TWO AND SHARE A
BE A HEAVENLY THE COULD SIGN THIRD
THAT A OR PRIDE HEADS SOMETHING
FIND THEY WILL UNCOVER YOU HELP THEM
WORLD A TO WAY OUTSIDE THE
WHEN BUT AT THE REMEMBER THIS SITE
AND IS RIGHT LEFT RIGHT IS THAT LEFT

Now, all he had to do was make sense out of what he had so far decoded.

At first he was unable to unscramble what was obviously a message. He could not find a connection between the lines, and in their current form they were meaningless. It did not take him long to find the key. As the incomprehensible jumble was from a children's book, he felt it was likely the proper sequence was penned in verse. And, if so, all he had to do was find the words that rhymed and place them at the end of their respective sentences. Once he had done that the other words could easily be arranged in an order that made sense. He soon discovered that there *were* rhyming words and his conjecture had been correct. In short time he had paired off square and share, pride and side and finally, site and right.

He jotted these down. When they were in place, he shuffled the other words around until each line had a coherent form. When finished, he had the following short piece of verse.

ONE IS A WELL KNOWN CANON
BUT NOT ON A BRITISH SQUARE
ONE KNEW A FINN AND A WOODMAN

AND TWO WAS A NAME TO SHARE
THE THIRD COULD BE A HEAVENLY SIGN
OR SOMETHING THAT HEADS A PRIDE
UNCOVER THEM THEY WILL HELP YOU FIND
A WAY TO THE WORLD OUTSIDE
BUT REMEMBER THIS WHEN AT THE SITE
THAT RIGHT IS LEFT AND LEFT IS RIGHT

Michael read what he had constructed. When he came to the last four lines he knew that he had confirmation of having discovered the means of escaping from the house. Now, all he had to do was establish what the rest of it meant.

The first two and the last two lines baffled him. but he knew the latter might make sense if he could reach the site to which they referred. To achieve that he had to solve the riddle posed by the rest of the poem.

He cracked the third couplet first. The, *something that heads a pride*, was easy to work out. It was obviously a lion, and as one of the, *heavenly signs* used by astrologists is Leo, the Latin word for lion, this was merely confirmation that he was correct in his presumption.

Putting his mind to the second couplet, he concentrated on the word, *two* on the second line, writing down all other words he knew that had the same meaning as it. When he had finished he had, brace, *couple, duo, dyad, pair, twain and deuce*. That didn't get him much further, so he switched his attention to the first line. After a bit more mental wrestling he gave up temporarily and moved to the first two lines of the poem.

Five minutes later he admitted defeat and returned to studying the variations of the word two on his writing pad. This time he carried out an exercise where he mentally paired each of the words he had written down with, Finn and Woodman, to see if anything stirred in his brain. And this time he made the association almost immediately.

Twain, Finn, Woodman; for Woodman read Sawyer. That led him to Tom Sawyer and Huckleberry Finn, whose creator was Mark Twain. Twain's real name was Samuel Langhorne Clemens, but he took the nom-de-plume after watching a riverboat man plumbing river depths on a Mississippi steamer. As the lead weight on the plumb-line hit the bottom of the river, the man called out the depth using terms such as, mark one or mark twain or mark three, whichever was appropriate. And in that moment, Samuel Langhorne Clemens changed his name and the author Mark Twain came into being.

So now Michael had two of the three answers required and he only had to determine the meaning of the first couplet.

At first he could not fathom this out and became increasingly frustrated. Without solving this part of the riddle he would be unable to comprehend the meaning of the last two lines. He was so close and yet the answer was tantalisingly out of his reach.

It was the word Canon that was throwing him, especially in connection with the phrase *British Square*. He was aware that a British Square was a military formation used in the Napoleonic wars and many conflicts thereafter. It consisted of a square formation of soldiers in two ranks, one kneeling with the other upright behind the first. On command, the kneeling soldiers would fire at the enemy, and then, while the standing lines of men discharged their weapons, their comrades in front would be reloading. The procedure would be repeated again and again so allowing the soldiers to keep up a continuous volley of shot in all directions. It was one of the most effective military techniques ever devised.

Sometimes heavier weapons, such as cannons, were positioned inside the square, and it was this military connotation that Michael could not get out of his head. The two words, canon and cannon, although meaning different things, sounded alike and were causing his fixation on things military. But perhaps this was not an accident and the originator of the puzzle had intended to sow confusion in the reader's mind when drawing it up. If so, the ploy was currently proving to be very effective.

Michael was stuck, and as had happened on a number of occasions before, words of his dad's came to him unbidden. *If a problem seems insoluble, try thinking laterally. When something seems too obvious, discard it and look for another way.* In the past he had been contemptuous of such advice, but this time, with his freedom and that of others at stake, he took it more seriously.

And indeed, to his surprise, it set him off on another tack. "What other definitions are there of Canon and square?" he mused aloud. "Canon can mean principle or rule or standard or convention or Priest. Square can mean to fix something, or fuddy-duddy or a geometric shape or someone true or conventional or an area in a town or city or right-angled or ethical. There were so many meanings his head began to reel. "There must be a connection between two of them," he muttered. "There has to be. Be methodical; pair one meaning of Canon with each of the meanings of square, and if nothing results, move on to the next meaning and do the same again."

It took a while, but by this painstaking process he finally hit upon a solution. A priest could be a Canon. If canonised, he could be admitted to the Canon of Saints. A square could be the confluence of streets within a town or city. If it wasn't a British square then it had to be in some other country. Put these facts together and he was looking for a foreign square with religious significance.

And then, of course, it was easy. The 'one' referred to on the first and third lines of the poem were linked. He glanced at them again just to make sure. *One is a well known canon, one knew a Finn and a Woodman.* Nodding in satisfaction, he carried through his thoughts to their logical conclusion.

Each one was a man's name. That name was Mark. He already had the second Mark, in Mark Twain, and now he had the first, which was in St. Mark's Square in Venice. Relief and a fleeting feeling of pleasure coursed through him. The answers to the three parts of the riddle were two Marks and a lion.

And he knew where he could find them. The site referred to in line nine of the poem was on the landing at the top of the first staircase. Here, facing down the stairs, was the painting of a lion, the symbol of Venice, and on either side, it was flanked by two views of San Marco, or St. Mark's Square, painted by Canaletto.

Pushing his scribblings to one side, he hurried from the room to the landing and took up a position facing the three paintings. He recalled the last two lines of the piece of verse; *But remember this when at the site, that right is left and left is right.*

What could it mean?

In turn, he raised the bottom of the Canalettos and peered behind them. In each instance all he found was a blank wall. He attempted to do the same with the painting of the lion, but the frame was fitted flush to the wall and fixed in such a fashion that it wouldn't budge.

He moved the right-hand Canaletto a bit to the left and the left-hand one to the right. He wasn't sure what he was hoping for, so he wasn't disappointed when nothing happened.

He decided to try something else.

Going back upstairs, he retrieved the ladder from the library and carried it down to the landing. Mounting this to the fourth step, he lifted the scenes of St. Mark's Square from the wall, one after the other. Then, careful not to damage them, he switched the right-hand one to the left of the lion, and the left-hand one to the right. Hardly had he the second frame in position when there was a dull rumbling sound and, to his astonishment and delight, the painting of the lion split in two with each half sliding laterally away from the other, halting only when they touched the Canalettos on either side. In the wall, where the painting of the lion had rested, an opening was revealed. It was the shape and size of a normal door, and beyond it all he could make out was darkness.

Michael's first thought was that the space in the wall was a Priest Hole, somewhere to hide when danger threatened. Most old houses in England had them, the practice of constructing Priest Holes stemming from the proscription of Roman Catholics at times of persecution in the 16th and 17th centuries. As it was a religious figure, St. Mark, which had been instrumental in leading him to it, Michael felt this might be apposite.

Climbing down from the ladder, he cautiously approached the opening. He peered into it.

Four steps were visible before the darkness swallowed any others there might be. Michael entered and began to descend. He had taken only three steps before he heard the familiar rumbling sound again. Turning swiftly he was in time to see the paintings sliding back into place. Powerless to prevent them, he found himself in a blackness so profound he might have been blind.

Seeking support, he reached for the wall. It was made of rock and felt cold and clammy. He tried to control a rising panic. Apart from the brief episode in the outlet channel of the park lake, he had never been in complete darkness before and the experience was unnerving.

"Being unable to see doesn't mean anything has changed," he said loudly in an attempt to still his nerves. "Everything that was here before is still here. There just isn't any light to reveal it."

The sound of his voice and his attempt at logic went some way to calming him, and after a few worrying moments when he thought he might lose control, his fears subsided to the extent that he was able to place a foot on the next step and move on downwards. This was the only thing he could do. Going back was no longer an option, for even if he found a way to prise apart the picture of the lion, he would only be going back into the house and admitting defeat. His challenge would be over.

Still with a hand on the wall, he made his descent, counting the steps as he went. He was up to fifteen before he reached the bottom, the same number as those on the first staircase. That meant he was on the same level as the ground floor.

At this point the ground flattened and, edging carefully forward, he eventually came to a divide where the tunnel split left and right. He took the left-hand fork, but after twenty metres or so, this proved to be a dead-end. Retracing his steps he tried the alternative route.

Still moving cautiously, he had gone a further thirty paces when he heard a faint noise ahead of him. He stopped, trying to fathom out what it was and whether it might herald danger. He edged forward, straining his ears. The noise was continuous and sounded familiar, but as yet, he could not determine what it was.

He continued, going even slower, the sound getting louder with every step he took. Twenty painstaking metres further on and he recognised what he was hearing. It was the sound of running water.

A couple of minutes later he was at the edge of a structure shaped like a well. He could make out the sides of it, for light was seeping in from somewhere underneath, and about six metres below him a little stream gurgled past from right to left, obviously from outside and appearing to run beneath the foundations of the house. A metre beyond the hole, the passage ended in a solid wall of rock.

As his eyes became accustomed to the faint light, he saw that metal spikes had been driven into the side of the well, providing a means of descent. Sitting down at the edge, his legs dangling into space, he leant forward and grasped the first spike. Searching gently with one foot for another one lower down, he swung out and began to descend. Seconds later he was standing in the stream with water up to his thighs. Here he took stock of his situation.

The light from outside was filtering in via a space between the stream and the upper wall of the tunnel through which it flowed. The space could not have more than fifteen centimetres high.

The opening was small and fairly round and not high enough for him to remain upright in order to wade through it. His options were limited. He would have to crawl or swim. Either way, by raising his head periodically above the surface, he could get air from the gap between the water and the rock ceiling. The thought was not appealing.

For some reason the water was very cold, the temperature more like you would find in mid-winter, and if it had not been running briskly, he was sure it would have frozen over. He began to shiver. He knew he would have to make a start or he would soon be freezing. If his body temperature fell, hypothermia could set in and he would be unable to function properly, if at all.

First he tried swimming, but the swift flow of the stream curtailed him and, although he made progress, it was slow. His clothes soon became saturated with water and held him back even more. And this wasn't the only impediment. The aperture through which he was swimming became narrower and he kept bumping against the sides. Added to this was the fact that it was only possible to do the breast stroke and the tunnel walls began to restrict his movements. He turned on his back and kicked his legs, hoping he could work up enough momentum to keep himself moving, but the current was too strong and this proved to be a worse alternative. Finally, he gave up and began to crawl.

He made better progress but his head was now under water and he had to stop every so often to take in air. The bed of the channel was uneven, and stones and debris, which he assumed had been washed in from elsewhere, scraped his knees, making them painful. He was sure they must be bleeding.

To make matters worse, he discovered that the farther he went the narrower the tunnel became, and as the stream was forced into a smaller area, the gap between it and the roof became steadily less. Soon there was little room for air and eventually he was forced to take stock of the situation.

He stopped, still on all fours, his mouth just above the waterline in about four centimetres of space. He was at the moment of crisis; did he go back or did he to go on? To turn back now meant defeat. To proceed might mean no access to air and the possibility of him drowning.

It did not take long for him to make up his mind. His old stubbornness became the deciding factor and he opted to carry on. His reasoning was that the tunnel might widen again, the stream become shallower and more air become available. Added to that was the fact that he was becoming colder by the minute and needed to get to a warmer place as quickly as possible. He started off again.

His hopes were soon dashed. Within a few metres, water was crashing off the roof and the remaining source of oxygen had been swallowed up.

He backtracked and thought again. To continue would be to risk death. He could give up now, or take a deep breath of air and hope it was enough to allow him to crawl to safety. He knew he had to be close to the entrance to the tunnel. Furthermore, he could not believe that the task was impossible. If so, why set it in the first place. His mind went back to the difficulties he had faced in the maze. Even when he had reached the centre and obtained the key, there was one last obstacle to be overcome before he was able to escape. He felt his present situation might parallel that.

He was fully aware that he wasn't brave by nature, and knew that to go on would not only be risky, but would test his resolve to the limit. Despite this, he felt there was only one course he could take. To go back meant failure and he wasn't ready to countenance that yet. He had got this far and hated to give up when he was so close to success. His reason told him to rely on logic and take his chances so, having convinced himself he was making the right decision, he drew as much oxygen into his lungs as he could and set off once more, trying to increase his pace, trying to ignore the numbing cold and a rising fear, and the pain in his sorely tried knees.

After about thirty seconds he felt an almost overwhelming desire to raise his head to search for air. He resisted the urge with difficulty and crawled on, eyes closed, attempting to eliminate all negative thoughts from his mind. Then his clothing snagged on a sharp stone embedded in the floor of the stream. He reached down to pull it clear. The offending piece of cloth was well and truly caught and, with little feeling left in his hand, he couldn't free it. Again panic gripped him. *I'm going to drown, he screamed silently. I'm going to drown.*

Again a voice spoke to him. *Calm down, calm down; go back; start again.*

Amazingly, his reason returned and he followed the voice's command. And almost instantly his clothing broke free. He continued to drag himself back until he was able to raise his head and take in air. Panting hard and with his head pounding, he remained where he was until his breathing steadied. But now he was becoming more and more conscious of how cold he was, and fearful that hypothermia was beginning to set in, he quickly filled his lungs with oxygen and set off once more, praying that the setback had not fatally damaged the chance to gain his freedom.

After another fifty seconds under water, there was a tight band across his chest and his resistance was beginning to weaken. Twenty seconds after that the tightness burned like a hot ring and his lungs felt as if they would soon burst. *Just five seconds more*, he thought, starting a mental count. *You can do it, you can do it.* But he couldn't. After two more agonising paces crawled, he lost control of his will and his head shot up involuntarily, banging against the roof of the tunnel. His mouth opened automatically to suck in either water or life-giving air.

It was air.

Dazed from the blow to his head, he miscalculated and gulped in some of the stream as well. Spluttering and retching, the worst twenty seconds of his life went by before water erupted from his lungs and poured down his nose and from his mouth, allowing him to breathe semi-properly again. And noisily he did, making sounds like an irate bull sea-lion whose harem was being threatened.

He remained where he was until his vision was no longer impaired by tears and his breathing had returned to something approaching normal, the icy waters of the stream breaking against his chest and shoulders. He peered into the gloom ahead, hoping to see the outside world, but still he was not at the opening to the tunnel.

Disappointed, and conscious that he could no longer feel his hands and feet, he submerged again and, breath held, doggedly continued his painful way forward. The next time he raised his head, he discovered that his torture was almost at an end. Not thirty metres in front of him was a half-circle of light, where the stream was broader and shallower and the current much weaker. At that point the tunnel was about two metres high and about five metres wide.

He was too weary to feel much elation, and when he tried to rise he found his joints had almost seized up. After a few awkward attempts, he was at last able to stumble to his feet and he dragged his throbbing head, his aching knees, his freezing body out of the tunnel and into the light.

He flopped on to the nearest bit of bank, shivering and utterly exhausted, both physically and mentally. There he lay, victorious, but unable, at that moment, to take any joy in the fact.

After the semi-darkness of the tunnel he found the bright light painful to his eyes, so he shut them tight and took consolation in the fact that he was still alive. When he felt enough time had elapsed to allow his eyes to acclimatise, he raised his head and looked about him.

He found that he had emerged some distance from the house. He focussed his attention on this, hoping to find the building still shuttered and dark. From his prone position he was unable to see it properly, so he struggled to his feet, panting with the effort. Then he wished he hadn't. As he came upright, blood suddenly rushed to his head. He felt dizzy, then nauseous.

A fit of coughing assailed him. It grew more violent. Water and bile spewed from his mouth on to the grass.

He staggered.

Still dizzy, his legs left him and he tumbled to the ground. Seconds later, his mind discarded all sensation and he blacked out. Above him, the brightness that had welcomed him a few minutes earlier went from the sky.

The day reverted to twilight again.

CHAPTER ELEVEN

Amazingly, when he came to his sickness had disappeared. His clothes were dry, his vitality had returned and the numbing cold of his body was just a memory. Spirits uplifted, he noticed the sky above was a beautiful azure blue.

A rough tongue on his cheek had roused him, and on opening his eyes he'd discovered Canis lying at his side. She gave a yelp of delight as he sat up and, once assured that he was all right, took off to chase something that could only be discerned by a dog's eye.

Someone must have moved him further along the bank, for he saw that the big house was now about half a kilometre away. Just at that moment he had little desire to enter it again.

He heard a sound and turned his head to see Jim Crow, Yuri and the twins watching him. They were seated by the edge of the stream a few metres away, seemingly giving him some space and a chance to waken fully. Sitting beside them, dressed in a green and red coloured sari, was the most beautiful girl he had ever seen. Eyes of liquid brown, set in an oval face, surveyed him calmly and with some curiosity. She was a bit older than the twins and he could hardly drag his eyes away from her.

When Jim Crow saw Michael was taking an interest in them he broke the silence. "Well done, Mikey," he cried, his black face beaming. "Two down, two to go." It was only then that the boy knew he had emerged from the house within the time set.

"Yes, well done," Yuri echoed. "Keep up this and we all soon be out."

Michael noted that Yuri was less ebullient than before and wondered if the Russian would regret having to leave this place if Michael was successful in completing the other two tasks.

The twins were grave and silent, their demeanour and lack of comment a message in itself.

"Come on now, Mikey, tell us how you did it," Jim Crow implored.

Michael wasn't too keen to relate what had happened, thinking that it might smack of immodesty, but Jim Crow and Yuri seemed so eager to hear that he acceded to their request. He realised also that he was pleased to see everyone, glad of their company after the singular trial he had just gone through. Feeling like that, he didn't want to disappoint anyone.

So, for the next fifteen minutes, he outlined the nature of the task he had been set, for it transpired that only Yuri was privy to that knowledge, and how he had gone about tackling it. He left nothing out, outlining his confusion, his mistakes, his inadequacies, his frustrations and everything that had caused his early inability to make progress. When he explained how he had made the first breakthrough, Jim Crow grinned and cried, "Attaboy," while Yuri clapped and the twins muttered secretively to each other. Michael wondered if they were saying something uncomplimentary. The newcomer said nothing, her face inscrutable. When he outlined how he had solved the riddle of the anagrams and the resulting piece of verse, Jim Crow shook his head in admiration and Yuri regained some of his old animation. The twins did not congratulate him. The Indian girl seemed to show more interest.

The rest of his tale was received in almost complete silence, his listeners obviously enthralled by his escape, especially the death-defying business of coming through the water-filled tunnel. When he had finished, everyone looked serious for a moment, then Yuri said quietly, "You very brave, Michael. Not many would take chance like that."

Michael shook his head. "It wasn't bravery, Yuri. That had to be the only way out, therefore it had to be negotiable. Whoever set the task made it difficult, not impossible. What would be the point in concocting it if it were too easy. I was almost certain I would have enough air in my lungs to see me through."

"Almost certain, yes, but not all over certain. That's why I say you brave."

Jim Crow reached forward and slapped him on the knee. "I agree with Yuri, buddy. You didn't know. That was quite a thing you did there."

Michael knew this might happen, yet he was still unprepared for it. His face went red with embarrassment at their admiring words, and immediately he took action to deflect the interest in him and shift their attention elsewhere.

Looking at the Indian girl, he said shyly, "I don't think we've met."

Yuri hit the side of his head with the heel of his hand. "Forgive me. I not mind manners. This is Rani. She lead you to next task."

The girl smiled, her teeth even and appearing very white in her brown face. "I am pleased to be meeting with you," she said, her voice gentle.

"Me too," was all Michael could manage, feeling a bit foolish. Then, to fill in the silence that followed, he went on, "Where are you from?"

"Bombay, originally, but before I was coming here, I was close by to Calcutta."

Michael wanted to continue with the conversation but was interrupted by Canis returning and flopping down in the middle of the group. Bright-eyed, she gazed up at Yuri and barked. Then she rose up on her hind legs and did a backward somersault before standing in front of him, tail wagging.

"I think, Yuri, old buddy, she's trying to tell you something," Jim Crow said.

Yuri smacked the side of his head again. "I very stupid this day. Michael, you hungry?"

It struck Michael that he was, having had nothing to eat since the test with the Paris buns, and that was a long time ago. So consumed with his problems had he been that all his other needs had been forgotten.

"Starving," he answered.

"Good. We all set then; all hungry?" he asked.

The others nodded.

Michael looked round him. "Where's the food?" he enquired, mystified.

Everyone laughed, even the twins.

I think you forget about wishes," Yuri said, his old happy self seemingly restored. "Now, Michael, you make choice."

Michael looked at Rani, and immediately he thought of the meals in the Indian restaurant he had enjoyed with his parents after nights out at the Opera or the Theatre. A wave of homesickness swept over him and he felt unusually sad. It was a sensation he had never experienced before and it surprised him. It meant he was missing his home life and he hadn't thought that possible.

The others must have noted a change in him, probably guessed the reason for it.

Yuri placed a hand on his shoulder. "Come, Michael, choose now; it will make you more happy. What you eat, we eat also."

Fighting off a sense of depression, Michael tried to remember as many dishes on the Tandoori restaurant's menu as he could. He thought if he listed a variety they could all help themselves. "Popadoms," he said, "and naan bread, and fried rice and curried chicken and curried lamb and Tandoori dishes, and dishes of Korma, Bhuna, Pasanda and Birani beef and prawn, and definitely not tikka massala anything" he ended emphatically.

The Indian girl's eyes lit up, Jim Crow and Yuri looked dubious, the twins emerged from their semi-comatose state and appeared pleased for the first time since Michael had awakened.

"And drink, Mikey, what do we wash it down with?" Jim Crow interjected. "We must have something to cool the throat after all that spicy grub."

"What would you like?" Michael asked, his spirits lifting and the thought of the appetising smells about to come causing him to look forward to the feast.

"Cold, cold milk for me," Jim Crow said immediately.

"Coke for us," shouted the twins."

"Could I have iced water, please?" Rani requested politely.

"And I have nice glass red wine," Yuri finished, "and maybe one glass vodka," he added in afterthought. "That is if nobody object," he added hastily.

No one minded.

"And you, Mikey." Jim Crow said. "What's your poison?"

"Coca-cola, like Paul and Paula – in a tall glass with lemon and ice."

"We'll have the lemon and ice too," the twins chorused, not to be outdone.

"Right, Michael," Yuri commanded. "Make wish loud."

Michael rattled off a list of all the food he'd thought of and then followed this by the different drinks the others had requested, not forgetting his own. He finished with the hope that they would appear immediately.

They did. A magnificent spread of dishes, laid out on a red and white spotted tablecloth, appeared on the grass beside the river, but there were no chairs, no table on which to set the food, and no cutlery. The al-fresco meal would have to be eaten using their fingers.

Just as they were about to begin Michael halted them. "We forgot about Canis," he said.

"Oh, she doesn't need anything," Paul said irritably.

"Why not?" Michael asked.

"She's only an animal. She shouldn't eat with us," Paula intervened.

"She's more human than some I could mention," Jim Crow remarked.

Michael turned to Yuri. "Can I extend my wish to take in Canis?" he enquired.

"Your wish, Michael. Can use as desired."

Michael called Canis who was still chasing around in a nearby meadow, and as the dog raced towards him he made his wish. She arrived just as a bowl of meaty scraps, a bone, several dog biscuits and a dish of lemonade materialised.

As she started in on the scraps, the others began their food, all with eagerness, except Paul and his sister, who donned sulky expressions at being overruled.

As the meal progressed, first Jim Crow and then Yuri began to relate tales about their boyhoods. Jim Crow took them back to his days on the plantation and then moved on to his experiences in the civil war in America. He recalled some of the battles in which he had fought, how he had seen men die, sometimes members of the same family, some who had fought for the federal army, some for the confederates. A certain sadness seemed to come over him as he spoke and no one said anything for a while after he finished.

Then Yuri raised everyone's spirits by recounting his years in the circus, the characters he had worked with and the people he had met in the various countries he had visited. He used his clown's gifts to good effect, pulling faces and acting out some of his routines. Soon all were laughing at his tales and antics.

When they had finished eating, Yuri said each of them must perform for the entertainment of the others.

There were instant protests, but he insisted, and said he would go first followed by the twins. When finished, each performer would have the choice of who would go next. Grudgingly, the others agreed.

Yuri sang a Russian folk-song, the Volga Boatman, his voice deep and mellow. Michael was reminded of a solo singer in the Red Army choir he had once heard and thought Yuri just as good. The song was poignant and was sung with great feeling, leaving Yuri looking sad when the last note died away.

Next it was the turn of the twins who, after a whispered conversation, chose to sing one of the great popular hits of the nineteen seventies, a Simon and Garfunkel number, Bridge Over Troubled Water. Their harmonies and pitch were perfect, and although Michael was loath to admit it, they were surprisingly good. They ended to a round of applause, and bowed extravagantly before sitting down with evident satisfaction.

After another bout of whispering, Jim Crow was rather spitefully named to do the next turn.

Michael assumed he would hear a negro spiritual, but Jim Crow astounded them by doing a decent impersonation of Eminem, and the rap rhythms had them all tapping their empty plates with their fingers in accompaniment. The words were Jim Crow's own and not the vulgar variety associated with the pop-star.

After another round of applause, the black man pointed at Michael, who went crimson at the thought of having to perform in public. He protested that he didn't know any songs and was told firmly by Yuri that, if he couldn't sing he would have to entertain them in some other fashion. He still tried to get out of it, but after some good-natured heckling, he thought he might satisfy them if he recited a poem. He felt something light-hearted might be appropriate and, searching his memory, he plumped for a nonsense poem either by Edward Lear or Lewis Carroll; perhaps, *You Are Old Father William*, or *Jabberwocky*. Then, for some reason he discarded the notion and decided to recite some of his own poetry.

When he was particularly unhappy at home he would pen some verse and this would help to dispel his wretched mood. So he made up his mind to give them the poem he had written just after a planned trip to the seaside had been cancelled by his dad because Michael had failed to analyse a Shakespearean sonnet properly. He had been looking forward to the excursion with the youth club for over a month and his hopes of a day away from the tyrant had been dashed. When he had written the piece he had imagined the person in it was his dad, first as a boy and finally as man.

The others were still waiting expectantly. "I'll give you a poem, more a bit of doggerel," he said. "I wrote it myself. It's about my dad. It's not very good but I think it says something about grown-ups." *At least, one in particular*, he thought. "It's called, *When he was young*." He stood up, took one deep breath, and began in a rather tremulous voice.

When he was young he took his bike
And cycled to the sea
He stood and marvelled at its size
Its shades and density.

He raced along its smooth washed shore

111

His shoes and socks in hand
And felt its wetness ooze between
His toes upon the sand.

He saw the light reflected on
The gently rolling waves
And heard them gush beneath white cliffs
In deep and shadowy caves.

He gathered up the speckled stones
Skimmed flat flints on the tide
Built castles at the water's edge
And watched their walls subside.

He delved in green and rocky pools
Caught tiny wriggling things
Then plopped them back to watery homes
Through ever-widening rings.

He sniffed the salty seaweed air
Heard gulls above him cry
Pretended he was Francis Drake
Never saw the time go by.

He found the gold in sunset rays
Blue sapphires in the sky
Great emeralds in the verdant depths
Each precious to his eye.

He gazed in youthful wonderment
Amazed by all around
His mind in love's euphoria
A paradise he'd found.

He's older now, he has a car
His time is seldom free
He drives along the coast each day
But he *never* sees the sea.

The others were quiet when he finished. They gazed at him uncertainly, not sure how to respond. Then, after a few seconds, they clapped politely.

Jim Crow was the first to speak. "That was great, Mikey," he said, trying to sound enthusiastic. "But I think it probably means more to you than it does to us."

"Our father's not like that," the twins said. "He's always fun."

"My father taught me first trick," Yuri remarked wistfully. He, great person."

Rani said nothing. She had a sympathetic expression on her face and somehow Michael knew she understood.

Jim Crow, sensing that the festive mood of the company might be lost, enquired quickly, Have you written any others, Mikey?"

Michael nodded. "A few," he replied, not willing to admit that he had penned quite a lot of unhappy verses.

"Another, then," Jim Crow said. "Give us another."

Michael thought of school and how he hated it. Apart from Maxie he had no friends there. He was constantly mocked and sometimes bullied by older boys who didn't like him for being smart. Maxie stood up for him, but even he couldn't offer much protection when the adversaries were bigger and stronger.

"I wrote one about the Sunday evening before I first went to school when my parents took me for a walk. I don't like school," he added. "I could recite that one."

"That would be good," Yuri said. "I not attend school, just learn about circus."

"There was no school for me either," Jim Crow said. "just work and more work."

Michael began to recite the second poem, his voice firm now that he had gained in confidence from his earlier rendition.

September eve so long ago
I walked in winding lane
Clutching the hands of parents tight
My heart a well of pain.

And in the quiet countryside
I heard the church bells call
A melancholy summons
Over field and garden wall.

Above me, parents murmured soft

On meeting lovers clasped
A smiling glance exchanged between
As slow the lovers passed.

I felt the warmth of dying sun
And smelt the scented air
So happy then I should have been
Instead, my lot was care.

No word could melt my misery
No act could change the rule
That freedom's lost on autumn eve
When first one goes to school.

Again there was silence when he finished, only this time it was soon followed by great applause, especially from Paula for whom the words seemed to have struck a chord.

"I can empathise with that," she shouted as the clapping began to die away. "I hated school too. I was ever so glad when we were taken away."

"You never told me that," Paul exclaimed, looking astounded.

"I don't tell you everything. Anyway, you seemed to be enjoying it so much I didn't want you to know that I wasn't."

"But I tell you everything."

"Everything?"

"Yes, everything."

"Well, now you know; women are different; they have to have some secrets.

"By heck, that's a first," Jim Crow said, smiling. "The twins having a row."

The others laughed, and the objects of their attention glowered.

"Right, Rani, you now," Yuri announced to draw attention away from the unhappy siblings. "You, only one left."

"I cannot sing, I know nothing of verse. I can dance; will that please?"

"That please very well," Yuri replied genially.

Rani stood up, very slender, very serene. She extended her arms above her head and moulded her hands into the shape of a bird's wings, then, back straight and head bowed, she bent slowly until she was resting on one knee.

She remained like that for a few moments, her body perfectly still.

Then she came upright in a slow, fluent movement and her hands began a dance of their own, wrists and palms and fingers moving in strange, delicate patterns. At the same time she took small steps, forward, back and side to side, swaying from the waist at times, at others moving her head to left and right while keeping her shoulders still. All her movements were sinuous and perfectly synchronised giving the impression that her body was flowing and swaying to some inner rhythm. Michael could almost hear the sound of a sitar playing in accompaniment.

Finally, in one lithe action, she again sank to her knee, her hands ceased their intricate movements and the bird's wings, now still, were placed high once more. Her body now motionless, she slowly bowed her head, hiding her face and presenting only a crown of the darkest hair to them.

She remained like that as everyone cheered, even the twins, and only when the noise had subsided did she look up. Then she smiled and murmured a thank you before sitting down demurely.

"Does your dance have a name?" Michael blurted out, then felt a bit foolish for asking.

"All dances have names," Rani replied readily. "That one is known as fluttering dove. It is a dance of peace."

"It's very beautiful."

"My mother taught it to me. She is very beautiful. Perhaps I will be seeing her again soon."

The quiet longing in her tone again reminded Michael of the responsibility that had been placed upon him. Others were depending on his efforts to succeed and he felt the weight of their hopes more than ever.

"I hope you do," was all he said, not wanting to raise anyone's expectations. He had been lucky so far in his endeavours, but with two tasks still to come, and given the problems he'd experienced with the others, he was under no illusion about their degree of difficulty. He could fail any of them, or even a qualifying test, and another period of purgatory would be ahead for all of them.

"Canis next," Yuri declared, interrupting his thoughts.

"Oh, no," the twins groaned.

Nevertheless, they watched as the Russian put the dog through a number of tricks he had taught her – jumping through a grass hoop, walking on her hind legs, somersaulting backwards and dribbling a round stone through a makeshift goal.

Everyone laughed and cheered, and good humour was restored all round. When the show was over, Canis grabbed her bone and dashed away to hide it somewhere.

Michael experienced a warm feeling of comradeship with his fellow exiles and realised that, apart from Maxie, this little band of odd people was the closest thing he had to friends. Adversity, or at least their peculiar circumstances, had given them a common purpose and brought them close together.

With the meal eaten, the remnants of food and the dirty plates vanished as mysteriously as they had appeared. No need for a dishwasher here, Michael thought.

Now that the entertainment was over, the group began to break up. Jim Crow ruffled Michael's hair and headed back towards the forest, while the twins wandered away in the direction of the garden. Yuri and Rani were left, and even Yuri took his leave once he had given the boy another bone-crushing embrace.

No words were exchanged.

Everyone was aware that the next task was about to begin and it was Rani's responsibility to outline to Michael the nature of the problem that lay ahead of him. Only she knew what that was and the others would not be told until he had set about finding a solution to it. There was no need for their presence.

CHAPTER TWELVE

Michael looked at Rani, not knowing what to expect. She rose and put out a hand. "Come, Michael, we are having a journey to make and miles to go before we sleep."

Michael recognised the truncated quotation, but could place neither its original context nor its author. He took the proffered hand and they started away in a direct line from the house towards a row of hills, which were just visible in the distance. At first he walked stiffly, conscious of the abrasions on his knees. But as his body warmed, his joints loosened and he began to walk more freely.

They followed roughly the same direction as the stream, which soon joined a larger tributary to form a fairly wide river. Sometimes the river was a hundred metres from their route, at others only a short distance away, as its meandering course took it hither and thither over a flat plain. In places, willow and silver birch lined its banks, while, in others, long stretches were devoid of plant cover other than grass, allowing them a clear view of its sluggish water and the land beyond. Occasionally a fish leapt, its scales glinting in the bright light. It was all very peaceful.

"You are not minding me holding your hand?" Rani asked, in her quaint way of speaking.

Michael shook his head, feeling a bit tongue-tied, but pleased with the physical contact. Having no sisters, he was a bit awkward around girls, especially those who teased him at school. They were monsters. But Rani was different. For a start she was older and he knew intuitively there was kindness in her. If she teased him it would not be with malicious intent.

"You are reminding me of my younger brother," she said. He must be nearly sixty now. He was wanting to be a Doctor. I am often wondering if that's what he became."

"Is he your only brother?"

"My only brother, yes. His name is Ranji."

"No sisters?"

"No sisters," she replied, sounding a bit sad. "I had one once, but she was after dying when she was ten. Malaria," Rani explained.

"Is that why Ranji wanted to be a doctor?"

It might have been having some influence on him, but I am thinking it was always in his mind. I am missing him, and my parents. I am hoping very much, Michael that you are going to succeed. I am wanting to see them all again."

Michael could sense the longing in her and it strengthened his resolve to try his hardest. If he failed it would not be for lack of effort. It would be because he wasn't good enough.

"Do you think your parents might still be alive?"

"I am hoping so. One can never be sure. If they are they have been living for eighty years and more."

Michael thought that if Rani's mother and father had survived until now they had probably been born high-caste. During the middle of the twentieth century in India, poor people, or those of low-caste, rarely lived to that age. As well as that, only those with position or wealth could provide their children with the education to enable them to enter a profession. If Ranji had hoped to be a doctor, then he must have come from that sort of background.

"Was your father a professional man?" Michael enquired, the curious streak in him overcoming his manners.

"My mother was a schoolteacher, one of the first women to be teaching in our district. My father was a diplomat and political advisor. We were originally from Bombay, but when India was gaining its independence from Britain in 1950, we were soon moving to Delhi to be at the centre of government life."

"Did you meet Mr. Gandhi?"

"Several times. My father was helping to shape the Congress Party, which ultimately was to take power. It was Mr. Gandhi's practice to be visiting our house. My mother would be feeding him when he wasn't fasting. To me it seemed he was always fasting. And when he was not, he was eating very little. He was very thin. When he was assassinated in 1948, he could not having been weighing more than forty kilos."

"It was a pity he didn't live to see India become a Republic."

"Perhaps his death was ordained. He might not have been liking the way things developed. As a pacifist he would have been hating the continual conflicts with Pakistan."

"At least he would have seen the achievement of his objective and Britain's withdrawal from his country."

"That is so. But he wasn't anti-British, you know. He acknowledged the good things the Raj had done for India – the setting up of a communication network, the administrative skills they were after passing on, the civil service they were establishing, second only to their own, and also a system of education that was giving much hope for better futures to millions of children. Indeed, Mr. Gandhi was liking the British. He was just wanting India to be ruled by Indians. In that respect he was like many others. My father was always quoting Rudyard Kipling and Robert Burns. He still was looking on England as the mother country even after India was being declared independent. He was taking joy in the fact that his country was still part of the Empire, or Commonwealth, as we are now calling it."

They walked on, Rani doing most of the talking, Michael learning things and storing them away in his memory. As they proceeded, the sky began to change colour again. The azure blue melding into a light purple which was less of a glare and easier on the eyes.

They rested at one point, close to the river and beneath the drooping leaves of a willow tree. Michael had never felt such contentment, and he began to believe that even if he did fail, a life here would not be so bad. And then he thought, with some shock, that he might be falling into a trap. The wizard, whoever he was, might be playing mind games with him, making the place so attractive that his will to escape would be sapped and unconsciously he might not try so hard to complete the next task. Perhaps that had happened to his predecessors and was responsible, in part, for their failures.

He sat up and said somewhat abruptly. "Come on, let's get on with this."

When Rani reached for his hand he pretended not to notice her gesture and kept it by his side. He wasn't sure, but she might be part of the plan to seduce him, lull him into complacency and so dilute his earnest intentions to escape from the place.

She didn't say anything, but he could sense she was hurt. They walked on in silence for some time, all the while the distant hills seeming to remain as far away as ever.

"Where are we going?" Michael asked at last.

"You will be seeing," she said, non-committal.

"Have we much further to go?"

"Many miles yet. You will be having another chance to rest before I am telling you what you must be doing."

Again they fell quiet, the easy companionship between them disturbed. A bit further on, when they were wading through a meadow of wildflowers, a lark, high in the sky and unseen, began to sing, There was a peculiar poignancy to its threnody. It was joined first by a thrush, then a blackbird, and then a myriad of smaller birds, wrens and finches and tits and many others until the air was filled with a symphony of warblings. It reminded Michael of home, of the dawn chorus when he was only half awake and of summer evenings just before sunset when the trees round his house were filled with the joyous cooings of ring necked doves and wild pigeons, comforting sounds before he went to bed. Once more he experienced a feeling of homesickness, an emotion which had been alien to him until arriving here.

Rani must have been feeling something similar for she began to quote some lines of Burns, her voice so soft the words might only have been for her own ears. They seemed appropriate, given their surroundings and what they were hearing.

Ye banks and braes o' bonnie Doon
How can ye bloom sae fresh and fair
How can ye chant, ye little birds
And I sae weary fu' o' care.

"That was a favourite poem of my father," she murmured.

There was so much sadness in her voice that Michael immediately felt ashamed for thinking she might have been party to a scheme to weaken his resolve. He reached for her hand and squeezed it, hoping to give comfort to both of them.

She smiled wistfully and the barrier that had been growing between them vanished. She squeezed his hand in return and Michael responded with a smile of his own.

So on they went, hand in hand, mile after mile, the landscape changing little, the hills seeming to go grow little in size, conversation flowing easily between them once more.

Rani asked Michael about his home life, and he told her about his parents. How his dad, who was a sales representative for a stationery company specialising in educational literature, visited schools with new publications, and how he was forever bringing home the latest text books and other up-to-date material for Michael to study. When she learned of the oppressive regime he was subjected to, and how little free time he had, she appeared horrified and asked why his mother did not intervene.

Michael, who loved his mother, knew that there was a good reason why she concurred with his father's stern ways; so he shrugged his shoulders and said that there was nothing she was prepared do about it. He just had to live with the strict life devised for him. He hoped to go to university when he was sixteen. Once there, they would seldom see him, and when he graduated they might never see him again.

Rani thought that very sad. Her home life had been completely different, her parents loving and protective, her father a figure to respect.

Michael was about to ask her how she had ended up here when there was a disturbance in the river, which had meandered close to them again. Two swans and half-a-dozen cygnets had been sailing serenely by when the cob suddenly reared up and dashed at something in the water that had come too close to its brood. All that was visible of the intruder was a sleek head which made Michael think it was an otter. The animal veered away in haste and, after its initial surge, the swan gave up the chase. With feathers still fluffed up and head swinging angrily from side to side, it returned to the head of the flotilla, which continued its sedate progress as if nothing had happened. The cob gave a couple of triumphant squawks to signal its victory over the animal that had dared to violate its territory and then allowed its ruffled feathers to subside and assume their proper shape again.

Rani and Michael watched with interest as the object of the swan's wrath headed for the river's edge. Once there, it emerged from the water and they saw at once that it was not an otter as Michael had surmised. Hair slicked flat, the animal looked half its normal size. Leaping up the bank it raced towards them, then stopped and shook itself so vigorously it sent up a great shower of spray. Laughing, Rani and Michael quickly distanced themselves from the deluge. Canis, for that's who it was, ran after them and again sent water flying into the air. Not satisfied with that she rolled on the grass until the hair on her body stood up and made her look more like her usual self. Almost dry, she trotted to where they'd retreated and, tail wagging, insinuated herself between them, head up, tongue lolling and intelligent eyes taking in their every movement.

Michael broke a small branch from a birch tree and fashioned a stick with a penknife he always kept in a pocket. An organiser in the youth club he attended had given this to him. It was needed quite frequently in the handicraft classes there.

When he had removed leaves and small twigs, he threw the stick for the dog to chase, taking pleasure in her evident delight in finding and retrieving the object.

He continued to throw the stick for some time, with Canis always bringing it back and dropping it at his feet, ready to fetch it again no matter where it landed. Finally, tiring of the game before the dog,

Michael casually flicked the stick into the river. That proved to be a mistake. Without hesitation, Canis dived in after it and was soon out with the piece of wood in her mouth and running after him. Knowing what was coming, Rani and Michael took to their heels, but they were no match for the dog. Soon abreast of them, she deposited the stick on the ground and proceeded to shake water out of her coat again, giving them a good soaking in the process.

Following that, she rolled on the grass as before, while Rani and Michael, both laughing, wiped themselves down with the palms of their hands. When all three were reasonably dry, the trek towards the hills was resumed.

After another few miles they finally rested. By then Michael had lost track of the time they had been walking. When asked, Rani informed him they had been on the go for six hours, adding that that was by his calculation of time.

On being told, Michael enquired why everyone worked out time for him as he knew it rather than the method obtaining in their own lives.

Rani looked thoughtful and then explained that until he failed a task he would not have entered fully into their world and would not age at the rate they did. That was why the two different calculations of time continued to be used. It was the same with hunger and thirst, she went on. They didn't need as much food as Michael because of a slower digestive rate. One day for them was much longer than his twenty-four hour cycle, so they only needed one meal in a period when he needed five or six. Their metabolisms were different too. The rhythm of the heart was also slower than his, around forty beats to the minute, and this put less strain on the other organs in the body. This meant the ageing process took longer, and anyone living here had a life expectancy similar to a giant turtle, something in the region of three to four hundred years.

Michael had already worked that out, but there was something that still puzzled him. If he was successful in tackling the four tasks and all the people incarcerated here were released back into his world, would they return to his time or their time, and had they any choice in the matter? He wanted to ask, but something held him back. If the others didn't know the answer, maybe they didn't want to. It might mean their having to face up to a situation they were deliberately trying not to think about. Some might want to go back to a time that was denied to them, and that would be a huge disappointment. Some might not be happy to return at all, considering their life here to be better than the one they had left. If that were the case they might have ambivalent feelings towards him, and a few might actually hope that he failed.

Rani broke in on his musings. "Time to go again," she said.

"How long before we get to our objective?" Michael asked wearily.

"About two hours. Then you can be eating and sleeping, and when you are waking, I will be letting you know what you must be doing."

Michael groaned inwardly. He was already tired and hungry, not being used to so much concentrated exercise. His feet were hot and aching and he had developed a blister on his right heel.

When he got to his feet he found the muscles in his legs had stiffened up. With his joints protesting and his painful heel causing him to limp, he started out on the final part of the journey walking like an old man.

Rani asked him what the matter was, and he explained about the blister.

She asked him to remove his shoe and sock, and while he was doing this, she collected the petals of a number of wild flowers. Crushing these in her hands, she produced a small amount of a sweet, perfumed oil which she smeared on the blister. Instantly it felt cool and a few seconds later it ceased to smart.

"There is camomile in the oil. It will be soothing to your hurt. Be telling me if it is bothering you again and I will be repeating the dose," she said.

With his sock and shoe replaced, Michael found he could walk easily again, although the thought of another two hours on his feet he found daunting. He had assumed that their objective was the distant hills, yet no matter how far they travelled these seemed to get little closer. At first he hadn't thought much about it, but now that only a quarter of the journey remained, the more peculiar this seemed to him and his mind began to dwell upon the fact more and more.

At last he raised the subject with Rani. "We've been on the move for more than six hours and yet the hills seem almost as far away as ever. Is this due to an optical illusion or is there something wrong with my eyesight?"

She smiled. "Strange, is it not. The more we are walking the more we are seeming to make no progress. A bit like Sisyphus, I am thinking; pushing that boulder downhill yet never being able to get it to the bottom because the bottom is always being just out of reach."

Michael was very tired, and for a moment he paid little attention to the allusion, accepting it as merely a parallel of their own situation. Then, with a jolt, he realised he had just been tested in the most natural of ways and had nearly missed the fact. Rani had spoken so gently, and in such a conversational manner, that he had almost been caught off guard and forfeited the opportunity to tackle the third task.

She had taken half-a dozen paces before he responded. She was gazing ahead and looking quite relaxed, as if her words had no significance out of the ordinary. "I think you got that analogy wrong," he remarked.

"Did I?" she replied, trying to look surprised.

"Sisyphus was the King of Corinth in the old Greek myth. He was punished in Hades for his misdeeds by having to roll a stone eternally, but not downhill to an unreachable destination, as you said. He had to push a stone, all right, but uphill, and every time he approached the top it escaped his grasp and rolled down to the bottom, so forcing him to start all over again."

"Perhaps you're right," she said, smiling. "Sometimes I am mixing these things up."

"Have I passed?" Michael enquired drily.

"With colours flying," she replied. "I thought, being tired, you might be falling off balance. You are keeping your wits about you very well."

Michael was a bit disappointed that Rani had tried to trap him. But then he thought she probably had no choice in the matter. The test had not been set by her, and the long trek had been an integral part of that test. It had been designed to weary him sufficiently to lower his guard and make him vulnerable. With the edge taken off his acuity, this would be the best time to slip in the literary rapier when he might not even see it coming.

From now on he would trust no one. Even though he had grown to like his new companions and felt that, apart from the twins, they liked him, he was also aware that they were part of the wizard's game. They set tests, and when he passed them they were pleased, but they also tried to make him fail. He didn't blame them for that, they were the wizard's puppets and could do nothing about their role in his schemes. He blamed himself for forgetting the fact, and would not do so in future.

"Look at the hills now," Rani instructed.

Michael looked, and saw they had grown enormously in size and were no more than three or four kilometres away.

"How did that happen?" he asked, still astounded by some of the things that occurred in this amazing place.

"Test being successfully passed, landscape back to normal."

Canis rubbed against his leg and he bent down and patted her head. Just an animal, he mused, but the only thing in the place I can put my trust in.

"Are we going as far as the hills?" he asked, tiredness making him slur his words.

"To their slopes. There I am telling you what you must be doing."

Now that their destination was relatively close, Michael, although bone weary, forced himself to increase his pace, eager to get there and rest. He didn't know if he was to be tested further, so, trying to ignore his protesting limbs, he made sure he kept his wits about him.

As his speed increased, the more his shoe rubbed against his heel and in a short time the blister was again on fire and he began to limp worse than before.

Rani soon noticed his discomfort and ordered him to stop and sit down. While he watched, she moved elegantly and serenely among the long grasses and wildflowers, exuding a self-possession he felt he would never attain. She plucked petals as before and this time he watched, interested in which types of species she collected.

On the marshy ground close to the river she plucked from Orchids and Ladies Slipper, followed by Ragged Robin, wild Iris and Queen Of The Meadow, while on the dry plain across which they had been walking, he saw her select Poppy and Dog Daisy and Cornflower and other plants he couldn't put a name to, although one of them must have been Camomile. Again she mulched the disparate selection of petals in her hands, and the tiny drop of oil produced soothed his offending heel and he was able to resume the trek without the previous hindrance.

How did you know which flowers to choose?" he asked, now proceeding more slowly.

"In India we are utilizing more than just modern treatments. It is traditional to be making use of the wild plants of the earth as remedies for many ailments. Proper medicines have not been reaching many places in the countryside and in the hills in quantities sufficient to meet people's needs. Old remedies are still having to be followed. My mother was taught by her mother and I have been learning from her."

"She must be very clever."

"Both my parents are exceeding clever. They have been teaching me very much."

"Do you get homesick."

"Every day."

"I wish I missed my parents as much as you do."

"In time I am thinking you will. That is," she added hastily, "if you are being here for some while longer. You might be resenting them now, but be thinking of what you have learned from them. Would you rather not be knowing the things you do, and would you have got as far as this without knowing them?"

Michael knew she had a point, and he also knew that the negative feelings he had about his father had lessened a little of late, but he still resented the fact that if he hadn't been forced to learn so much he wouldn't be here in the first place. He doubted if his bitterness would ever fade away completely.

Rani seemed to read his thoughts. "You were telling me why your father is making you work at your studies so much, but not why he is as he is."

Michael was silent, not sure that he should disclose family business.

"Perhaps I should not be asking you this," she added hastily. "It is just that you are seeming so unhappy."

She looked troubled by this, and her concern seemed so genuine that it helped him to make up his mind. She was someone who would never be able to discuss what he told her with anyone who knew him, so there was little point in remaining silent about the matter.

He collected his thoughts. "There was a tragedy in the family," he said slowly. "My twin sister, Lucy, died when she was eight. I don't think my parents have recovered fully from this."

"You have no other brothers and sisters?"

He shook his head.

She looked puzzled. "Why then is all this affecting your father that he is so hard on you?"

"I think what happened to Lucy disturbed him so much that he wants me to be in the best position to confront whatever befalls me. He stuffs my head with all sorts of things that will never be any use to me, without considering that I might be tough enough and clever enough to deal with any pitfalls that I might encounter. He feels he is preparing me for life ahead. I suppose he means well, but he can be very tiring."

"And your mother; why is she allowing him to do this?"

Michael hesitated, a bit reluctant to talk about his mother. Then he sighed and continued.

"She had a nervous breakdown after Lucy died," he said softly, his mind going back to the time the condition first became manifest. "It took her a long time to get better, and to this day she has moments when depression still affects her. Because of that, even if she believed my dad was being too strict, and at times I think she does, she would not interfere. To do so might mean confrontation, and for the sake of her health, she avoids anything that might be stressful."

Rani looked at him with sympathy, a slight glint of tears in her eyes. "Thank you for telling me," she said simply.

The stood awkwardly for a few moments, then she reached out and took his hand again and they went on in quiet comradeship, the one taking solace from the other's company, while all the time the hills got closer. By now, Michael was so tired he could have lain down and slept on the spot. In contrast, Rani looked as fresh as ever.

As the journey came close to its end, Michael was able to make out wooded slopes on the hills and little streams running down to meet and merge with the river below. It was all so beautiful – the well-leafed trees, the shining waters, the great fields of grass and flowers. As he gazed at the scene, he was reminded of Beethoven's sixth symphony, the Pastoral, and remembered snatches began to slip unbidden into his head. Rani heard him humming some of the melody and didn't speak, content to leave him to his inner rapture.

At last they came to the foothills and to a circle of close-cropped grass surrounded by trees growing close to the river. A number of mountain goats, which had been grazing on the patch, fled at their approach, bounding upwards with sure-footedness over indentations and rocky outcrops into a belt of pine trees.

They were pursued by Canis, whose ambition to run them down was not hatched by her speed or agility and soon she was trailing a long way in their wake. When her quarry disappeared, she stopped and barked at the trees in frustration, before returning hesitantly and exercising more caution on the way down than she had when ascending.

"We will be stopping here and you can be sleeping again," Rani announced.

Thankfully, Michael slumped down with his back against the nearest tree, weary almost to the point of exhaustion.

Rani was gazing round her as if trying to spot something. "Any more tests?" he enquired weakly, not sure if he should relax his guard.

She seemed to find what she was looking for and turned to face him, her expression content. "Perhaps, perhaps not, she answered. "But certainly not before you are taking your rest."

Michael was relieved to hear that. He didn't think he was capable of reasoning properly anymore.

Rani settled down close by and, as she did so, the birdsong that had accompanied them all the way to their present spot ceased as if by magic and, at the same time, the mauve-coloured sky deepened in colour, making it seem almost like nightfall.

"That was clever," Michael remarked drowsily.

"I could be making it black more, if you like," Rani suggested softly.

Michael shook his head, her words coming to him as if from a distance. "It's dark enough," he responded dreamily.

Then he relaxed, and within a minute he was fully asleep.

CHAPTER THIRTEEN

The first sight Michael had when he awoke was of Rani. Her face was in profile, her hair loose and tumbling, shining and black and strangely lustrous in the purple light. She sat, cross-legged and straight-backed, a slim figure gazing towards the open countryside, pensive looking and rather sad. He felt a pang of sympathy for her obvious unhappiness. So preoccupied with her thoughts was she that she had failed to notice he was awake.

He lay for some time watching her, thinking again how beautiful she was, but not just beautiful – composed, serene, and, to his mind, not the least fragile, otherwise, how would she have been able to cope with such a long separation from her loving family. There had to be steel in her also, a strength of mind that allowed her to keep hoping that some day she would see her loved ones again and allow her to make the best of her situation until she did.

He was loath to break into her meditation, but curiosity at last spurred him to do so. He coughed, and when she turned her head and smiled, he asked, "Why were you brought here, Rani? You seem so different from the others."

She reflected a moment before she answered, as if not quite back to reality. "I am not sure," she answered eventually and rather hesitantly, still trying to focus her mind on the present. "Like you, I was having to do some tests, but I was poor in my attempts and soon failing. I can only be thinking that I was selected, not because I was special, but because someone knew of my circumstances and was taking pity on me."

Puzzled, Michael said, "But you love your parents. Weren't you happy at home?"

"Very happy. But it was not from home that I was being taken."

"I don't understand."

"I will be making all plain. My family, and all our relatives who were able, were making a pilgrimage to the great Pitcher Festival, the Maha Kumbh Mela. We were travelling by slow train and for two days were picking up pilgrims. Then we were disembarking and walking the forty odd miles to Allahabad. There we would be praying and bathing in Mother Ganges. Allahabad is five hundred miles to the east of New Delhi.

"By the time we are reaching it there are many, many persons. It was said there were fifty million, all there to wash away their sins in the holy waters.

"I had never seen so many different sects. There were many holy men and many castes from very high, like the Brahmans, down to the very low like the Untouchables, for whom Mr. Gandhi was a champion. The high caste women were very rich and were wearing much gold and beautiful silk saris and fine Pashmina scarves made from the underfur of goats. They had luxury tents to stay in.

"The people of low caste were very poor, the men just in dhotis, the women in simple cotton saris. All were barefoot; many were ill and very thin. I was feeling sorry for them.

"Everything was seeming so strange. There were always crowds, always noise – drums and cymbals and the chanting of mantras, and always dust, thrown into the air by so many feet.

"And there were many beggars and thieves, and we were having to be careful not to be robbed. There were entertainers and jugglers, snake charmers and fakirs, all plying their trade.

"Some of the religious sects were very strange. They were coming from all over India, many with dialects I was not understanding. There were many holy men, some with heads shaven, some with hair plaited. Others, like the ascetic, Naga warrior sect, had long, flowing beards and ash-covered bodies. They were running naked into Mother Ganges, invoking her blessing and waving swords and tridents and spears in the air as they went. They were immersing themselves to the knees at the Sangram, which is the spot where Mother Ganges is converging with the Yamuna and the mythical underground Saraswati river, which embodies true knowledge. They are believing that immersion is accelerating the road to illumination for mankind. Other sects were believing that bathing there during the festival ensures nirvana. Another group was lighting incense and praying for the great river to bless them. As for the members of my family, we were believing that just being there was ensuring good karma for all of us.

"Many pilgrims wore flowers and garlands, and when it came time for them to bathe, they were casting them on the water. All was colour and confusion. Robes and saris and scarves and head coverings were of many different colours; green and gold and saffron and vermillion and simple white were just a few of them."

"How did this festival come about?" Michael interrupted, wondering where the narrative was going.

"It is a very ancient tradition. It traces its origins to a great battle between Hindu gods and demons over a pitcher containing the nectar of immortality. During the fight, Garuda, the flying steed of Lord Vishna, who was carrying the pitcher, was resting at four places in northern and western India and spilling nectar at each spot. One of these places was Allahabad.

"It is one of the holiest times for Hindus, who are believing that bathing in any of the four places guarantees immortality. They are making a great occasion of it, praying, and burning incense and herbs and marijuana.

"I did not like being there. There were too many people; the crowds were enormous, larger than any of us had seen before. We were always being pushed and jostled. It was very hot and very dirty, with dust everywhere, and the smell was not nice – peoples sweaty bodies and the stench from the ablutions. I was frightened. I was only eleven years old and had never been away from home before. The festival was very overwhelming for someone of my age.

"Then I got lost.

"I was watching a poor, crippled man who was having only stumps for legs. He was pushing himself along on a little, flat trolley, trying to avoid bumping into those around him. When I was looking up, my father and mother and all my relatives had moved on.

"I went running in the direction I was thinking they had taken, but the crowd was very great and I could only see a few yards ahead. I was jostled here and there and, in a very short time, I was not knowing where I was, or which way to go, and I became very frightened.

"I was sure they would soon be discovering they had left me behind and would come looking for me. I was close to a man who was performing conjuring tricks and who had made a little space for himself, so I decided to stay close to him, hoping they would come there.

"But they did not. After some hours the conjurer stopped and went away and the crowds were closing the space up again. At that stage I was panicking and beginning to rush here and there, but it was of little use. I could not find them.

"I must have seemed very distressed for a kind man came over to me and was enquiring as to the matter. I was telling him I had lost my parents and he asked me my name. When he was informed, he said he would help me to find them. He was telling me that he knew of a place where all people who had misplaced children went. If someone was finding a lost child like me they were taken there and being reunited with their family.

"I was so happy I went with him willingly.

"We went away from the crowds to a hilly area overlooking the great river where there were many tents. Here the pilgrims were cooking and the smell of lamb and goat and herbs and curry was lovely.

"I thought it was to here I was being taken. But I was wrong. The kind man held my hand and soon he was leading me through this place to a higher one where there were very few people. I was very tired by now and it was growing dark, so I was asking him if we could stop for a rest. But he said no, as the place where lost children were brought was very close.

"I insisted, and he hit me. It was then that I was realising he was not a kind man at all. Some people close by saw him do this, and I was shouting to them for help. But the man said I was his daughter, Rani, and I was misbehaving. They were believing him and he dragged me on.

"A short time after that he was being joined by another man, who took my other arm and they brought me to a hut in the hills where we were all alone. They put me inside and locked the door. It was very dark in the hut and I was able to see nothing. I was so tired by then that I just lay down and cried myself to sleep.

"I was wakened by the sound of voices outside. It was the two men talking. They were discussing what they should be doing with me.

"One man was saying I should be sold to a rich house as a servant, the other was wanting to put me on the streets as a beggar. The man who was wanting to make me a beggar was saying that he would cut off my nose and ears so that people would look at me sympathetically and give me more money. He was considering cutting off my toes as well so I could not run away. They were arguing for some time, but eventually it was agreed they would be taking me to Calcutta and a decision would be made there.

"I was very afraid. When their voices were silent and I was assuming they were asleep, I tried to escape. But the hut was made of strong wood and there was no way to get out except through the door, and it was locked.

"Next morning we set out for Calcutta, which was many days walk away.

"From then on we stayed away from villages and people, and anytime we were meeting someone, I was warned not to say anything.

Once I did try and was beaten for my temerity. The men were walking quickly and I had to keep up with them. If I was lagging behind, one of them would hit me with a stick.

"We were walking for twelve days. I was fed very little, just some rice, now and then. Each night they were tying my hands and feet so I could not escape. It made sleeping very difficult.

"On the thirteenth day the men were arguing again. One did not want to be proceeding any further. The other was insisting they continue to Calcutta, which was another eight days walk away. I could see they were growing tired also, and was afraid they would be changing their plans and killing me.

"The squabble died away, but I could see the man who was not wishing to continue was most unhappy.

"We were walking in the foothills, where it was cooler, and a few hours later we came upon a large house. It had lovely gardens, with flowers and fountains and a place with fruit trees growing.

"When the men were seeing the house they were beginning to argue again. The unhappy one is saying they should try to sell me here.

"After a time, when it seemed they were about to be fighting, the other man is giving in and they are tying me up while they go up to the large house.

"A short while later, one of them returned for me and I was being brought to the back of the house and given to a serving girl not much older than myself. The serving girl took me to a room and told me to wash. She took away my silk sari, which was dirty. When she was returning, I was given a cheap, cotton garment. I am not seeing my beautiful sari there again.

"The owners of the house were from England and they had bought me. I was to be their servant. I was learning from another servant some time later that forty rupees were given to the men."

Michael, who had been listening to all this in horrified fascination, broke in. "Did you not tell them how you had been stolen and brought there against your will?"

"All the time I was there I was never being permitted to speak directly to the mistress of the house and I was rarely seeing the master. He was away for long periods travelling about the country. He was a senior civil servant and advising on the transition to complete Indian autonomy."

"Did they treat you well?"

"I had to work very hard, usually from dawn until dusk. Every day I was having to clean each room in the house and polish the furniture. There were four other servants. One was a cook, two were setting tables, serving meals and washing dishes, and one was a gardener. They were mostly kind to me, especially the gardener, but the cook was beating me once for being in her kitchen. I was not told I should not be there."

"Had the owners any children?"

"Two – an older girl and a boy about my age. They were horrible to me. They would be calling me names and bullying me. When I had tidied a room, they would be messing it up so I had to be doing it again. Sometimes they would strike me."

"Did the mistress know about this?"

"She was seeing them on many occasions, but was just tut-tutting and telling them not to be mischievous. They had private tutors, but when they were not being instructed they made me very unhappy. I would not cry for them, but at night I was shedding tears many times."

Michael felt for her. "Did you not try to escape?" he asked.

"I was not allowed from the house, so I had no opportunity to run away. And where would I be going if I was getting away. I did not know where I was and I had no money. How would I be living? One time, in my mistress's room, I was finding a writing set and a fountain pen. I wrote a note and put it in an envelope with my parents address. I gave it to the cook, who was not living in the house. I asked her to put a stamp on it and post it for me. But she was taking it to the mistress, who was accusing me of being a thief. The master beat me with a cane on the back and shoulders until I was bleeding. As an extra punishment I was given no food for two days.

"I was still having to carry out my chores. I was in very much pain for some time and the boy and girl were striking me on the back when they saw me. They were very cruel."

"How did you get away?" Michael asked, feeling anger at her treatment.

"It was exceeding strange how it happened. It was on my twelfth birthday and I was longing a lot for home. It had been a terribly bad day. The children were being at their worst, teasing and tormenting me for hours. They were throwing food on the floor, and when I had cleaned it up, they were throwing more down where I had cleaned. They were punching my arms and pulling my hair; they were dragging the bedclothes from the beds, and when I tidied them, they were doing it again. Everything I did they were after spoiling. The boy was even leaving a pool of urine on the floor of the bathroom for me to be cleaning it up. I got more and more tired and unhappy as the day was wearing on, and it was almost midnight before I had everything done. It was the day of my birth, yet it had been one of the worst days' of my life.

"My bed was just a rattan mat on the floor of the hall near the front door and I was feeling very miserable when at last I was lying down on it. I was not crying any more, for I had learned it was doing no good to cry. I just was closing my eyes and trying to sleep. I did not think I could, for my mind was full of the injustices I had suffered. But I must have been managing to, because I was awakened by the sound of a great storm. The wind was howling and blowing so hard that the house was shaking dreadfully and pictures were crashing down off the walls. It was very frightening. I was hearing doors banging and people screaming and I was thinking the end of the world had come.

"Suddenly the front door was blowing open and a small dog was standing in the entrance. It trotted over and tugged at my sleeve. I got up and followed it from the house.

"Outside, it was very strange. There was no wind, yet inside I had heard it howling and I was feeling the house rocking on its foundations. As I looked, the roof was blowing off and pieces of stone and wood were starting to fall from the sides.

"The dog began to run and I was running after it. I must be confessing that I was not feeling sad for those I was leaving behind.

"When we were some way from the house it was beginning to rain. It rained very heavily and I was thinking I had never seen such heavy rain, even in the monsoons. Soon the water was streaming down the hillside. We came to a stream. It was a torrent. Suddenly a great gust of wind caught me and blew me into the water and I was swept downstream. I should have drowned, but the trunk of a tree came alongside me and the dog was sitting on it. I took hold of a branch that was sticking out and was able to keep my head above the tumult.

"All was well until we were coming to a series of rapids. With the water thrashing about in a fury, we negotiated the first three, but the fourth was very steep and we were seeming to be falling for a long time. So long that my head was getting light and I must have blacked out. The next thing I was knowing I was in this place and the dog was sitting beside me and licking my face. And do you know, I was wearing my beautiful sari again."

"Wow," was all Michael could say.

The dog in question, which had been absent during Rani's tale, now trotted into the clearing and stopped a short distance from her. It looked at her steadfastly and raised one ear. Distracted, the pain engendered by her remembrances cleared from her face.

"She is telling me I am speaking enough of myself."

"I suppose that means the time has come," Michael said, his mind still partly on the amazing events the girl had outlined. As she had spoken, his admiration for her had grown enormously.

Rani nodded.

Michael felt the muscles in his neck stiffen and a nervous tension begin to well up again. Rani had placed extra pressure on him. Such were the terrible experiences she had gone through, he felt he had to get her out of this place and back to where she would only be really happy.

As he waited for her to speak, he felt a surge of adrenaline, and was surprised to find that he was actually looking forward to the challenge. *Success must breed confidence*, was the thought that entered his mind. And then, taking a more cautious view, he hoped his optimism wasn't misplaced.

"Any more tests?" he enquired.

"None at this time. You have proved yourself fit to continue.

"What must I do?"

"It is quite simple. You will be entering a designated place. You will be spending some time there. When you come out, you will be telling me of something special you have seen. If you are not seeing this thing, then you will be failing and your challenge will be over. You will be staying here with us.

"Mystified, Michael asked, "Is that all you can tell me?"

"That is all you are needing to know."

Rani could see that Michael was bursting with other questions. She put up a hand to stop him saying anything further. "Before leaving, I am saying two things. Firstly, be remembering everything I have been telling you on the way here. There will be something in my words that will help you. Secondly, you will be finding a cow's horn. Change it so it can make a noise."

Her points made, she pointed to a spot where a track left the clearing. It was where she had been looking just prior to him falling asleep. "Take that path. It will be leading you to where you are needing to go."

And with those enigmatic instructions, she leaned forward and kissed him on the cheek. "Do well, Michael. I am praying with all my heart for you to be succeeding. I am speaking for everyone when I say that. Now I must go. Use the talents that the gods' have given you and be bringing me back what I am wanting to hear."

Having no more to say, she turned away and, with Canis trotting beside her, she left the clearing. Michael watched her go, his mind working hard on what she had told him, and making little sense of it.

With a sigh, he gave up the mental struggle for the moment, hoping that everything would fall into place in due course. The path beckoned and he started out towards it. He left the clearing, feeling quite calm now and looking forward to whatever lay ahead. As he did so, the sky turned to a dusty pink.

CHAPTER FOURTEEN

The path was narrow and green with moss, making it slippery in places and suggesting few, if any, feet had trodden upon it. Before long the thin fringe of trees on either side thickened to the extent that, although Michael could hear the river to his left, he could no longer see it. Soon the well leafed branches of mighty oaks and chestnuts began to join high above him forming an arch through which long, pink beams of light filtered downwards, reminding him of his little church at home when the sun's rays streamed through the stained glass windows on summer mornings during Sunday service.

As he walked, the path began to rise, imperceptibly at first and then with an increasing gradient. Only the sound of birdsong accompanied the tread of his feet. He puzzled over Rani's parting advice as he went along. She had said much during their journey and he wondered if he could remember the parts that would help when he needed them. As for the cow horn, he would worry what to do with that when he found it – if he found it.

He continued for half an hour, the trees around him becoming increasingly sparse, all the while the path continuing to ascend and becoming so steep in parts that small steps had been cut into the earth to facilitate the walker. At the end of that time the trees died away completely and he came to a spot where he could see the land ahead.

He found himself at the edge of a cliff. Before him lay a valley through which the river meandered like a bright ribbon. A great sward of pastureland covered the land on either side of the water and he could see animals grazing in the distance. They were too far away for him to determine their species.

On the far side of the river beyond the grassy area, the land rose in a long escarpment. All along its length it was covered in pine trees. On the side of the river where he now stood, the ground was mostly bare of vegetation, consisting of rocky outcrops and areas of shale. Scrub and sage brush grew at intervals, clinging stubbornly to the hillside, their roots shallow in the sparse soil of the impoverished terrain. Half a kilometre from where he stood, a rushing stream had cut a channel into the rock face. It tumbled down the hillside, messily tossing up spray, as if eager to join the river in the flatlands below.

The valley was like something out of a western novel, written perhaps, by Zane Grey or Louis L'Amour. Michael half expected a herd of cattle to emerge at any moment, driven along by lariat wielding cowboys.

The path ran along the edge of the cliff for thirty metres, before turning left and taking a precarious route down the rock-strewn hillside towards the lush area below. He decided to follow it rather than set out across the top of the higher ground. The valley would provide a better surface for him to walk on and he could explore the area there quicker and more easily. And as he would be searching for something special, that seemed the best place to start.

It took him some time to reach the valley floor. The path disappeared in places where the cliff face had crumbled leaving layers of scree. He slipped and slid through these until he reached firmer ground, where he continued at a faster rate until he hit the next patch of rock fragments and had to repeat his precarious performance. On one occasion his feet left him and he had visions of sliding all the way to the bottom. Fortunately he was close to some sage, which he was able to grab and hold on to, so halting his downward progress.

From there on the surface was more stable and he had no further alarms, and, after another ten minutes carefully negotiating the pitfalls of what was now only a rough track, he reached the verdant pastures below.

Making his way to the edge of the grassy area he gazed back the way he had come. Only then did he realise how steep the descent had been, and how dangerous. He didn't fancy the idea of climbing back to where he had started and wondered if there was another way out.

He quickly banished the thought from his mind. Leaving the place was a concern for the future. The present was the only thing that should be occupying him. It meant solving something which wasn't obvious, which might not be tangible, and which he might never find.

He began to walk through the grassland, following the line of the river, looking at everything in the immediate vicinity, hoping to see something, anything, that might seem out of the normal.

At first, the only thing that struck him as odd was the contrast between the opposing hillsides. Apart from a few shiny leafed shrubs, the one that he had struggled down was barren, while the other was covered in healthy looking trees. That meant there was sufficient earth for them to root and grow. How could that be?"

The solution came easily to him. There was nothing strange about it at all: what he was seeing was the legacy of history. In school he had learned about the ice age and glaciers that moved and created valleys such as this. They gouged sections out of the earth's surface, and when they melted, they distributed the sub-soil they had collected along their path. This was done haphazardly, and often all that remained of their presence was a river valley where one side was short of soil while the other had it in abundance. On the bottom of the indentation, rich moraines would be deposited, where grass and plants could grow. Man could either till this, or graze animals on the rich pastures. It was obvious that this was what had happened here. The different landscapes on either side of the river had nothing to do with the answer to his problem. They were not in the least unusual.

The valley was a micro example of what was left everywhere a glacier melted. In this instance it was like something the pioneers in America would have seen as they moved west to open up the vast tracks of unexplored country.

Seeing nothing that would help him, Michael continued with his exploration.

A few kilometres further on the valley swung to the right in a gentle curve. As he followed its contours he thought he heard a sound. At first he believed he had imagined it. Then he heard it again. It sounded like a faint drumming and it seemed to be growing louder. He had no idea what it could be or what might be making it.

The valley had narrowed at that point and feeling exposed in the open, he quickly moved to the side of the hill he had descended. He clambered up about ten metres and hid himself behind a boulder. All the while he was moving upwards the sound grew in volume. Something ahead was charging towards him and he felt he might be in danger.

Popping his head up he kept his eyes on the spot where the bend took the remainder of the valley from his sight. This lay about fifty metres from his hideout. Whatever was making the sound was now close to that point. He crouched lower, making sure he could not easily be seen, a sliver of fear coursing through him.

Louder and louder came the drumming, muffled by distance and the hill, and then, suddenly, it was sharper and easily identifiable. He recognised what it was before the herd of wild mustangs swept round the bend and into his view, their hooves pounding on the firm ground of the valley floor.

They were led by a stallion, a muscular palomino, whose golden mane and tail swished aggressively at it ran. As they neared his vantage point the stallion checked and the following herd of mares slowed. These would have been the grazing animals Michael had seen in the distance when first he had gazed into the valley from his vantage point on the escarpment.

Something had disturbed them.

The palomino was agitated. It brought its harem to a halt almost opposite the spot where Michael had taken refuge. It sniffed the air, shook its head, snorted and whinnied. Michael began to think it knew he was there and got ready to flee farther up the hillside.

But he wasn't the source of the animal's disquiet. The stallion moved behind the mares, and nipping at their rear legs and buttocks, sent them trotting on down the valley. A hundred metres further on, realising their leader wasn't with them, they slowed and then came to a halt, some to graze, others to mill about nervously.

The stallion stood stock still facing back the way it had come, head raised and mane fluffed up, trying to make itself as large as possible. It waited. The mares waited. Michael waited.

Again came a faint sound of drumming hooves. The noise grew in volume and around the bend raced another stallion, a pinto and clearly younger than the palomino. It stopped when it saw its path to the mares was blocked. It snorted, pawed the ground, tossed its head and gave every indication that it wanted guardianship of the herd. It was here to displace the older animal.

Now the palomino took action. With a great snort of anger it charged at the newcomer. The pinto stood its ground and the two mustangs reared in the air, hooves clashing. In the background the mares over which they were fighting moved farther away.

The contest seemed to last an age. Hooves and teeth and heads were used as each animal attempted to gain supremacy over the other. The fight moved back and forth, churning up the grass and ground, sweat soon beginning to glisten on the necks and flanks of the antagonists. Still it went on with neither animal flagging, each biting violently at the other's withers or turning round to aim vicious kicks with their back legs, trying to wound or maim.

Michael watched all this hardly daring to breathe.

Squealing and rearing and pirouetting and charging, both horses inflicted damage on the other, and blood began to mingle with sweat and dust and dirt as the conflict went on and the ground became even more churned up beneath their whirling hooves. The younger animal was game, but it had not yet the strength or cunning of the palomino and gradually it was driven backwards towards the bend. Finally, after receiving one telling kick to the flanks, it whinnied and retreated, and with the older mustang pursuing it and trying to get in one final bite, it fled from the arena leaving the field to the victor.

The palomino slowed and then stopped, watching its adversary until the other horse was out of sight. Flanks heaving and nostrils blood-flecked and steaming, it turned and trotted back. When it reached a spot opposite to where Michael was crouching, it halted and, wild eyed, glared straight in his direction. Then, rearing up until its front legs were high, it kicked the air like a victorious boxer saluting the crowd, while at the same time emitting a great squeal of triumph. Three times it performed the ritual, then, turning, it raced towards the rest of the herd, which began to run before it. Hooves thundering on the dry ground, the mustangs galloped away down the valley, the golden mane of the palomino streaming in a breeze of its own creation.

Michael, part fearful, part fascinated, watched until he could see the wild horses no longer. Only then did he reflect that he had been holding his breath for periods when the conflict was at its fiercest. He realised he had just learned a lesson. Despite looking benign, this was a savage land and from here on he would have to be careful. He knew the stallion had sensed his presence. If the animal ever felt he presented a threat, it would have no hesitation in attacking him. And there was also the pinto. It was somewhere up ahead, injured and untamed. It too provided a threat and was probably more dangerous than the palomino. He would have to be on the look-out for it and take evasive action if it ever appeared.

He knew he could remain where he was no longer, even though there might be perils lying ahead. Something significant was out there somewhere and to free himself and the others from the wizard's bondage, he would have to take risks in his quest to discover it.

As he rose from his shelter, an oblong object, partly wedged beneath one of the nearby rocks, caught his attention. He scrambled closer and at once realized that this was the thing Rani had spoken about. Bleached almost white, the cow horn looked as if it had lain there undisturbed for a long time.

Poking it from its resting place with a thin piece of shale, he found the horn to be quite light. The reason soon became obvious. He expected it to be solid. Instead, it was hollow and rather brittle looking. It curved to quite a fine point.

Change it to make a noise. Rani's words came back to him. He studied the object, trying to decide how best he could do that. He would have to be careful. The shell was so thin that any undue force might shatter it.

After giving the problem some thought, he sat down with his back against a boulder and took his penknife from a pocket. Opening the blades in search of the one with the finest point, he settled for the corkscrew, which had a fine, sharp tip. He closed the other blades.

Drawing his knees up, and wedging the cow horn between them, he used the corkscrew to work on the pointed end, trying to bore a hole. He proceeded slowly and carefully in order not to damage the thing.

Like an egg, the horn was stronger at the point than elsewhere, and quite hard. It took him some time to make a significant impression, but eventually an opening appeared no bigger than the head of a pin. He raised the object to his lips and blew into it using the hole he had created.

Not a sound came.

He enlarged the opening fractionally and blew once more.

Still no sound greeted his efforts, but the air flowed through it better.

He worked on the object some more, using the knife gently in a circular motion. When he was satisfied that the hole was again slightly enlarged, he tried a third time and was rewarded with a screechy whistle.

Encouraged, he gave the point of the corkscrew three soft revolutions, making the hole larger by a minute amount. This time, when he blew into the horn, he covered the open end with his hand as a trumpeter does when he wishes to restrict the air going through his instrument in order to produce a muted effect; and he was delighted to hear a strong note emanating from its mouth. He blew twice in quick succession and synchronized this with a cupping and uncupping of his hand. A wah-wah sound was produced. Happy with that, and not wanting to lose what he had achieved with more tinkering, he tucked the horn into his jacket and rose to his feet.

Making his way down to the grassy area, he set out cautiously towards the bend in the valley from whence the mustangs had emerged.

As he proceeded, he pondered on the other comment made by Rani before he had left her. She had intimated that there were words somewhere in the conversations she had had with him on their long walk which would be of help to him in finding the mysterious something she had spoken about. Fortunately, he had a good memory and he was able to recall almost everything she had said. But try as he might, he was unable to think of anything that would give him an indication of what he should be looking for.

Still thinking about the problem, he followed the curve of the valley, always cautious, always conscious that he was exposed and vulnerable to any animal that wished to attack him.

When the contours straightened once more, the area on either side of the river widened again and the narrow strip of grassland grew broader; the bordering hills gradually diminished in size and began to slope gently downwards to a distant point where they met the ground. Here, the valley came to an end and a wide plain came into view. There was no sign of the pinto and he hoped it had galloped out into the flatlands beyond.

The remainder of the valley was empty of livestock, although, at the river's edge, he noticed the droppings of other animals, possibly cattle or caribou. The signs of the mustangs were there also. Twice he came upon the stripped carcass of an unknown species, which suggested there were predators in the area that attacked their prey when they were watering. Each time he saw the bleached bones he glanced uneasily around, but there was nothing to be seen. Nevertheless, he did not relax his guard, sensing there was danger nearby.

At this point the valley was much like the area where he had witnessed the stallions fighting. The only thing of major difference he could see was the stream that tumbled down the hillside to his right. It entered the river about two hundred metres ahead of him and, when he reached it, he found it so shallow that he could wade through easily. Small fish darted around his feet as he crossed, seemingly unperturbed by his presence. He thought this must have been what the American west was like before the pioneers moved across from the east to populate and develop it – an abundance of grassland and game, with only the native Indian to witness the fact.

On the other side of the stream, he saw the spoor of a large cat close to the water's edge. Perhaps it drank there or preyed on animals that did. The direction of the spoor suggested that the animal came from the hillside to hunt. As there were no signs of remains, its victims must be carried back to a lair somewhere among the rocks before being devoured.

Hurrying on, he soon put some distance between himself and the cat's trail. The area along the river looked idyllic, but was probably where countless, unsuspecting animals had met swift deaths. He shuddered at the thought of it.

A further hour's walk took him to the farthest point of the valley. Here, with the bordering hills petering out, he could now see clearly the extent of the plain. It was enormous, stretching away in three directions as far as the eye could see. Under the dusty, pink light, the landscape looked peaceful and inviting. The river, which had broadened to a sluggish crawl, served only to enhance this perspective. But Michael knew this was deceptive. He was certain there were animals out there that killed, and his sense of danger was stronger than ever. He did not want to become one of their victims.

Another thought that struck him was the lack of other creatures on the plain. If there were predators here, then there had to be food for them. But then, nothing in this place followed normal lines of logic, so he wasn't surprised by the absence of both grazing herds and beasts that hunted them.

Before making the return journey, and tired of his wanderings, he sat down for a while to muse on the things he had seen and to try and find a link between them and Rani's words. It did not take him long for him to realise he couldn't see one. Either he was being stupid or he had not yet encountered the object or scene that would act as a catalyst and change the way he was thinking. When that happened, he would be able to make the connection. If he had already seen this unknown thing and failed to recognize it, then he was in trouble, but he didn't think he had, for at no time did anything he had passed suggest it was other than it was. Nothing seemed of greater importance or interest than anything else. Everything was in its proper place and in harmony with its environment.

With a mounting sense of frustration, he got to his feet and kicked angrily at a mound of scree in front of him. Some of the loose stones scattered. He lashed out at those that remained, but the feeling of dissatisfaction failed to lessen. He was not used to failure and his inability to make any sort of progress with the task was like an itch he couldn't scratch. It left him feeling irritable and helpless.

He began the return journey again thinking about his various conversations with Rani, mulling over for the umpteenth time what had been said. The clues had to be there, but he just could not identify them. A bit despondent, and sensing failure, he trudged along only half conscious of his surroundings. But not for long. He squared his shoulders and raised his head. Depression didn't solve anything and he knew he could not give up. Rani and his new friends were depending on him. Once more he began to take an interest in all that was around him, and immediately felt the better for it.

Galvanised by his new found determination, he had only gone a short distance before he realised that from this angle the valley had taken on a new perspective. Nooks and crannies and small indentations in the hills, which had been obscured on his original approach, were now visible. His interest quickened further. All was not lost. He had not inspected everything and there might still be something close by which would lead to a stirring in his mental stagnation.

And there was.

He had missed it in his haste to get away from the spot where he had noticed the cat's spoor. If he had looked up, he would have spotted a tumbling cataract on the upper reaches of the hillside. Its waters fell steeply for about forty metres, landing on a shelf of rock in a cloud of spray before forming the stream he had waded through. It was cut into the hillside to such an extent that, forty paces on either side of where he stood, anyone looking upwards would not have been able to see it. More importantly, it provided the vital clue for which he had been searching. In an instant he had identified the parts of Rani's conversations that were relevant. They were contained in the Robert Burns poem she had quoted and her offer to darken the light before he slept. Elated, he thought he now had the answer to finding the something special, but not for long and he was soon aware that his problems were only starting.

The beginning of the cataract was near the top of the hillside, at least eighty metres above the spot where he was currently standing. And he had to reach it, for he was certain it held the key to the task given to him. The difficulty was that, when he reached the shelf on to which it fell, the area round it was almost sheer. If he had to climb above this, then from his angle, he could see no way of achieving the feat.

But he didn't give up hope. There might be a route which wasn't visible from below, and the only way to find out if this were so was to start climbing.

He began to follow the path of the stream and, at first, his ascent was straightforward. Although the ground was uneven, the gradient was gentle and posed no great impediment to his progress. He was able to walk the first part of the climb quite easily and was halfway to his objective before things got a bit more problematical.

At that juncture there was a bulge in the hillside, with a narrow crevice at its centre through which the stream was compressed. So steep was this that there was no way up, either in or out of the water. The bulge extended for thirty metres on either side of the torrent and it was immediately obvious that his only hope of getting higher was to circumvent this. He moved sideways under the shadow of the convex mass of rock until he had left it behind, only to find a further difficulty presenting itself.

On this section, the hillside had suffered the ravages of the weather, resulting in a scree slope. Above him lay a mass of loose rock and shale. He tried to scramble up through it, but after he had slid back three times, grazing his hands and knees and releasing a small avalanche of dust and stones in the process, he accepted that there was no further progress to be made at this point.

He retreated.

Making his way back, he followed the course of the stream down to where the slope was less defined and the rush of water less severe. Finding a spot with some useful stepping stones, he crossed over and climbed back up to the bulge on that side. Moving round it, he found the hillside here was firm underfoot; furthermore, a rough track, snaking its way up through rock and gorse in the general direction of the summit, was revealed. Thinking it was probably made by wild goats, he breathed a silent prayer of thanks and set out along its twisting course.

At first his path took him away from the cataract and into a cleft in the face of the hill. By the time he had reached a spot level with his objective, his view was obstructed by a wall of rock, the only evidence of the cataract's presence being the sound of water crashing on to the ledge. But then his luck changed. After another thirty paces, the track took a sudden turn and he found himself edging towards the tumbling water along the face of the hill, the open side falling away steeply on one side. The track here was a mere metre wide. One slip and he would be over the edge, with a resulting fall of twenty metres before he landed. To complicate matters, the ground beneath his feet was covered in a layer of the shale, making underfoot conditions hazardous.

He inched along, nervous now, hearing the roar of the falling water grow louder with every tentative step he took, aware he was close to the source of the sound.

Progressing ever more cautiously, his nose suddenly caught the odour of something peculiar, heavy and unpleasant. Surprised, he could not think what it was, at first, for it was a peculiar place for any sort of smell to be present, the immediate area where he was now perched being completely barren. Then, with a flash of insight, he realised what it could be and the hairs stood up on the nape of his neck. His first instinct was to retreat immediately; but he knew, couldn't. There was too much at stake. No matter what lay ahead of him he had to go on.

Half a dozen faltering steps and he reached a bend. Stopping for a moment to stiffen his resolve, he moved slowly round it. From there he could see the cataract, no more than twenty paces away. He was opposite the mid-point of its cascade and the track seemed to disappear into the falling waters. He took this in at a glance, his mind concentrated on something else that was located halfway between the cataract and where he stood, and from which the fetid odour was emanating.

It was a cave in the rock, which could not be seen from below. Even as he assimilated the fact, there was a movement in its depths and a grayish-brown shape emerged from the entrance. His sense of danger was confirmed. The shape was a mountain lion, and it had scented him. The cat's mouth opened in a silent snarl exposing yellow fangs. Its long tail began to swish ominously.

He froze. His muscles seemed to contract and he felt his legs sag in sudden weakness. The beast's ears went back and its fur stood up menacingly. It sank back on its haunches, its rear end beginning to waggle, and Michael knew instinctively it was getting ready to spring. If it did so, he was at its mercy. He was completely defenceless, caught on a narrow ledge down which he could not retreat at any speed and with a long drop on one side. If he tried to run he would be caught in seconds and dead in a couple of minutes.

Galvanised by the imminent danger, his muscles and his mind returned to life. With trembling hand, he reached frantically into his jacket and hauled out the cow horn, almost dropping it in his haste to extract it.

The mountain lion's muscles had tensed and he knew that within seconds it would launch itself upon him. Hand now shaking almost uncontrollably, he raised the horn to his lips, and not bothering to cup the mouth, he blew into it as hard as he could, praying it would respond as he hoped. A great WHAAAH came roaring out, much louder than the last time. The cat, momentarily startled by the unexpected noise, flinched and then rose uncertainly to all fours. What followed next Michael considered to be a miracle.

The sound he had made was trapped in the valley and began to echo up and down between the two ranges of hills. He blew again, even harder than before, and the combination of his efforts and the responding echoes made it seem as if twenty people were making the commotion.

The mountain lion, bewildered now, and not sure what it was facing, half turned as if to flee, no longer concerned that its territory had been invaded. Michael blew a third time, and with the other reverberations still sounding out, the increased din was sufficient to deter the beast from attacking him. To his immense relief he saw it turn away, still snarling and showing its fangs, and then, with a defiant roar, it loped off towards the cataract, where it vanished into the curtain of water and spray.

Feeling drained, Michael sagged against the rock wall, the racket he had created still ringing and counter-ringing between the close-set hills. It continued in decreasing volume for some time, until, eventually, it faded away. Now he knew why Rani had given him the odd instruction about the cow horn. It had turned out to be his salvation.

He stayed slumped where he was for a while, trying to steady his frayed nerves, trying to regain his composure. So terror-stricken had he been that he was thankful he hadn't wet himself, or even worse, messed his trousers.

He continued to wait, unwilling to follow the path the cat had taken, wanting it to get well clear before he went on. He didn't think his heart could survive another encounter with the beast. It was still beating too rapidly and he felt sick and breathless and very weak at the thought of his narrow escape. He shuddered at the memory of it and what would have happened if the animal had pounced. He breathed a silent prayer of thanks to Rani for his survival.

Eventually he managed to get himself under control, his nerves now reasonably steady and his heart back to a near-normal beat. The feeling of sickness had disappeared and, although still reluctant to resume his journey, he knew the time had come to proceed, there being no good reason for him to put off the moment any longer. Two deep breaths, and with the horn clasped tightly in his hand ready to use if necessary, he pushed himself away from the wall of rock and set off in the direction taken by the mountain lion.

He went slowly, his near escape making him extremely cautious, praying he was not walking into further danger. He edged past the cat's cave, hoping it didn't have a mate lurking in the dark recesses.

The stench coming from the opening was almost overpowering and he had a vision of skin and bones and the putrefying remains of animals killed and devoured by the beast. He held his breath until he was past, but the sickening odour continued to follow him until he was almost at the spume filled air of the cataract.

The track led directly to the cascade. Such was the spray being thrown up by the water dashing on to the shelf below that before he got close to the spot where the mountain lion had disappeared from view his clothes were wet through. Edging closer and shielding his eyes with a hand, he was able to see that there was a gap between the rushing water and the rock over which it tumbled. The gap was a continuation of the track he'd been following and had clearly provided an escape route for the mountain lion.

Pressing close to the hillside, he ducked through the spray and water and emerged into a cavern behind the cataract. The instant he was inside he became aware of a change within himself, a feeling of calm, and more, a sense that he was at home in this place. At first he could make nothing out. Having stepped from bright light into gloom his eyes took a few moments to adjust. But when his sight returned, he saw that the cavern was about six metres across and about four metres high. The floor was flat and appeared to have been worn down by something other than the elements. He tried to analyse the feeling that gripped him, and decided it was one of awe. There was something cathedral-like about the atmosphere. Instinctively he knew the cavern was very old, and more; it could well have been holy ground for an ancient people. If so, it deserved respect. He felt almost as if he were intruding and hoped he wasn't desecrating anything by being there. If he was, he was sorry for the fact, but it couldn't be helped. He had to explore further, for his task was not yet at an end.

As he looked around, he realised that the light seeping into the place was not wholly the result of the cataract's translucency. There was too much of it for that. He came to the conclusion that there must be another opening somewhere, otherwise the big cat would have been trapped and would be waiting for him.

He edged deeper into the cavern, moving away from the pounding water, treading cautiously, the cow horn at the ready. But there was no sign of the beast. With every step he took the air grew lighter. Soon he saw an opening up ahead. He stopped.

Now he could see everything clearly – the floor, the walls, the low roof, and he knew for certain that he was not the first human to have walked in this lofty vault. There must have been many. Perhaps with wood and stone implements they had levelled the floor, started fires by striking flints, eaten the animals they had hunted and killed with spears or bows and clubs. The walls spoke to him. He could hear the sound of voices from people long gone, strange tongues from a dead race, incomprehensible to him. Ghosts walked here. He could sense their presence. A psychic legacy from unknown forbears stirred within him; and certainty consumed him. They were benign.

He did not know how long he remained there, but something held him. He walked between the narrow walls, studying everything that was there, and as he moved he became aware of strange stirrings in the air, heard soft whisperings in his ears, sensed rather than saw little eddies of dust around him and knew that others were walking with him. He felt safe. As long as he remained within these walls he would come to no harm. He felt a strange affinity for the place and the long-dead tribe that had used it. It seemed as if they had accepted him as one of their own and were sending out messages to tell him so. Perhaps these were the spirits of his ancestors. If so, he welcomed the communion with them, at peace in their presence.

Close to the entrance he came upon a circular indentation in the stone floor. Peering into it he saw a flaky, white substance. Dropping to one knee, he dipped in a hand and discovered ashes and tiny bits of charred wood. His earlier surmise had been correct. This was the spot where the ancient people had heated the cave and cooked their food. Strategically located near the mouth of the cave, the smoke could escape and keep the air clear of noxious fumes.

He sat beside it. Cross-legged, he pictured the scene that must have occurred many centuries before. Native Indians, no doubt, would have rested here after a day's hunting, enjoying the food they had killed. They would have kept the flame alive throughout the winter, slept round it covered in skins, raised their children by its warmth. In the long, dark evenings they would have made and honed weapons, shaped implements, carved bone for decorative purposes, or simply for amusement; told stories of fierce warriors and great hunters who had gone before them. He felt a great sense of belonging. As he sat, the sounds around him stilled, as if the spirits rested also, as if they accepted his presence, as if they were content in his company.

He gazed at the walls surrounding him, so different from those in his own home, but somehow comforting. They told him more than any modern structure could. He sat for a long while, imbibing the unique atmosphere, unwilling to leave.

Finally, and with great reluctance, he rose. He had dallied longer than he should have done. Almost in a trance, and certain that he was among friends, he dragged himself away, his will in danger of being overwhelmed by the forces around him, both mystical and uplifting. The mouth of the holy place beckoned. He was almost sorry when he reached the opening, such was the bond that had been forged between him and the spirits of the people he was about to leave.

He gazed outward. The land lay below, the hill at this point stretching away in a gentle slope. It was covered in trees – spruce and birch and pine and the mighty redwood. It melded naturally into the wide plain. But now the plain had changed. Unlike before, the vast landscape was now dotted with grazing animals. At first he could hardly believe what he was seeing. But there was no doubt. The huge heads, the characteristic humps, the great, hairy bodies were not figments of his imagination. There were thousands of the beasts, stretching away into the distance as far as the eye could see.

Buffalo.

In this peculiar land they were far from extinction. As he gazed in awe upon the scene, he felt privileged to be in their presence.

There were other animals too, but in lesser numbers. Caribou, and young mustang stallions running together; no mares, the young horses neither mature enough nor strong enough yet to fight for, and win a harem. The pinto might well have been one of them.

And in the natural order of things there were predators also, lurking on the fringes of the great herds, seeking to bring down the sickly and the old, or steal newborn calves from their mothers. He saw coyote and wolf and even his adversary, the mountain lion, slinking near the trees, eyes fixed on the mighty beasts as they grazed and slowly moved on.

Mesmerised, he stood for long minutes knowing that he was looking at something that he would never see again, a spectacle that only the native Indian and the early settlers in America would have witnessed as they pushed west. He did not know what Power had brought them here. He did not care. He only knew, that in his lifetime, it was a sight that would never be surpassed.

At last, and with great regret, he made the decision to move on. He hoped he had the information to satisfy Rani. If not, at least he would have the consolation of an unforgettable experience.

One last look into the sacred cavern and he turned and began to climb the tree-studded slope around it. He did not want to return the way he had come, and something was telling him that this was the way to go. Some sense within him was saying that he was safe, some supernatural force guiding his footsteps and assuring him he was not alone. It was strangely comforting

The climb was relatively easy, and when he reached the top he found himself on a long plateau. With the plain behind and to his left, and a ridge rising at right-angles to the plateau on his right, he started back to seek the spot where he had taken the precarious route down into the valley.

Although rocky in places and containing small pools of clear water, the uneven surface proved little impediment to his progress. When he had walked for a further two hours, the cow horn back inside his windcheater, and all the while conscious of another unseen presence as a companion, he spotted the wooded area through which he had come. That part of his quest now seemed an age ago.

Tired now, he could have rested, but with the blissful state he had experienced earlier largely dissipated, he wanted the journey to be at an end, so he continued walking.

Close to the trees, and with the path through them visible, the ridge which had obstructed his view to the right, ceased abruptly and the river came back into view.

He halted at that point, unwilling to go on, knowing that his quest was almost at an end. He could hear a voice in his head, soft but insistent. The words being spoken were in a tongue foreign to him. That didn't matter. He understood everything that was being said. The voice was telling him that he must mark the experience, make a gesture of respect. There was no further instruction, but, instinctively, he knew what he had to do.

Taking the horn from his jacket, he laid it in a small hollow at the centre of the plateau. Gathering a number of rocks, he placed them round the little relic and built a cairn over it. The horn must not leave this place. It belonged here. It was part of the area's history.

When the last rock was in place, he chose a smooth-sided one set near the top and scratched his initials on it with his penknife. If anyone came this way again they would wonder who he was. Such a mystery was befitting of the place. And a part of him would be left there too. And that seemed right also.

When he had finished, he rose and looked back the way he had travelled with his unseen companion. With the plain and the animals spread out to the front and right of him, and the river valley to his left, he raised his arms in silent supplication. Closing his eyes, he thought for a few moments of all those who had gone before him in this hallowed land, and gave thanks for the privilege that had been bestowed upon him.

When he opened them again, he found that the sky had changed from dusty pink to brilliant yellow, and the presence that had accompanied him from the cavern was gone. And so too had the animals. The great plain was empty – not a buffalo, not a mustang, not a coyote, not a vulture anywhere. The vast stretch of land had returned to the state in which he had first observed it. The fact didn't bother him, and somehow he was not surprised. He knew that some external force had permitted him to see it as it once had been, and for that he was grateful. He hoped that the memory of it would always remain with him.

He turned and, taking a steep track down the edge of the plateau, the plain now hidden from his view, he made his way back through the trees and on to another world, a place just as bizarre as the one he had left behind.

CHAPTER FIFTEEN

When Michael reached the clearing Rani was there. Canis was asleep beside her, head resting on her front paws. Rani was seated in the lotus position, back straight, eyes closed, meditating. In her composure she looked serene and beautiful.

The sense of contentment that Michael had been experiencing since first entering the cavern was still with him and, not wishing to disturb her, he sat down on the spot where he had slept and kept a watching brief.

As he waited for the end of her meditation, the others joined her. First the twins who, strangely for them, were quiet, then Jim Crow and Yuri, who entered together, and lastly, to his surprise, the Victorian gentleman.

No-one spoke, each being content with a nod in his direction. They arranged themselves behind Rani in a semi-circle, and each, in their turn, adopted the lotus position, even the Victorian gentleman, who looked decidedly uncomfortable. Like him, they waited. In deference to the Indian girl, they made no sound.

At last, Rani stirred. She opened her eyes and looked at him. Simultaneously, Canis raised her head and sat up. On seeing Michael she began to bark.

"Shush, Canis," Rani chided gently. The dog quietened and lay down again, tail thumping the ground. "You are back, Michael," she said, turning her attention to him. "Were you being successful?"

The others looked on with interest.

"I think so," he said.

"Did you find a wonderment?"

"It was all a wonderment," he replied, using her quaint term. "I saw wild mustangs fight; I chased away a mountain lion with a cow horn; I found a cavern behind a waterfall, and I saw thousands of buffalos grazing on a plain that seemed to stretch to infinity."

"And which was proving a rapture to you?"

"All of it. But mostly the buffalos. They were majestic – one of the finest things I have ever seen. It was as if they had never been on the verge of extinction."

A shadow of disappointment crossed Rani's face. In the

background the twins perked up, Jim Crow looked concerned and Yuri, along with the Victorian gentleman, remained inscrutable.

Rani spoke again. "And this is the special thing you are returning to tell us about?"

"Not that," Michael replied, teasing her. "I built a cairn over the cow horn on a plateau overlooking the great plain and a river valley. I thought it belonged there. It was my way of saying thanks for the experience to those who had gone before me."

Rani's voice was sad. "So you are telling me this was being the most special moment for you."

Michael looked past her at the others. The twins were grinning, Jim Crow's face wore an expression of despair, and even Yuri looked perturbed. Only the old gentleman remained unmoved.

Michael felt like laughing. If his eyes could have twinkled they would have done so. "I didn't say that," he rejoined, managing to keep a straight face.

"You were finding something else?" Rani asked, her tone cautious.

Michael decided to put her out of her misery. "Something quite astounding," he said.

Rani's countenance brightened visibly. "You will be telling us now?"

"I will be telling you now." Michael halted for a few moments, putting his thoughts together. When he spoke again he had gone back a couple of stages to where Rani had given him the enigmatic clue to help him in his search.

"When you told me to remember everything you had said, at first I could make no sense of this. I walked the length of the valley with it gnawing in my mind, but could neither find nor see anything to help me make the connection with your words. It was only on the return journey, when I saw the cataract, that everything fell into place.

"You had quoted a piece from Robert Burns – *Ye banks and braes o' bonnie Doon*. Just before I went to sleep you asked me if I wanted the sky darkened further, but you used a strange phrase. I was drowsy at the time and didn't pay much attention. Later on, when I remembered this, the odd construction of your words became crucial."

He paused, noting that everyone was now eyeing him intently. When he had first come here he would have been nervous addressing a group of people so much older than himself. Since then, however, with each success, he had felt his confidence grow and now he was able to enjoy the experience. He continued.

"The sky had just changed from mauve to a deep purple and you asked me if I wanted it black more. At first I put this down to your individual way of saying things, but, eventually, I realized that, even with your odd syntax, this was so clumsily put that it was not how you would normally have phrased it. If you want to deepen the colour purple, it would be more proper to use the word darken, not a reversed comparative of the word black. That made me think that the wording was not unintentional and led me to concentrate on this and the poetic reference, *Doon*.

"It didn't take me long to realize that neither were right in the context in which they made sense. But a simple tweak corrected this. *Doon* became *Doone* and *black more* all one word, and a proper name, to boot. Nothing is ever simple here and I know now these differences were to make things more difficult for me. In short, you were pointing me towards a novel – *Lorna Doone*, written by *RD Blackmore*. In the book, the hero, John Ridd, climbs a waterfall on to Doone land, where he sets eyes on Lorna Doone for the first time. Knowing that, I also knew that the solution to my problem lay somewhere beyond the cataract, and like John Ridd, I too would have to climb it in order to complete the task."

"And will you be telling us what you found?" Rani broke in almost impatiently.

"Now you will know," Michael said, deciding to keep them on tenterhooks no longer.

"As I mentioned before, there was a cavern behind the falling water. The moment I entered it I knew I was in a holy place, a place that an ancient people had used, probably native Indians. The spirits spoke to me from the walls using a tongue I didn't understand. But I knew they welcomed my presence. Don't ask me how, I just knew. I seemed to have a rapport with them. Perhaps they were aware of my quest, perhaps they sensed I shared their understanding that man and nature are interdependent. Destroy one and the other is destroyed. All this came to me as if in a trance and I felt honoured to be in their midst.

"They bestowed a great favour upon me. They showed me the great herds of deer and buffalo that supported their existence. They allowed me to witness the great beasts grazing, cropping the pastureland, leaving their droppings to fertilize and enrich their feeding grounds so that there would be food in abundance for them on their return. I saw the predators that lived off them, the coyote, the mountain lion, the vulture. All they were doing was fulfilling the law of nature, where one animal dies so another might live. I saw the cycle of life and death in the wild and, like that ancient tribe, understood the need for it.

"And when I looked back after building the cairn for the cow horn, the great herds were gone, and I knew then they had never been there. They had merely been a vision telling me that they were wiped out, and in that act of sacrilege, the tribes that had depended upon them for meat and hide and bone, were rendered extinct also. Another larger tribe, whose aims were rooted in greed and selfishness and who had no concern for the balance of nature, had seen to that. The white man had not the nobility of the native Indian."

Rani interrupted his preaching, her voice quiet. "And is it this mystical experience that you are believing is the answer to my request?"

Michael shook his head, aware of how he must have sounded. "In part only. There is one other thing. Lorna Doone had a brother who hated John Ridd and his family. His name was Carver Doone. When I saw the inside of the cavern I knew I had completed my task."

"And how was that so?"

"The ancient people were great whittlers, especially of wood; but they were more than that. They were carvers; carvers of bone, carvers of implements, carvers of stone. They had even carved pictures of animals into the walls of their holy place – deer, buffalo and wolves, and caricatures of tribesmen hunting with bows and arrows and spears. To see these was just as special to me as my communion with the spirits or witnessing the great herds."

He paused, and then said softly, "This, I think is the final piece of what you want to hear."

Rani looked at him for a long moment. Michael held his breath. The onlookers watched her. When she smiled suddenly, all except the twins smiled with her. "Michael," she said, unable to keep the relief from her voice, "it is you who are being special. You have kept our hopes alive."

Hardly had she uttered the words than the others rose to congratulate him. Canis beat them to it, and laughing, he had to fend her off as she jumped all over him in her excitement.

When the back thumping and the hand shaking and the kisses on the cheek from Rani, and even Paula, were over, they wanted to know more about his adventures, so, for the next half hour or so, he described his journey and all that had happened to him. Many questions and a lot of admiring comments later, he was allowed to end his narrative and relax.

At that point the Victorian gentleman brought a more serious note to the proceedings. The others immediately deferred to him, which made Michael think that he was the eminent person in the group.

In his slightly old-fashioned way of speaking, he said, "You have done exceeding well, Michael; certainly much better than I expected. I have to profess that on our first meeting I thought you would not go far. You seemed angry and resentful and ill-fitted for the trials that lay ahead. I was of the opinion your personal problems would inhibit you and lead to early failure. Thankfully, you have proved me wrong. You have mellowed, become more adult and less self-centred. I believe you are now a better person than you were when you arrived. I now have to tell you that you are only the second contender in this cycle of tasks to have reached this stage. And, of course, it goes without saying that no one has successfully tackled all four tasks."

Michael glanced at his other companions. Their faces gave nothing away, and he could not tell who had been in this position before him.

The Victorian gentleman read his thoughts. "The person who made it through to this juncture is not in our company. I hope you will meet him soon, but, for now, that is not possible."

"Will he instruct me on the nature of the final task?"

The Victorian gentleman shook his head. "Unfortunately, he is not in a position to do so. That duty will be performed by me. But enough of that for now. I would be doing you a disservice if I sent you out on the final challenge immediately on the back of the previous one. You must have a chance to relax and recharge your mental and physical powers. You shall eat and sleep, but before then you need something to take your mind off the hardship to come. Tell me, what would you like to do?"

Michael didn't like the sound of that. The previous tasks had been difficult, but nobody had referred to them as a hardship beforehand, and he wondered just what might be different about the last one to warrant such a comment.

His new friends were staring at him, awaiting a reply to the question. Noting their impatience, and rather than dwell on the point, he put all thoughts of the future to one side for the moment. He would have plenty of time to dwell on the Victorian gentleman's words at a later stage. For now he needed to think of the others. They gave the impression of being in limbo, waiting to see if he could free them. *They* also needed some form of recreation in order to stop them dwelling on his possible success, or probable failure.

He kept them waiting a while longer, trying to think of something they could all do. Then his mind honed in on a game played at his house with his parents and some of his relatives on Christmas night, when everyone else he knew was probably watching television. At least he considered it to be a game, but it wasn't really, more of a diversion.

He said, "I would like you all to take part in telling me a story. Any of you can start. He or she can speak for a few minutes until I stop you, then someone else, nominated by the first speaker, has to continue. When that speaker is stopped, he or she chooses the next one and so on until each has had a go. This will continue until everyone has spoken five times. The fun is in seeing how imaginative you can be, and in creating problems for the next speaker.

When he finished explaining the rules, he felt it all sounded a bit lame and thought the twins would refuse to take part, deeming it to be beneath their intelligence. But, to his surprise, they greeted the suggestion enthusiastically and Paul even insisted on going first.

Brimming with self-confidence, he made them all sit cross-legged in a circle. Then, he stood in the middle, posed theatrically, and began to speak, his hands waving expressively as his tale unfolded. He created a character who got himself into all sorts of scrapes and, when Michael halted the dialogue, the hero of the story was chained to a chair in a room slowly filling with water.

As Michael had stipulated that each storyteller could select the next person to continue the tale, Paul chose Yuri, who immediately put himself in the position of the person trapped and, using an old Harry Houdini trick, which he described in detail, managed to release himself and escape through a skylight when the water was high enough, but not before he had built up the drama of the situation with a will-he, won't-he, element in his discourse. He continued the process of placing the hero in a well-nigh impossible situation and, when Michael stopped him, he passed the serial on to Jim Crow, beaming with delight as he did so.

The black man naturally transferred the action to the southern states of America and introduced redneck sheriffs and the Ku Klux Klan as the villains of the piece, before giving way to Rani, who, in turn, developed the tale along different lines, but with no less enthusiasm. Paula ended the sequence with a series of twists and turns that spoke well of her imagination and even outdid her brother for ingenuity. Paul, eager to get going again, started the next round.

Amid much raillery and good-natured banter, the storytelling got more and more eccentric and more and more outrageous and soon had Michael laughing so much his sides got sore. It soon became clear that the twins thrived on the idea and their invention at times was brilliant, causing immense problems for those following them. Some, who could not plausibly extricate the hero from the predicament he was left in, used the scenario of, *one bound and he was free*, which brought good-natured booing and protests from the other players, but at least had the value of allowing the whole thing to continue.

The Victorian gentleman, who had elected himself as adjudicator, took no part in the proceedings. But he watched with interest, and, from time to time, betrayed his enjoyment with a small smile. He had reverted to a normal sitting posture and seemed more comfortable. There was so much fidgeting and jiggling around by the others in the excitement of the contest that only Rani now continued to sit cross-legged.

Such was the extent of the fun they were having that the condition stipulated by Michael of five rounds each was exceeded by far, and it was left eventually to the Victorian gentleman to bring the entertainment to an end, causing much groaning, and beseeching from the participants to allow it to continue for a while longer. He declared Paula to be the winner by a short head from her brother, which brought good-natured protests from the others and smug looks of triumph from the twins.

Despite their disappointment at his decision, he remained adamant, declaring that Michael must be in the best possible condition to tackle the final task. That meant that he had to eat and sleep, and the time for that had now come. As a concession to the others, and as they hadn't had a meal since the last feast with Michael, when they'd all had Indian food, he would allow them to stay and eat with the boy. This time, they could choose what they wanted.

That pleased them, and when Michael asked for cod and chips in paper, it materialised immediately. Salt and vinegar was an extra. His companions, not having eaten such lowly food before, looked at him in surprise. But Michael was happy with his choice. Not allowed this at home, and only experienced illicitly when he was out with Maxie, he took the opportunity once more to savour the forbidden.

Surprisingly, the twins also opted for modest fare, selecting hamburgers and French fries, followed by ice cream consisting of four different flavours. The latter dish came in huge quantities, making the others wonder how they could possibly eat it all. But eat it they did, smacking their lips with relish and scraping their plates to secure every last drop.

Yuri asked for some strange, meat concoction and a glass of vodka, while Rani had a Tandoori dish of curried lamb, which she placed in her lap and ate daintily and with great absoption. Jim Crow chose sweet potatoes, fried pork and black-eyed peas.

The Victorian gentleman abstained, explaining that it was not long since he'd had a repast. A short time later he changed his mind, feeling he was being unsociable. He decided to have a roast beef sandwich, with a glass of wine to wash it down. The wine was a fine Bordeaux, and he sipped it before saying that he had chosen red because modern thinking was that it was good for the heart. Paul immediately suggested that he should send some to the wizard.

Ignoring the gibe, the older man glanced at Michael and asked mischievously, "Who invented the sandwich?"

"Is this another test?" the boy mumbled in reply, his mouth full of food.

The Victorian gentleman smiled. "Not this time. I'm just curious to know if you know, that's all."

Michael didn't even have to think. "The Earl of Sandwich," he replied.

"Which Earl?"

"I think it was thought of in the 1760s,' Michael mused. Probably the fourth, but I could be wrong."

"You could be, but you're not. What a load of facts you have crammed away in that head of yours."

"Mostly trivia," Michael muttered modestly, and went back to concentrating on his fish and chips.

"Sometimes trivia is more important than you suppose. You never know when you might need it," the Victorian gentleman remarked ominously.

When the meal ended, they sat chatting for a while, and Michael marvelled at the speed at which he had made friends with them all, even the twins, who seemed to be mellowing. Their worst excesses were nothing in comparison with the bullies and teasers who abused him at home. Here, he was treated as an equal. He was liked, not looked on as a freak. He felt a warm glow of pleasure in their company. Again the thought crossed his mind that if he failed in the final task, this would not be a bad place to be. He was happy here.

But then he looked at the others and was once more struck by how much some of them wanted him to succeed. For their sake he had to do his best. They were depending on him. His stomach tightened. Their hopes were a burden, one that he was not sure he wished to carry. He shrugged the thought away, but not entirely, and he was left with the uneasy feeling that maybe too much was being asked of him.

Soon afterwards their voices became a pleasant drone on the edge of his consciousness, and as much as he would have liked the occasion to continue, the excitement and physical excesses of his day began to take their toll. Tiredness enveloped him. He yawned, feeling drowsy, and his head began to nod. Seeing this, his new friends slipped away one by one, leaving only the Victorian gentleman behind them.

"Take a good rest, Michael," he advised softly. "When you wake I will let you know what you must do to complete the final task. It will not be easy." And with a pat of the boy's shoulder, he too was gone.

Michael fell asleep harbouring no worries, no anxiety, the self-doubt he had experienced earlier quite gone. What happened when he wakened was of no consequence at present. At that moment in time he was content.

CHAPTER SIXTEEN

Once again the landscape had changed utterly.

First he had encountered a tropical rainforest, then lush pastureland, followed by a river valley with glacial features. Now he was faced by a desert.

The Victorian gentleman had led him a short distance from the clearing along a route at right angles to the one by which he had arrived. In no time at all they were standing at the edge of a barren land. The hills were still in view to their left and still the main feature of the landscape, but they had slipped down in a series of gentle gradients to ground level. To their right and front the land was sandy and arid, with scrub rather than grass appearing infrequently. There was no wildlife to be seen; no birds, no bees, no butterflies. Apart from the odd rocky outcrop of sandstone, the area upon which they gazed was a wasteland, empty and uninviting.

The Victorian gentleman spoke. "You must go out there and find someone."

"Who?"

"The one I spoke to you about. The last person to reach the fourth task. He was sent out to find an answer to something. He did not return."

"How long ago was this?"

"In your time, approximately seventy-five years."

But I thought this was a short while ago," Michael exclaimed in amazement.

"You are forgetting, the ones chosen to attempt the tasks are from different generations, usually twenty-five years apart. If we count the twins as one, then three have tried since then, and that includes you."

But why hasn't someone been sent to find out what happened to him before now, that is if it's a he we're speaking about?"

"It is indeed a he. And the answer is simple. No person is permitted to enter an area designated for a task unless he or she has qualified to do so. This has been laid down. Therefore, as no one else reached this stage since he did, no one could go in search of Orwell Thomas."

"Orwell Thomas; Welsh, is he?"

"I believe that is so. A relative of the fellow who wrote *Animal Farm* and *1984*, I am told."

"He could be dead," Michael said worriedly, ignoring the reference to George Orwell.

"The Victorian gentleman shook his head. "He is not dead."

"How can you be so sure?"

"I have been told. The birds sing it, the wind whispers it, the river growls it out as it passes."

"Why do you hear these things when no one else does?"

"I have been here the longest. I am the oldest. Because of that, the dubious honour of hearing things that others cannot has been bestowed upon me. I say dubious because it has its sadnesses. I am the first to know when someone has failed. I am the one who is aware that the light of expectation on the faces of the others will soon be extinguished. I am the one who has lived with the knowledge that Orwell Thomas is still alive and awaits someone who has reached this stage, someone who may be able to discover what has befallen him and bring him out."

Michael's shoulders sagged as if an even greater weight had been placed upon them. Now, not only did the hopes of Rani and the others rest with him, but he was expected to go into the unknown and effect a rescue of someone he hadn't met, from a situation he knew nothing about.

"Take heart," his companion said gently. "You have much enterprise. If anyone can do this, it is you."

"I wish I had your faith."

"We must all have faith? After all, it is faith in the ability of our fellow beings that keeps our hopes alive. Can't you see it in Yuri and Jim Crow, in Rani, and even the twins, though they try hard not to show it? All have faith in you. Hope springs eternal, you know, and you must never forget that."

Doubts about his ability still assailed Michael, despite the man's fine words. He should have been comforted by them, his resolve should have been strengthened, but all they did was magnify in his mind the magnitude of the task that lay ahead and his inadequacy to tackle it.

"What was Orwell Thomas asked to find out?" he enquired weakly.

"Why the sky changes colour."

"And the answer lies out there?"

"That, I am led to believe."

"That sounds as if you don't know."

"This is the final task. I am a cautious man. I have thought many times over the years that Orwell Thomas might not have been destined to succeed. Perhaps there was no answer to that question and the wizard meant him to fail. Perhaps he intends to keep us here forever. He is cruel. He raises our hopes knowing that ultimately they will be dashed."

"Where's your faith now?" Michael asked, unwilling to accept the Victorian gentleman's hypothesis.

"It is still with me. But it is natural to have doubts, and I sometimes question the wizard's motives. Even if I am right, I can always pray he will change his mind. And, of course, I can always hope my doubts are groundless. By coming this far you have given me the chance to determine if they are."

"Are you the wizard?" Michael asked suddenly.

The Victorian gentleman laughed. "Oh, if only that were the case; I could release everyone in an instant. Unfortunately, all I can do is relay his thoughts and his wishes."

Michael noted he hadn't actually denied that he was and wondered if his companion was being deliberately disingenuous. But he felt it better not to pursue the subject.

"Have you a test for me before I begin?" he asked.

"Do you want one?"

"Perhaps I should say yes, then I could fail it and wouldn't have to go."

"Would you want to do that?"

"I suppose not. That would be the coward's way out."

"It would indeed."

"Is there one?"

"Why do you ask?"

"There has always been one before."

"Not this time. Anyone who reaches this stage has proved to be more than worthy of tackling the final trial. You are in that category, a credit to your upbringing."

Michael could hardly believe his ears. His parents were being praised for the person he was, or the Victorian gentleman believed he had become. That came as something of a shock. He was not sure he liked the idea, for he hated to give his parents credit for anything, especially his dad. But even as he maligned them mentally, the thought struck him that perhaps he was being a bit unfair. Without the knowledge he had attained from his dad's draconian methods, the

Victorian gentleman and his newfound friends would not now hold him in such esteem. And he had to confess their opinion meant a lot to him. So, perhaps, it was time to reassess his view of his parents. But not now: now he had more important things to think about.

"Have you any advice for me?" he asked, hastily dismissing the uncomfortable thought from his mind.

"I always have advice," the Victorian gentleman said, smiling. "I will say two things to you. Do not trust appearances, and remember your Homer."

"Can you elaborate?"

"I'm afraid not. That is all I am permitted to say. If you heed my words, it should be enough to see you through."

Michael felt the nervousness build in him and thought it a good sign. He always seemed to perform better when he was on edge. "Then there is no reason to wait?"

"None at all. Go now. Find Orwell Thomas, if you can, and discover why the sky takes on so many colours. You know our thoughts are with you."

"I know," he replied. "I just wish I were only doing this for myself."

"You have a power in you, Michael. Use it well. And never forget, with power comes responsibility. That is your cross. It always will be."

Michael wasn't sure what to say to that, so he let it pass. "See you soon," he muttered, feeling not a whit comforted."

"I hope we do."

Those being his last words, the Victorian gentleman turned on his heel and headed back towards the trees. As he did so, the others appeared to see Michael off.

"Two minutes," he called to them as they passed his retreating form.

They didn't take two minutes.

Jim Crow, his face serious, clapped him wordlessly on the back.

Expressionless, the twins wished him good luck. As ever, he wasn't quite sure if they meant it.

Looking emotional, Yuri clasped him in his arms and then ruffled his hair. When either of his parents did this at home he would turn his head away in irritation. But, with Yuri, he felt the gesture was so natural, and done with such affection, that his only reaction was a feeling of pleasure.

Rani was the last to approach him. She took one of his hands in both of hers and gave it a gentle squeeze. Like Jim Crow, she did not speak and, unlike the twins, there was no need for words. Michael could not mistake the encouragement in her eyes.

When she turned away, the rest followed suit, and within seconds they were swallowed up by the trees. Michael watched them until they were out of sight. All at once he felt very alone, and a bit afraid. *Be positive*, he thought, *be positive*. Then, angry with himself for again adopting his father's mantra, he set off into the wilderness, and into the unknown.

At his first step, as if to remind him of his task, the sky turned to a muddy brown.

CHAPTER SEVENTEEN

A reddish dust lay everywhere. He disturbed it as he walked and soon a thin film of grime overlay his trainers and clung to his clothes. At first the temperature was pleasant, but as he progressed, it began to rise, making him feel uncomfortable. The sky appeared to be lower than before. Yellow, before he started out, the change to brown seemed to have had a catalytic effect, increasing its density and creating the impression of a low ceiling, which compressed and held in the heat.

The air was dry and hot and it wasn't long before he felt it beginning to irritate his throat and lungs, making him want to cough. Instead, he began to sneeze, once, twice, three times, and on and on until his nose and eyes were streaming. Forced to stop, he took a handkerchief from his pocket and tied it over his mouth and nose hoping that whatever was causing the problem would be neutralised. His action had the desired effect and, with a final minor explosion, the paroxysm ceased. He realised that he should have brought some water with him, but when he'd started out, he hadn't envisaged the escalating temperature he was now facing. Already, he was soaked with sweat and losing moisture rapidly.

Walking wasn't easy either. Beneath the dust the surface was like hardpan and impervious to moisture, making it difficult for plant life to gain a hold. It was hard on his feet and, already hot, he feared they would soon be blistered. To Michael, the whole area seemed to be like the surface of the moon. It was as if a great climatic change had taken place, with the temperature rising so rapidly and precipitation being reduced so drastically, that vegetation could no longer survive. The ground had become iron and desiccated – uninhabitable.

Evidence to support his reasoning came a little further on when he discovered the remains of a large animal, ribs and skull lying bleached in the hot air. Soon he came upon others of different shapes and sizes, indicating that the wild life of the area had been wiped out, probably because of the lack of food and water.

He laboured on, hot, sticky and increasingly uncomfortable. The land stretched ahead, unchanging and inhospitable, a place where no one in his proper senses would want to go.

As he progressed, he thought of the advice given to him by the Victorian gentleman. *Don't trust appearances*, the old fellow had said. Well he knew that already. This world was like a hall of mirrors, constantly changing and distorting what seemed normal until it appeared to be something entirely different. He had learned to look beyond the obvious.

The reference to Homer disturbed him more. The blind, Greek poet had penned so much that Michael was not sure if his knowledge would be sufficient for him to recognise any situation that might be paralleled in the man's writings. He hoped too that he was not about to play the role of Ulysses who, after the Trojan war, had been forced to wander for many years before being able to return to his wife Penelope and his faithful dog in his homeland of Ithaca.

Michael's fear was that this had been the fate of Orwell Thomas and was the reason why he had never come back from the wasteland. That or, with nothing to sustain him in this blighted place, and contrary to what the Victorian gentleman believed, the boy was dead. If the latter situation were the case, then his bones might be slowly disintegrating out here somewhere and there would be no way to determine if he were dead or alive. He would just be another fleshless carcass among many.

With those morbid thoughts whirling around in his head, Michael began to dwell on his own possible fate. Perhaps the wizard did not want anyone to succeed and the problem set in this last task was insoluble. Perhaps this was part of the wizard's cruel game, and Michael's reward for getting this far was to wander like Ulysses, beset by misfortune and despair or, worse still, end up on some barren patch of ground, dead from hunger and thirst, his flesh providing a meal for vultures, if there were any.

He shuddered at the mental picture he was painting. Then something else struck him. Perhaps he was meant to think like this. If so, he was doing himself no favours. He was depressing himself so much he was reducing his ability to think clearly, and rational thought was probably the best weapon he had in his armoury. The moment he realised this he gave himself a good scolding for thinking so negatively. His other tasks had been difficult and he had come through them successfully. There was no reason to question his ability to do likewise in this instance. Determined to remain hopeful, he cast all doubts aside and continued on his way with renewed vigour.

Trying to ignore the heat and dust, which was beginning to sap his energy and making him long for a cool drink of water, he put his mind to the fact that he had now been walking for an hour with nothing to guide him. When he looked back to get his bearings, he discovered that the trees he had walked through with the Victorian gentleman could no longer be seen. The hills were still in vision, but were now merely a faint outline and they seemed to have moved further to his right. This suggested he had not been taking a straight line, and that worried him. Without landmarks it was very easy to end up walking in a circle and getting nowhere, and he was in the middle of terrain so flat that no part was distinguishable from any other.

Then three things happened in quick succession.

A dust-devil appeared, zig-zagging towards him. It raced past, a whirlwind in microcosm. "That shouldn't be," he said aloud, as much wanting to hear the sound of a voice as commenting on the strange phenomenon. "There's no wind." He closed his eyes, thinking his senses were playing him tricks. When he opened them again, he looked in the direction the whirling dust had taken. It was still there, moving just as rapidly away from him.

Hardly had the dust-devil disappeared when a black bird materialised. It dropped down out of the dusky sky, swooped and settled on the stunted remains of a long dead tree. At first he thought it was a crow, then a raven, but, on closer inspection, he saw it was too large for a crow and not large enough to be a raven. It was sitting at right angles to him, and he noticed its bill was long, downward curving, and red. Its legs too had a reddish tinge. That struck a chord with him and he was reminded of a newspaper article he had read recently about species which were becoming rare in the British Isles. The bird that had just landed was one of them. It was a chough and was native to parts of Europe, Asia and Africa. Obviously used to heat, it would be at home in its present overly warm environment. As he drew close, it cocked its head and eyed him brazenly. When he was about ten metres away, it gave a loud caw and flapped awkwardly into the air. Flying ahead of him, it landed on some animal bones lying somewhat to the left of the line he had been taking. Curious, he changed direction and headed towards it. When he was close enough to admire its shiny, black feathers and fine head, it again took off, only to settle on a lump of sandstone even further from his original track.

When the bird repeated the procedure for a third time, Michael concluded that it was leading him somewhere. By now he could feel his face burning and rivulets of sweat were rolling down his back and legs. Despite the heat he had not yet removed his windcheater, concerned that his exposed arms would be burned to a frazzle. But soon he could stand the discomfort no longer and peeling the garment off, he tied it round his waist by the sleeves. Stooping, he gathered up a handful of the red dust and smeared it on his arms and face. The sweat helped it to stick patchily and, looking like a cross between an ancient Briton plastered in woad and an aborigine daubed with ceremonial paint, he soldiered on.

The chough watched all this with great interest and then was on the move again. Michael was content to follow and the stop-start procedure was repeated so many times that he lost count of the number. All the while he got farther and farther from his original path. Finally, the bird remained airborne, and with a farewell squawk, it rose high in the air until it became only a dot and was finally lost against the dark texture of the muddy coloured firmament.

As it deserted him, he became aware of shapes in the distance. At first he wasn't sure if they were real. The heat was now such that it rose in shimmering waves over the desert-like floor. He knew he was starting to become dehydrated and became increasingly concerned that his ability to think straight would soon be impaired. The things that had appeared ahead of him in the distance might only be a mirage and, in reality, there was nothing there. Perhaps the dust devil and the chough had merely been figments of his imagination and he was already in the first stages of delirium. If that was the case, then, if he didn't get a drink soon, he could well lose his reason.

But his fears were not realised. He was still rational.

Another fifty metres and he could see the configuration was genuine. As he continued, it took on form and substance. He found he was approaching a small settlement, and what he had first glimpsed was the outline of buildings.

He limped towards them, his feet sore and, as he had anticipated, blisters on soles and heels. Each step was painful, and this time there was no Rani to apply a soothing oil to the affected parts.

As he got closer, he could see the settlement was small, not even worthy of the description, hamlet. The main thoroughfare had a few shops, a bank and a cinema, all poorly constructed. Small houses bordered the surrounding streets. The buildings were made of wood and of a shape and design that suggested they were seventy or eighty years old. There were no inhabitants. The roofs of the houses had caved in; doors and windows gaped; beams and debris lay heaped inside. The all-pervading red dust covered everything. The town was derelict.

Michael hobbled his way down the main street, stopping now and then to peer into some of the buildings. A shop, which had obviously combined a grocery, hardware, and liquor trade, still contained a selection of bottles in its glassless window. Michael reached eagerly for one, hoping there was liquid inside, but he was disappointed. It was doubtful if they had ever contained anything, being there merely for advertising purposes, the labels on them now faded and illegible. Inside, a poster so dry and sere it would have crumbled at his touch, declared that BRASSO IS BEST. Empty shelves, some still in place, told their sad tale of a livelihood long abandoned.

The bank, a stronger structure, had survived almost intact. A counter with a number of metal, cashier grills a few metres apart, still stretched the length of the main room. Behind it, built into a wall, a Chubb safe lay open and empty. An office behind the counter was doorless and it too contained nothing, giving no hint of the financial transactions that its former occupants might have transacted.

Seeing no point in going any further along the main thoroughfare, he turned into a side street and explored some of the houses. He found nothing of interest. Apart from the odd broken chair or stool, and in one instance a rusted bedstead, there was little in them. In the last house he entered he saw a tiny, cloth doll, arms missing and crudely made. It lay beside a picture book, torn and faded. Somehow Michael felt moved by the sight of the pathetic little items and he wondered what had happened to the children who had played with them.

Knowing he would never find the answer he moved on, hoping to locate some water, hoping to discover some trace of Orwell Thomas. He was unsuccessful on both counts, his only comfort being that he was in shade for most of the time and the temperature was more bearable.

When he reached the last of the buildings, he came to an area where nothing had been built. Beyond this there were a couple of isolated shacks about a hundred metres away, and beyond that, the open desert. He did not feel like venturing into the heat again, but knew that he had to find out what the buildings were doing there and what, if anything, they contained. When he got there, he discovered the raison d'être for the town. The shacks had been used to store equipment. Racks and shelves were still there, as were an assortment of shovels and pickaxes and chisels and sledgehammers and cutting tools. Whoever had used them had not thought it worthwhile to take the implements with them when abandoning the place.

Close to the shacks, in a hollow hidden from the settlement, he noticed the remnants of old mine workings. He decided to investigate.

Beside mounds of clay and rubble torn from the earth, he discovered two shafts, both open. One contained a pulley system, rusted and broken, with buckets still attached to it. The piles of debris, and the remains of an old sluice nearby, suggested it was either gold or precious stones that had been mined. The other shaft was empty. It was wider than the first, and beside it lay cables attached to a steel cage. It was clear the cage had been used to transport the miners underground.

At the end of the workings there was a dry riverbed. When running, the water from this would have been used in the sluices. It might even have generated electricity to raise and lower the cage. A rise in temperature would have brought drought. With drought, the river would have dried up and the means to wash out the gold or stones would have gone. When that happened, the mine would have been abandoned and the settlement along with it.

Michael made his way about carefully. The ground beneath his feet was probably riddled with mineshafts, making the area unstable. The last thing he wanted was to fall through the crust and end up buried thirty metres deep. Even if he survived, no one would know what had happened to him and he would never be pulled out.

He wondered if he should try to get down below, see if Orwell Thomas, or his corpse, was there. Further inspection told him the idea was impracticable. There was no safe way to reach the workings underground. The shafts were black holes going straight down for who knew how far. There was no light to show the way and he hadn't a torch. There might have been candles in one of the shacks, but even if he found one, he had nothing with which to light it. If there had been a ladder embedded in the sides of one of the shafts, he might have chanced a descent. As it was, they were only death traps waiting to catch the unwary and he would leave them like that. If Orwell Thomas was at the bottom of one of them then he was there for eternity.

He turned his back on it all and, keen to get out of the heat, headed back to the town, concentration beginning to slip and his blisters smarting painfully. To date he had been singularly unsuccessful in his quest and, unlike the previous occasions he had been put to the test, he felt his will to continue being sapped by increasing fatigue and the physical discomforts he was suffering. He hadn't quite given up yet, but he knew that that point could not be far off. Thirst and tiredness were taking their toll on him and if he didn't make a breakthrough soon, he would be forced to abandon the search and return to the others. Delay too long in doing so and he would be so dehydrated he would neither have the strength nor reason to complete the journey.

Back among the hulks of the buildings, he slumped down in the shade of the first house he came to, his heart beating too strongly and his lungs working too hard to inhale the heat-seared air. *Half an hour*, he thought, *half an hour at the most. If I find nothing significant in that time, I go back.* He didn't want to. He hated failure. But he was aware an excess of stubbornness on his part and he might not live to regret it.

He rested for five minutes and felt no better at the end of that period. His body was overheated and was telling him to give it time to cool down. He wanted to comply, but he could wait no longer. He got stoically to his feet and made for the main street. As he reached the part that he hadn't explored, he noticed a graveyard. It was at the end of an alley running between the cinema and the remains of a hardware store. Something tugged him in that direction.

A picket fence, surprisingly still standing, surrounded the little burial plot. He let himself in through a fragile gate, which scraped the ground as he pushed it open. Not all the graves had headstones. Of those that had, few were still upright, others were slanted sideways at varying angles, suggesting the dry soil could no longer hold them firmly in place. Those without headstones merely had simple, wooden crosses sunk into in piles of stones, which made Michael think that those who had interred the bodies were not prepared to labour much at the hard ground. The proper graves had probably been hacked out of the unforgiving earth with picks and shovels. The headstones were crude sandstone blocks. Each had a name, followed by both a date of birth and a date of death chiselled roughly into it. This was in contrast to the wooden crosses on the other graves, which only had names, some of which were miss-spelt. Others only had forenames, others still, only surnames, cut into the wood with varying degrees of expertise. Who knew who they were, or where they came from? Probably not even those who had erected the simple crosses were privy to that information. Once covered by rocks and stones, the buried ones were forgotten with none to mourn them.

Michael wiped some of the legends on the headstones clear of dust. Most of the dead buried here were adults, probably miners or their wives, but the occasional one was a child, boy and girl. In all probability they had succumbed to malnutrition, or diseases such as smallpox and scarlet fever.

In a rectangular patch of ground slightly apart from the other graves, wooden crosses had been driven into the hard pan. These were empty of names and Michael was astonished to see they were a tribute to the fallen of many wars. Each carried a simple inscription and, unlike the poor script on the other crosses, this was done neatly in block capitals. It said simply, TO AN UNKNOWN SOLDIER. Underneath were the name of a conflict and the dates of its duration. The first one he looked at was the Great War, 1914-1918; the next the American Civil War; 1861-1865; the third the Crimean War, 1853-1856. Others in the patch of ground were, the Russo-Japanese war, the Boer War and the American War of Independence. There were many more, some he was aware of, others of which he had little or no knowledge. Each had its cross and simple inscription. The dates on the last one were 1939-45. After that the record stopped, suggesting that whoever was responsible for the memorials had either died or moved away when the mining ceased.

It was a strange thing for someone to do, but no more strange than many of the things that had happened in this strangest of places.

Michael wanted to leave, to go back to the green coolness of the clearing he had set out from. Despite the handkerchief he had placed over his mouth, his lips felt cracked and his tongue was beginning to swell. He was feeling more unwell by the minute and his desire to continue was being gradually eroded. But he was about to discover that he could not leave yet.

As he began to make his way back out of the graveyard, he found that his feet had developed a will of their own. He wanted to go one way, they took him in another.

Despite summoning up every bit of mental energy in an attempt to regain control of his recalcitrant limbs, he was drawn relentlessly to the end of the graves marked with the headstones. The pull on him ceased as he reached the last one. It was nothing remarkable, just like all the others, covered in the all-pervading red dust.

He bent down and brushed the rough surface with his hand; and discovered that it *was* different. The stone was not as weathered as its companions, and whereas the inscriptions on some of them were hard to read, this one was neither worn nor badly written. Cut cleanly and boldly into the headstone was the legend, ORWELL THOMAS. There was no date of birth or date of death, but the fate of the Welsh contender was now no longer a mystery. Here was confirmation of what Michael had feared. The youth would not be accompanying Michael back to the others. Orwell Thomas had made his final journey and the Victorian gentleman's belief in his continued existence had been sadly misplaced. It might be that the wizard had intended this also, misinformation being a part of his great game. If so, it seemed to serve no purpose in this instance and Michael was too weary to dwell upon it.

Despite his own mounting problems the boy felt a sense of sadness. The only other person to reach stage four, and he had died in the attempt to succeed and so free himself and his trapped companions. Orwell Thomas had deserved a better fate. Feeling it was the right thing to do, he said a small prayer for him; and then he left.

He would have liked to remain longer, but his body was telling him to leave immediately. To linger would increase the likelihood of him perishing here like the Welsh boy. And he still had to solve the conundrum of the ever-changing sky.

As he hobbled back down the alley between the buildings, he thought he could hear someone speaking. He stopped to listen. There wasn't a noise. That disturbed him and, afraid he was beginning to hallucinate, he pressed on, trying to stay rational.

When he reached the main street he heard the voice again, and this time, to his relief, he was certain he wasn't imagining things. It seemed to be coming from the cinema.

Much as he wanted to ignore the sound and go on his way, he knew there might be a purpose behind it and that meant he had no alternative but to investigate. With the greatest of reluctance he pushed open the door, which, surprisingly, was still in place, and found himself in a small foyer. Straight ahead of him was a cubicle with an opening halfway up. A sign above it said, ENTRANCE FEE – 1-shilling. A curtain on a rail hung over an open doorway beside it. Pushing this to one side, he stepped through into an auditorium, which sloped gently away from him and housed row upon row of tip-up seats. The place should have been in darkness, but it wasn't. It was lit by an ever-changing beam of light coming from a point high on a wall at the back of the building. The beam played on a large screen at the bottom of the room and, to his utter amazement, he saw that it was from this the voice was emanating.

He knew the voice. It was the familiar growl of Winston Churchill. As Michael watched, the old war leader finished speaking and the screen went blank. The room was plunged into darkness. Michael looked back and up and almost immediately the flickering light from a projector shot from an aperture in the wall of an upstairs room. The screen was lit up again.

Michael soon found he was watching an old Movietone News feature, which was relaying a wartime broadcast by the then British Prime Minister. It was December 1941 and a perilous time in Britain, with every likelihood that the conflict would be lost. Churchill was trying to raise the morale of the people with his speech. Almost mesmerised by the stirring rhetoric and the deep cadences of the speaker's voice, Michael nearly missed the significance of his words. As he had in the first run of the newsreel, the politician had rounded off his oratory with some poetry. Michael knew the piece vaguely, having had it quoted at him once by his father when he was at his most frustrated by yet another increase in his reading quota.

The lines were from a poem by Arthur Hugh Clough titled, *Say Not the Struggle Naught Availeth*. Churchill had used the last two verses in a radio broadcast shortly after the United States had entered the war as Britain's ally. He listened to the words again, certain that they were of significance in his present situation.

> For while the tired waves, vainly breaking,
> Seem here no painful inch to gain,
> Far back in creeks and inlets making
> Comes silent, flooding in the main.
>
> And not by eastern windows only,
> When daylight comes, comes in the light,
> In front the sun climbs slow, how slowly,
> But westward, look, the land is bright.

Michael cared little about home problems now, for the moment he heard the final line, his mind cleared miraculously. *BUT WESTWARD, LOOK, THE LAND IS BRIGHT*. Galvanised, and for a few moments even forgetting his painful feet, he dashed outside and looked up.

Even as he watched, the sky turned from its dull brown colour to a splendid orange. In that instant he knew the answer to the Victorian gentleman's question.

He re-entered the foyer intending to watch the newsreel again just to make sure he had heard right.

He never got the chance.

This time, when he went through the door, he saw that the roof gaped open and the place was filled with rubble and broken wood. The ticket booth had collapsed and the curtain at the entrance to the auditorium was tattered and torn, allowing him to see through holes in the fabric. The seats were no longer there and the screen had disintegrated into a rotting heap at the bottom of the slope.

Leaving the deserted area, he climbed a set of stairs, careful not to fall through gaps where the steps were missing. Off a narrow landing at the top, he found and entered the projectionist's room. It too was in a sorry state, with wooden beams protruding from the wreck of a ceiling and dust everywhere.

There was no projectionist to be seen.

Baffled, and beginning to wonder if he had imagined the whole thing, he worked his way back down the decrepit stairs and out of the building, once again conscious of his weakened state.

He looked up. The sky was still orange.

That heartened him, and with nothing more to do in the desolate settlement, he finally and thankfully turned his back on it and started off on the arduous journey back towards the shady clearing and his friends.

CHAPTER EIGHTEEN

Michael had intended to use the footprints he had made in the dust on the outward trek to guide him back to the cool haven of the clearing. When he set out from the settlement he could find no trace of them. It was then that he remembered the dust devil. In its whirling, sweeping motion, it must have followed the path of his tracks and wiped out all traces of them.

That meant he had a problem. The buildings behind him would provide a steer for a while, but when they were lost to view, and with the hills not yet in sight, he would be in a flat expanse of wilderness with no point to aim for. Until he saw the hills, he would not know if he were proceeding in the right direction.

Yet he had no choice. He had to go ahead. To remain where he was, with no food and especially no water, would mean eventual delirium and a painful, gasping death. Even now he was becoming more dehydrated by the minute. If the condition got bad enough, his muscles might begin to cramp for lack of salt and prevent him from walking. He had to set out immediately.

The heat, if anything, seemed worse. Despite the dust he had plastered on to them, his arms, and the part of his face that was exposed, were burning. Making a quick decision, he discarded his armless sweater and donned the windcheater, working on the theory that, being looser on him, it would keep air circulating round his upper body, so reducing the warmth. Arabs with their flowing robes worked on the same principle. If he wore no clothes at all, his skin would be exposed and whatever moisture it still retained would be sucked out all the sooner.

He laboured on, every so often checking his position in relation to the settlement until it had almost disappeared in a shimmering haze of heat. All around him was a vast stretch of unbroken wasteland, consisting of dust and a surface of unrelenting hardness and populated only with withered trees and the bones of dead animals. He felt utterly alone.

He continued to glance back until the buildings in the settlement were just about still visible. He knew that about here on his way out the chough had deserted him, its job done. To get to this point the bird had caused him to deviate from the route he had been taking. He paused to consider what he should do next.

After giving serious consideration to the dilemma, he made his decision. If he made the assumption that his present position was a point on a compass and he took north to be dead ahead, then he reckoned that by taking a direction, nor – nor west, he should be retracing the path along which the chough had led him. Making a leaden, mental calculation, he judged that the distance from the spot where the bird had appeared, to where it had flown away, was about a kilometre; a thousand good paces for an adult, eleven hundred for him.

He found difficulty in coming to this reasoning. He was finding it hard to concentrate. So much had his strength been drained by the heat and the long slog his body had endured, that every step he took was now an effort, distracting him from the task ahead.

But once he had made the judgement, he automatically made the adjustment to his route and set off again. Every ten paces or so, he looked back to check if his footsteps were continuing in a straight line. He counted out his steps as he went. Always in the back of his mind was the thought that if he could get back to the point where he had first spotted the chough, then he might be able to see the outline of the hills. Once they were in view, he would be able to take a line on them and have something tangible to aim for.

On he went, finding it harder and harder to summon up the energy required to continue. The handkerchief still covered his mouth and nose, but was now less efficient and dust was beginning to filter through the fine divisions in the fabric making breathing more difficult. And if that wasn't bad enough, the heavy sky had dropped again and was now so low it was condensing the air available and creating even more heat. The hardpan beneath him grew hotter by the minute, exacerbating the pain of his blisters and giving rise to the thought that eventually the rubber on the soles of his trainers might begin to melt. As time passed he found it increasing difficult to put one sorely tried foot in front of the other. As a distraction from his discomfort, he began to conjure up pleasurable images of home.

Lucy was the first to emerge from the murkiness of his mind, face pert and cheeky. She was splashing water at him, cold and invigorating. It was Saturday morning. They were in the shallow end of the local swimming pool. Their father was attempting to teach them to swim; he smiled indulgently at her antics; he was a different person in those days. Sighing dramatically, he left them to their horseplay and swam a few lengths in the deep end. Then, using the high diving board, he split the water, his tall frame causing hardly a ripple on the surface. Michael found that he was smiling. Then he remembered. It was the last time the three of them were together there. Lucy died a week later and his world became a different place.

His mind reacted quickly to the disturbing memory and his thoughts switched elsewhere.

He saw himself walking through green fields sparkling with morning dew. He was on his way to visit Maxie. The cows were being milked when he arrived, Mr Dummigan, Maxie's father, supervising the task, the creamy liquid swishing frothily in the mechanical milkers. A line of churns was being filled. They would not stand for long. A lorry would arrive within the hour and the contents emptied into the long tank on its back, prior to being delivered to a nearby creamery for pasteurization. He could see the churns being tipped, hear the gurgle of the liquid as it landed in the innards of the larger container. He could taste the contents of the full glass Mrs Dummigan always gave him before the milk was driven away, the creamy wetness of it warm on his tongue.

Later, he was walking back through the fields, now soaking wet. An autumn rain fell steadily. It drenched his clothes and ran in rivulets down his face and neck. He was warm. He turned his face skywards and opened his mouth. The rain trickled down his throat, cool and refreshing. He reached the orchard behind the house. The trees were heavy with fruit, windfalls littering the ground. He picked an over-ripe plum, the core so fat it had split the skin. Giving it a rub, he bit into it, its succulence immediately producing a stream of purple juice. It spurted down his throat and down his chin. What ecstasy!

Three gulped plums later and he was in the house. His clothes dripping, he was standing at the kitchen door watching his mother make wheaten bread. She was unaware of his presence. She was kneading dough. A jug of buttermilk sat on the table beside the baking board. From time to time she poured a little of this on to the mixture, then added a little more flour, fingers searching for some mysterious consistency that felt right to her and which only she could ascertain. He didn't like the taste of buttermilk – too sour. He had tasted it once and spat it out without swallowing. Now, if a full jug were in his hands he would have quaffed the lot of it and asked for more.

His exercise in mental chicanery ended abruptly.

A sudden pain in his head caused him to halt. He felt dizzy, then weak. His legs sagged and he slumped to the ground. Breathless, he fought the sensation. There was no immediate improvement. He vomited; a thin trickle of food, severely devoid of liquid, hit the burning ground. Feeling no better, he drew his knees up to his chest and put his head between them. He pulled off his windcheater and covered his head with it. He sat like this for some time, heart pounding. Gradually the pain in his head began to ease. His heart steadied and he began to breathe a little easier. His ability to think straight returned. He got to his feet, staggering a little as he regained his balance.

Off again he went, head still covered, mind returning to his plan which he had been neglecting. He looked back at his tracks and was thankful to see that his path had been reasonably straight. He began to count aloud each step he took. This helped him to focus on what he was doing and, although his progress was slow, and got slower by the minute as his energy faded, he managed about five hundred paces before things began to go awry.

His head still pounded, the dizziness came and went, the feeling of nausea never completely left him. This took its toll and without him realizing it, his ability to concentrate on what he was doing was seriously eroded.

He looked back and was surprised to see that he was beginning to wander off line. He couldn't understand the reason for this, for he was sure he was doing everything right. He conceded that he might not have been checking every ten paces or so, and sometimes he might have missed out on a count, but his dereliction was minor and shouldn't have led to him being as far out as it seemed. He made a correction and focused again on what he was doing. Convinced that he would get things right from now on, he continued pacing and counting.

The next time he looked back, he saw he had wandered again and the length of his stride appeared to be decreasing, so throwing out the number of steps he was supposed to take. He made another correction, vowing it was the last mistake he would make.

And so it went on. His concentration lapsed, he found he was off line; his stride was still too short; he made further corrections. Soon he forgot his count and began to make guesses as to the distance he had travelled. Another correction, and then another when he lost his count again. This continued until he was no longer sure how far he had gone or if he was still on the path he wanted to take. By now his sight was becoming blurred and his ability to think straight seriously eroded. His body was betraying him, pain in every part of it, his tongue so swollen that it seemed to be filling his whole mouth. And then there was the thirst; it was becoming unbearable, his lips so parched that they were beginning to crack.

Visions of slaking it began to intrude more often on his thought processes, impairing his ability to make decisions. As his body rebelled, his mind no longer subjected itself to his will. The more his being cried out for liquid, the harder it became to think about what he should be doing.

With increasing frequency his head became filled with images of water – always cold, always available.

He had a vision of the park at home where he had taken the rowing boat on to the lake. He saw the rushing stream that he had swam through to escape from the big house. He experienced again the walk along the riverbank with Rani, when Canis had drenched them by shaking her sodden coat. He felt the spray of the cataract as it cascaded in torrents down the hill as he bypassed it to the hidden cavern. Water, water, water – icy and refreshing; finally it was all his mind would dwell upon. All other considerations became secondary. The attempt to walk in a straight line was forgotten. All thought of returning to the others was abandoned, as his whole being began to scream out for something to drink.

And then, to compound his mental chaos, he heard something that was entirely at odds with his surroundings. It was music; a sweet lilting air which he thought familiar, but couldn't quite place. It seemed to becoming from somewhere to his left. Then he recognised the piece. It was part of Handel's Water Music. Struggling to make sense of the fact, he turned slowly and half-limped, half-dragged his protesting limbs in that direction, a still surviving curiosity urging him to seek out the source of the beautiful composition.

As he stumbled towards the sound, it seemed to act like a drug; it soothed him; it swept away his pain. No longer was he conscious of his terrible thirst, his enlarged tongue, his aching body, the terrible heat. The music brought peace. Its calming strains lured him on.

And then he spotted it. The most welcoming sight he had ever seen. A fountain, with water shooting high in the air and falling so gently that it appeared to be descending in slow motion; a million droplets landing in a ring of spray, only to be sent skywards to fall again, every movement of every bead seeming to keep time with the music.

He forced his body towards it, desperate to throw himself beneath the glorious cascade, desperate to open his mouth and savour its

184

wonderful cold, wetness; desperate to drink and drink and drink until his thirst was completely quenched and the torment of his burning body was washed away.

But the fountain kept moving away from him, just as the music did. No matter how hard he tried, they never seemed to get any closer. But yet he persevered. He had to reach those tumbling waters. They were his salvation. Once there he could regain his strength and continue his trek to the clearing. He *would* get to them. They were so near. Just another effort would take him there. But still they remained just beyond his reach, tantalisingly so, tempting him, taunting him, leading him further from the path he had been taking.

And then he stumbled and fell, banging his temple against something hard.

Lights blazed in his head, and as if a switch had been turned on, for precious seconds his sanity returned. His mind cleared and he found he was lying against the object his head had struck – the dessicated remains of the tree where he had first seen the chough. And with the moment of clarity, into his consciousness came the sound of the Victorian gentleman's voice, fierce and urgent, exhorting him to remember his Homer.

And in that instant he did remember his Homer.

He remembered the hero of Greek mythology – Ulysses.

He remembered the tale of the siren sisters, the strange hybrids that were half bird, half woman, who lured sailors to destruction by the sweetness of their songs. He remembered that they were to be found between Aeaea and the rocks of Scylla, with some legends having it that they were the daughters of the sea god, Phorcys, others the offspring of the river god, Achelous.

He remembered Ulysses' encounter with them, and how he took the advice of the sorceress, Circe and plugged the ears of his crew with wax so that they were deaf to the seductive music. He remembered that Ulysses could still hear their singing and how he had made his crew tie him to the mast so that he would not steer the ship off course and on to the rocks and to their deaths.

And in his remembering, Michael understood the meaning behind the Victorian gentleman's words.

The Water Music was still filling the air and he knew he hadn't much time before he fell beneath its spell again. Propping his back against the trunk of the tree, he tugged the handkerchief from his face. Bringing it to his mouth, he bit into the hem, trying to ignore the searing pain that resulted. Tearing it at the spot where he had made the incision, he ripped the piece of cloth in two. Quickly wadding each half, he stuffed a piece in each ear as tight to the eardrum as he could manage. Then he filled any remaining gaps with dust. Struggling to his feet, he shaded his eyes with a hand and gazed ahead at the shimmering landscape. At first he could see nothing, and then, as his eyes became accustomed to the long view, he found what he was looking for. The outline of the hills came slowly and blurrily into view.

CHAPTER NINETEEN

Rani was the first to see him. Some hours earlier she had taken up a position on the edge of the trees, with the flat landscape stretching out ahead of her. There she had commenced a series of yoga exercises, followed by a period of meditation. When this was completed she remained where she was, seated in the lotus position. Canis lay beside her snoring gently. She was hoping that Michael would appear.

The desolate plain sent up waves of hot air and more than once she thought she saw something move in the midst of the unrelenting haze that covered the red earth. But each time she was mistaken.

When once again she spotted a movement, she was not sure if this was another false alarm or, at last, her gaze was playing her true.

When the disturbance was repeated, she squinted and shaded her eyes, straining to bring the thing that was out there into focus. Whatever it was appeared and disappeared, each time remaining a little longer in her vision when it was in view. Eventually, it materialised as a dark dot, which remained constant for a short time and then gradually emerged as a human shape. She could make out no more than that, but of one thing she was sure. Someone was in trouble. They kept wandering about drunkenly, never in a straight line for more than a few steps. They fell over and lay prone for seconds at a time. Then they struggled up, and swaying alarmingly, staggered forward again on their wayward path. Finally, after falling over once more, the figure began to crawl on hands and knees, before finally collapsing and lying still. The someone had to be Michael.

Canis came awake and took off. Rani waited no longer. Her heart pounding, she called for the others. When they arrived, she explained breathlessly what she had witnessed.

Not waiting till she had finished, Paul, Yuri and Jim Crow raced out into the wilderness towards the distant figure, which seemed almost to have been swallowed up by the red dust. Canis stood beside the prostrate form, whining and nuzzling it in a pathetic attempt to help.

Yuri reached him next. As the others arrived he was turning the boy over on his back. With his face swollen and caked with dust they could hardly recognise him. Yuri felt for a pulse. Finding one still beating faintly, he gently lifted his young friend, and with Jim Crow and Paul walking anxiously beside him, he carried the unconscious boy back to the cool haven of the clearing. Here he placed him in the shade of the tree where Michael had last slept. The girls, concern etched on their faces, gave little gasps when they saw his face. The Victorian gentleman watched as this was being done. Although secretly appalled at the state the boy was in, he did not permit himself a display of emotion. Instead, he quietly gave orders.

While Jim Crow and Yuri eased off Michael's clothes, Paul and the girls were despatched to the river with cotton cloths and a container, which the older man had conjured up. When they returned, with the container full of water and the cloths soaking in it, Jim Crow washed the dust and sweat from the boy's feverish body and pulled the makeshift plugs from his ears. The Victorian gentleman noted these with interest. When Michael's trainers and socks were removed they saw his feet were badly blistered. Where the blisters had burst, the flesh was raw and bleeding. So bad were they that Yuri wondered angrily aloud how Michael could have walked at all. Jim Crow cleaned them as best he could. Leaving them, Rani went out into the meadows beside the river and brought back a selection of flowers and herbs. She began to prepare a concoction that was both soothing and medicinal.

As she did so, the others attempted to bring Michael's temperature down by applying wet compresses to his head and body. While they were working on him, their patient began to mutter and lash out in delirium. Yuri was forced to hold his arms and Jim Crow his feet, as the twins continued to lay the cold, wet cloths on him. After a while he settled, but still he muttered wildly, sometimes incoherent, sometimes lucid. He spoke croakily of graves and goldmines, of a cinema and Winston Churchill, of the searing heat and a great fountain, his voice hoarse and distorted by his swollen tongue. At times they couldn't make him out, and when they could, his ramblings made little sense to them. They didn't try to understand what he was saying, being too busy ministering to his physical needs.

Gradually, as his body grew cooler, they gave him sips of water, a little at a time, not wanting to cause his stomach to cramp, or to risk him vomiting the precious liquid back up again.

At last he seemed to sleep, and with Paula continuing to keep his forehead cool and Jim Crow waving a leafy branch over his unconscious figure like a fan, they watched over him, none more so than the Victorian gentleman, who believed he bore some responsibility for the boy's wretched condition.

Now that Michael was still, Rani applied her balm to his bleeding feet: then she bound them gently in soft, cotton cloths. She would repeat this at four hourly intervals over the next two days until the healing process was well advanced.

After that, they all took turns at applying the compresses or waving the leafy branch until the Victorian gentleman was satisfied Michael's temperature had fallen and he would survive his ordeal. Only then did they draw back, and with one of them always close by in case he wakened or his fever returned, they were at last free to ponder on how he had arrived in such a state and how he had fared on his mission to liberate them. Some of them felt guilty at harbouring such thoughts while he was still so ill.

Paula and Rani continued to moisten his cracked lips and trickle tiny quantities of water down his parched throat at regular intervals.

For the next forty-eight hours he moved in and out of consciousness, never quite lucid enough in his waking periods to account for the condition they had found him in or tell them if he had completed the final task successfully. During this time he was able to take greater and greater amounts of water, with the girls eventually being able to feed him other liquids such as cold soup or fruit juice. Easily eaten food, like ice cream, was also spoon-fed to him.

The wild ranting with which he had first greeted them manifested itself with decreasing frequency, its content never changing. It was always about graves, or Churchill, or one of the other things initially mentioned in his ravings.

On the third twenty-four hour cycle of days, he wakened and looked around him. His clothes, washed and dried, sat in a neat pile by his side. He found he was wearing a long garment like a nightshirt. His eyes were alert, and when he spoke, it was clear his normal self had returned. His voice was still hoarse and croaking, but his tongue had returned to almost its proper size and, although weak, he recognised his companions who were close by.

They crowded round, dying to hear what had happened to him. Again they had to wait for their curiosity to be satisfied.

After a brief account of his outward journey and how the temperature had risen and risen, when he got to the part where the dust devil and the chough had appeared, he grew tired and asked to be allowed to sleep once more. Paula tried to press him further, but the others, although eager for him to continue, shushed her to silence, aware that he could have a relapse and it might be days before they could speak to him again. So, not wanting to tax his strength further, they withdrew and waited for him to waken once more.

When he did so, he was much stronger. They gave him a little chicken to eat and a drink of cold milk with which to wash it down, trying not to seem too impatient for him to continue his story. After he had finished the food, he satisfied their desires to know what had occurred.

Still speaking with difficulty, and in a halting voice, he described how he had begun to dehydrate, and warned them that what he had experienced might not always be reality, for he was sure there were times when he was hallucinating. When he voiced that caveat, he noticed the Victorian gentleman nodding.

Then he went on to relate how he had been led to the derelict settlement by the chough and how he had discovered the nearby mine and then the graveyard with its homage to the dead of many wars. He made a point of emphasising that the last war recorded was the 1939-45 conflict, which he felt sure was there for a reason and one he would explain to them in a moment.

When he told them about finding the undated grave of Orwell Thomas there was a gasp from Rani and expressions of shock from the others. Even the Victorian gentleman, who was normally inexpressive, looked perturbed. No one had died before, which showed their existence was not as safe or as cosy as they thought it was.

Seeing their concern, he moved quickly on to tell them of the cinema that was and then was not, and how he felt the grave for the 1939-45 war was a link to what he saw and heard inside. For he believed he had seen up on the screen there the great war leader Winston Churchill broadcasting to the British people in 1941 when things were at their most perilous, and exhorting them to take heart for the future was bright. He added that he was aware he wasn't in complete control of his faculties by that time, but something happened to sustain him in his belief that what he had witnessed was real, and it was only later that the heat and thirst affected his senses to the extent that he could not distinguish between what was genuine and what was not.

When he described the journey back and how, due to the terrible effects of the heat and the dehydration he was suffering, he had lost his bearings, Rani became agitated. She rose and said she couldn't listen anymore. No one else left. They were too engrossed in his tale.

After she was out of earshot, he continued by saying that by this stage on his trek, not only had he lost his way, but he had lost his reason as well and so could not stand over what he was about to relate to them, for it was possible he might well have imagined it all.

Then he went into greater detail about how, as his thoughts became more and more centered on images of water until finally he became utterly obsessed with finding it, he had abandoned his plans to find a way back. Where he was and why he was there no longer had any relevance for him.

When he came to the part where he thought he heard music and saw the fountain, the Victorian gentleman took an even keener interest in what he was saying. And when he informed his listeners about how he was seduced into trying to reach the tumbling waters and couldn't, because they kept moving and were always just out of reach, the older man broke into his narrative.

"Did you recall what I told you?" he asked intently.

"I did, but only because of good fortune. By then I was incapable of remembering anything you said, but either by good luck or outside intervention, I fell and hit my head. That brought me to my senses temporarily and it was then that your words about Homer came back to me and I made the connection between Ulysses and myself. He heard the songs of the siren sisters, I heard the music. In the few moments of lucidity the bang on the head gave me, I realised the fountain was an illusion and the music was not guiding me towards water but further and further into the wilderness. Like Ulysses and his crew, I was being led to my destruction; for once I was lost and with my mind gone, I would never be able to find my way out of the desert."

"And that was why we found the pieces of cloth in your ears?"

Michael nodded. "I knew I would soon succumb to the music again so I had to shut it out. I used my handkerchief to make ear plugs and that allowed me to act rationally and take stock of my surroundings. I discovered that the object I had knocked my head against was the tree stump where the chough had sat when I'd first seen it. Somehow I was back to my original path. From there I could see the outline of the hills."

"Very fortuitous," the Victorian gentleman said dryly.

"Indeed it was," Michael replied earnestly, missing the nuance. "I now had a target to aim for and it was only a matter of keeping going in that direction. How I managed that I don't know, for I was soon feverish and lost all track of time. After that, I don't remember much of the journey, or how I got here. A voice inside me kept insisting that I put one foot in front of the other, and when I could no longer do that, it told me to keep going whatever way I could. That's why I ended up crawling. I just followed its instructions until my strength gave out."

"Rani saw you first," the Victorian gentleman explained. "Then the men went out and brought you in; just in time, I might add. You were in a poor state, unconscious and covered in dust. Strangely enough, that protected you to some extent. Your skin was largely burn free and only part of your face and arms were affected, and, of course, your tongue was badly swollen. But all that was largely superficial and could be taken care of with liquids. More serious was the fact that you were completely exhausted and your body was burning with fever. We had to get your temperature down, and quickly, otherwise you might have died of heat stroke. We all worked at that. When you were cool, you slept, and your fever gradually abated. It took quite a time for you to recover, but here you are none the worse for your experience.

"Who took my clothes off?"

"Oh, the girls, of course," Paul said innocently.

Michael went scarlet and everyone laughed.

"Can we call Rani back now?" Jim Crow asked to ease his embarrassment.

"I presume you want to know if I completed the task?"

"We all do," the large black man replied quietly. "Our fate is in your hands."

Rani was summoned and she took her place with the others. When she had settled into her accustomed lotus position, the Victorian gentleman spoke.

"As you are all aware, it was laid to me to advise Michael before he set out. I alone knew the nature of the task he had to accomplish. I asked him, on the instruction of the wizard, to discover why the sky changed colour, as the answer was out there somewhere. Additionally, I wanted to know what had happened to Orwell Thomas, so I also requested Michael to find him and bring him back. Well, we now know of Orwell's fate, but we have yet to hear the result of the primary purpose of Michael's quest. So I will ask him once again, why does the sky change colour?"

Michael didn't reply immediately and, when he did, he sought clarification of something that had been puzzling him. "Before I answer that," he said slowly, "there is one thing I have to know. When you asked me to find and bring out Orwell Thomas, was that also part of the wizard's task?"

The Victorian gentleman considered the question for a moment.

When he answered he sounded subdued. "No, my boy, it wasn't. I have always wondered what happened to him, and as I was charged to set him the same task as yours, I have always felt responsible for my actions. I'm afraid I exceeded the authority given to me when I placed that extra burden upon you. I feel now that that was a mistake, for the task you were given was onerous enough without my adding to it. I may even have put your life in danger. If so, I crave your forgiveness."

Michael studied the man, who he considered to be a friend, and saw regret and sadness etched on his face. "There is nothing to forgive," he answered quietly. Looking for Orwell Thomas took up such a small portion of my time it made little or no contribution to the condition you found me in. That was down to my failure to prepare properly for my ordeal. I didn't know how long I would be out there and should have brought provisions with me. Even one bottle of water would have been sufficient to keep my thirst at bay and stave off the effects of dehydration. So don't punish yourself. The blame is all mine."

"Thank you," the Victorian gentleman said. You have a most generous nature."

Michael smiled wanly. "Only when it is right to be generous; you should hear me when I think I've been wronged." As he said this, he was thinking about his dad. And then he was surprised he could joke about his situation at home. He had never been able to do that before.

"I think you are more forgiving than you think you are."

The Victorian gentleman was about to say more, but he didn't get the chance. He was halted by a tetchy voice. "What is this, a mutual admiration society," Paula said impatiently. "When are we going to hear if we're on our way out of this awful place, or not?"

"My apologies," the Victorian gentleman said, somewhat taken aback by the girl's irritation. "I forgot how eager you all are to hear if your sojourn here is over. Now, Michael, for the last time, why does the sky change colour?"

"Because we make it," the boy answered simply.

"And how do you know that?"

"Because of Winston Churchill."

"I think I know what you mean, but for the benefit of the others would you elaborate?"

"He was the key to my understanding. When I saw the film clip, I realised he was not only trying to raise the morale of a war-weary people, he was also telling them something."

"And that was?"

"Not to give in; to keep contributing to the war effort; to keep supplying men to fight, and to keep producing the equipment to fight with. By so doing they would influence the way the war was going and ultimately have a large say in winning it. He exhorted them to look to the future and better times."

"But what has that to do with our sky changing colour?" Paul asked.

"Everything. As I said before, he finished by quoting a verse of a poem, the last line of which said, *But westward, look, the land is bright.* By that he meant the skies would clear over Britain when the war was won, and the people would have caused that to happen."

"And can you change the colour of the sky here?" the Victorian gentleman enquired.

"We all can. Apart from Rani, we do it unconsciously."

"*We* can't," the twins chirped.

"Nor I," said Yuri, and his words were echoed by Jim Crow, while Rani and the Victorian gentleman remained silent.

"Yes, you can," Michael insisted gently. "Only you're not aware of the fact. It only happens when there is a dramatic change in your emotions – when you're angry or frightened or under stress. You all live here stress free and mostly in harmony, that's why you haven't noticed the connection between huge swings in mood and the type of sky you see. You could all be seeing a different colour if your moods were different. For instance, I have just wakened from a peaceful sleep and the sky is purple. I wonder what the rest of you see, especially as most of you are excited, expectant, hoping to hear I've set you free. Yuri, what do you see?"

"Yellow," he said.

"Paul and Paula?"

"Yellow," they answered disbelievingly.

"Jim Crow?"

"Yellow."

"Rani?"

"Purple," came the quiet reply.

"I don't need to go on, do I?" Michael said.

"What colour is associated with each mood?" Paula asked, still a bit skeptical.

"I'm not entirely certain of that. I can only speak for myself, but in my case, bright colours are synonymous with excitement and danger – yellow, green or red; anxiety and tiredness bring on darker hues; sanguine moments create something in between."

"You can prove this?" The Victorian gentleman pressed.

"Only if you believe what happened to me after seeing and hearing Winston Churchill."

"And that was?"

"The sky turned colour. Up until then I was tired, worried, dehydrated, and I had just found Orwell Thomas's grave. Prior to my trek there the sky was a bright yellow. Discomfort and my anxiety about what lay ahead turned it to a muddy brown. But Churchill changed that. His words excited me, filled me with hope. I felt they might just have given me the solution to your question. I rushed outside and discovered that the firmament was no longer drear. Now it was a glorious orange, in tune with my mood. That was proof enough for me that the two things were connected."

But still the Victorian gentleman was not satisfied.

"If we are to believe what you've said about the variations in the sky being due to our unconscious emotions, how is it that you exclude Rani in this hypothesis, and why is she seeing purple now when everyone else is seeing yellow?"

"Simple. Unlike the rest of you, Rani has not really adapted to living here. I think she is sad a lot of the time and that means she tends to live under skies of muted colours. And, by the way, she isn't the only one seeing purple. Don't forget, I'm seeing it too."

"I see. Do you think Rani would agree with your analysis?"

Michael looked at the girl, who smiled wistfully and nodded.

"But that only answers part of my question. If we are to believe your assertion that we affect the colour of the sky by how we feel, how is it that Rani can override her own change of mood and select whatever colour she wants? You *are* saying that, are you not?

"I'm not certain. Perhaps only she can answer that. I only know that just before I went to sleep before commencing the third task, she offered to darken the sky a bit to give me a semblance of night. You should be aware of that because I've mentioned it before."

"Do you have an opinion?"

Michael glanced at Rani, hoping for her to intercede, or at least to give him a sign that his thinking was soundly based. But her features remained impassive.

· Seeing he was about to get no help, he continued. "I think it stems from the fact that because she has lived mostly under subdued light up until now, that, on the rare occasion she did feel happy or uplifted, the accompanying change in the sky became more obvious to her than everyone else and, when she realised why this occurred, she set out to find a means of controlling the phenomenon. I don't know how she manages it, but I think it's got something to do with her meditation. She might live on a higher plane to us, which gives her more control over her mind. From there it's a short step to producing a certain emotion at will and this enables her to effect changes in the sky when she wants to."

"Is Michael correct?" the Victorian gentleman asked.

Everyone looked at the Indian girl. "Perfectly," Rani acknowledged, smiling.

"More to the point," Michael interjected, "do *you* believe I'm right?"

The world seemed to go still, breaths were held and all eyes focussed on the Victorian gentleman. Their fates depended on his answer; was it to be freedom, or another long, interminable period of time until the next contender arrived?

He kept them waiting, seeming to consider all that had been said, his face serious and his brow seemingly furrowed in concentration. At last his face cleared; then he smiled. "My questions are over," he said. "Congratulations, Michael. At long last we have someone who has successfully completed the four tasks."

The clearing erupted in sound. The twins danced up and down, Jim Crow and Yuri hugged Rani and then each other, Canis leapt around barking and rolling over, and everyone except the Victorian gentleman cheered. Although smiling, he maintained a proper decorum.

Yuri made a beeline for Michael and was just about to haul the hero up to embrace him when he remembered the boy's weakened state, so he made do with pumping a hand up and down while repeating, "Well done, little one," over and over again.

When Yuri had exhausted his congratulations, Jim Crow, grinning broadly, ruffled Michael's hair, and Paul, followed by the Victorian gentleman, who was now beaming, also shook his hand. Paula and Rani kissed him on the cheek, Paula with much more enthusiasm than the last time. Much to Michael's chagrin his face went red again. Embarrassment was something he had not yet learned to control.

When the mayhem had subsided, everyone wanted to know what would happen next; would the wizard keep his word; how long would it be before they were whisked away from there? Their enquiries were directed towards the Victorian gentleman, who stilled their voices by raising a hand.

"I know you are eager to be away," he said solemnly, "but as this situation has never arisen before, I am just as ignorant about what will happen as you are. Settle yourselves and I will take a walk by the river. There I will hear what is being whispered. When I know that, I will impart my gleanings to you."

The twins groaned, unable to hide their impatience. The others settled round Michael and asked him more about his experiences, while Rani dressed his feet again. It soon became obvious that their interest in his hardships was only half-hearted and they were simply killing time until the Victorian gentleman returned. An air of anxiety now began to pervade the group, with each member beginning to wonder if, despite Michael fulfilling the demands of the four tasks, they would be permitted to leave as promised. None was sure that the word of the wizard could be trusted.

The Victorian gentleman took some time to reappear and, while he was absent, their nervousness grew. This was manifested in different ways.

The twins talked incessantly and became an irritant to everyone else. Jim Crow grew unnaturally quiet and answered only in monosyllables when addressed. Yuri turned to Canis and began to teach the dog new tricks, but he soon grew tired of this and began a series of strengthening exercises, press-ups and the like, which punished his muscles until they shone with sweat.

Rani coped best. She retired to a shady spot beneath the trees and, in her favourite lotus position, began to meditate, remaining in a state of relaxation as she waited for news.

Michael, still recuperating, fell asleep.

At last the Victorian gentleman emerged from the trees. He walked deliberately to the centre of the clearing, his outmoded attire now so familiar to Michael that it hardly impinged on his consciousness. His demeanour told them nothing. Rani returned and everyone, except Michael, crowded round him, an air of expectancy apparent. He removed his hat to reveal a head of greying hair. He placed the hat upon the ground.

He looked into their faces one by one, as if trying to fix in his mind what they looked like. Only when he had completed the little ritual did he speak.

"Is there anyone who wishes to stay?" he asked quietly.

Michael immediately glanced at Yuri and saw his face was a

picture of indecision.

"Not us," the twins answered instantly.

"Nor I," Jim Crow said fervently.

Rani also indicated that she wished to leave, which left Michael and Yuri, both of whom were slow in answering. The rest looked at them, mostly in surprise at their hesitancy.

"Michael?" the Victorian gentleman enquired, raising his eyebrows in bemusement.

Michael had a problem. He discovered there was a certain appeal in the thought of staying. Here, he would be away from the suffocating influence of his parents and would be free to do what he wanted. But, opposed to that, if the others left he would be on his own and was bound to be lonely. A few days ago, given such a choice, he would have opted to stay, even if he were alone. Now, he wasn't so sure. He had to admit that if his dad had not insisted on him making the most of his gifts, he would not have been able to meet the wizard's challenges and set everyone free. He also found that his resentment of the harsh regime imposed upon him had eased considerably, for he recognised it was nothing in comparison to the tribulations he had experienced here. But still he hesitated, unable to make up his mind.

Seeing he needed more time to consider, the Victorian gentleman did not pursue the matter less it put pressure on the boy to make a hasty answer. "Yuri?" he said, turning to the Russian.

Yuri nodded his head and then spoke slowly and soberly. "Choice not easy; while here I spend many times thinking about this moment if it come to pass. Sometimes, I sure I go; sometimes, I sure I not go. Now, I have to decide." He hesitated and the others waited, all of them hanging on his words. He nodded again as if something had come together in his mind. At last, he spoke. "As said, choice not easy; I had hard life in Russia, hard climate too, and it wonderful here. But now it time to go back to circus. I miss it, despite hard times." With the choice made, his face relaxed into a smile.

The Victorian gentleman inclined his head slightly in understanding. Only Michael was left. "Now, my young friend, have you come to a decision?"

Michael admired Yuri and his analysis helped the boy to make up his mind. If Yuri was prepared to return to the old world knowing his life would be harsher there, then Michael's objections to going home were trivial in comparison. His thoughts crystallized. "I'll go home," he said.

As soon as he had uttered the words the others broke into a

delighted chatter.

"One more thing," the Victorian gentleman said, silencing them. A sombre expression and the strangeness of his tone captured their attention. "Michael has only been here a short while and will go back to his own time quite seamlessly. The rest of you have a choice to make. Do you wish to return to the period before you came here, or to the twenty-first century like him?"

There was a hush. This was something they had not envisaged, expecting to go back automatically to the friends and families in the era they had left. They looked at each other as if hoping someone would help them with their choice.

"If we go back to our own time," Paul said thoughtfully, "would we still retain everything we have learned about the world since coming here?"

"You're thinking you might use that knowledge, especially the new technology, to make yourself rich and famous. I think not. You go back with no recollection of your stay here. It will be as if you never left your proper time."

Paul looked crestfallen. "In that case, Paula and I will wait for the twenty-first century to come in due course."

"I wish to see my family again," Rani said gently. "It is something I have been dreaming of since I was lost. That will make me very happy."

"I too return to old life," Yuri said. "New world too frantic and not enough circuses; only choice for me." With each decision he made he looked ever more content.

"I have to find my sister," Jim Crow said simply. "She is the only family left to me. I will take care of her and we will no longer be slaves."

"What name will you take?" Michael asked, "now that you're a free man."

The black man's face split in a great grin. "You remembered. No more Jim Crow, that's for sure. From now on I shall be known as Lincoln Brown. How do you like that, Mikey?"

Michael laughed, acknowledging the amalgam of Abraham Lincoln and John Brown, the abolitionist leader hanged for leading an unsuccessful rebellion of slaves at Harper's Ferry in Virginia. "Very appropriate," he replied. "I like that. I like it very much."

"And you, sir?" Paula asked the Victorian gentleman. "What choice have you made?"

The older man thought for a moment before he answered. When

he spoke, his voice was quiet and slightly hesitant, as if he were considering his words carefully.

"I have been here a long time and, consequently, I have been able to study the world above me at leisure. I have noted the changes that have taken place in the last century and a half, the great inventions that have revolutionized the way people live; the aeroplanes, the motor cars, the remarkable technology that can take men and women to the depths of the oceans, or into space, even to the moon. I have seen the great strides that have been made in the field of medicine, the lives that are now saved in ways that would have been unthinkable in the Victorian era. I am impressed by the quality of the lives lived now in what is called the developed world. But I have noted that not everyone gains from these beneficial factors. Two thirds of the world's population still live below the poverty line. People still starve; people are still persecuted; people are still tortured on the orders of despotic rulers and the agents of governments,' and, more often than not, the rich nations and those with the greatest influence do nothing to help, leaving altruism and good works to a few saintly organizations or individuals. I am not so naive as to believe that things were any better in my age, when the weak and the poor were also exploited; but times were more unenlightened then, and although this is not an excuse for the way the helpless were treated, it helps to explain why it was so. With the technology at the disposal of the powerful nations, there is no reason for that to happen today. With the ability to harness the great resources of the earth, no one should be without shelter or food. Yet, that is not the case. The capitalist system, which has largely vanquished socialism in all its forms, has placed profit before welfare, greed before financial equality, and the have-nots can be counted in their hundreds of millions. It seems that for the poor, the more things change the more they stay the same, and that those in positions of power have not learned this particular lesson of history."

He paused at that point and looked a little pensive. His audience waited raptly for him to continue. He seemed to look inwards for a short time, and then he went on.

"No, I do not like the world as I see it today. Like Yuri said, it is too frantic, and more, it is too selfish, too cruel. Common courtesy seems to have been replaced by intolerance and bad manners. I would be out of place in it and I feel my values would be mocked. Therefore, I too shall return to the England in which I was born. It has its faults, and they are many, but I will feel more comfortable there."

"Here endeth the lesson," Paul muttered, and was startled when his sister's elbow dug painfully into his ribs. He swivelled his head to see her glaring at him. Chastened, he turned his attention back to the Victorian gentleman, who, if he had noticed the altercation, chose to ignore it. His mind seemed to be elsewhere again.

Everyone was staring at him, giving consideration to his words, a bit startled by the heartfelt nature of them, for they had always thought of him as someone lacking in emotion.

At last, Rani broke the silence. "When shall we be going?" she asked gently.

The Victorian gentleman seemed to start. Collecting his thoughts, he gave a wry smile. "Forgive me," he said. "I was indulging in personal convictions and ignoring your pressing concerns. When shall you be going?" he mused. "The answer is, soon; but as we will have to get used to the twenty-four hour day again we will wait that length of time to allow Michael to recuperate fully. That will also give us a chance to reflect on the decisions made today and the opportunity for a change of mind if anyone wishes to do so. You can say goodbye to your favourite places and we will meet here at the same time tomorrow. But not all of you can go. One must stay to keep an eye on Michael. We don't want him to relapse with no one to help him."

"I will do that," Rani said. "I am not sure I have a favourite place. I am just happy to be leaving."

Michael nodded his thanks. Then he looked thoughtful. "You've changed," he remarked.

"In what way?"

"You're English is perfect now. What happened to your old speech patterns?"

"Rani smiled. "I think you know."

Michael wasn't sure that he did, but, as usual, he underestimated his abilities. Seeking an answer, he cast his mind back. And it came to him swiftly and easily, as most things did. He remembered the curious looks his other companions had given her when first she had spoken to him. It now seemed ages ago.

"It was only a subterfuge," he responded slowly. You were trying to conceal the clue you gave me about RD Blackmore in a maze of convoluted syntax, If you had been speaking naturally the pointer would have been too obvious, so, aware of that, to make the puzzle more difficult for me to fathom when it was eventually presented, you adopted a false dialect from the moment we were introduced."

"Just like a stage Indian," Rani remarked dryly. "You know what that is?"

"First cousin to a stage Irishman."

Everyone laughed.

When the amusement died, Paula brought them back to the moment.

"I think we should all stay with Michael," she said, surprising them all. "This is our last time together and I don't think we should waste it. I know we've had our differences from time to time, but all that should be forgotten now that we're leaving, and I'm sure that Michael could do with the company."

"I agree," Yuri said.

"Paul, and the newly named Lincoln Brown, on hearing how Paula and Yuri felt, also concurred.

The decision was not unanimous, however. The Victorian gentleman had one other important piece of business to attend to. He did not yet know how the journey to their respective homelands and individual eras was to be effected. So he left them without disclosing his destination, accompanied by the ever present Canis.

With their impatience now largely under control, the others settled down to await his return. An air of excitement and anticipation prevailed.

CHAPTER TWENTY

Michael felt much better when the twenty-four hours had elapsed. His mouth no longer bothered him, his feet were nearly healed, and his old strength and vitality had almost returned. Finding himself in such an improved condition, he could not help but think that healing time was much shorter here than in his normal environment.

He found he was still wearing the shift. As his clothes were still beside him, he rose and went into the woods to change into them. Someone had retrieved and washed his sweater and, miraculously, it now had its sleeves. Some things still amazed him.

On his return to the clearing he saw the sky was now a brilliant blue. It was in perfect harmony with his mood.

In his absence, the Victorian gentleman had arrived back. Michael joined his friends, who had been awaiting his return and, with mounting expectation, they gathered to hear what the senior figure had to say. When he spoke, the quiet excitement in his voice was not hard to notice.

"Has there been a change of mind among you?" he asked.

No one said a word. As he had done previously, he looked fixedly at each of them in turn as if testing their resolve to stick by their decision. No one quelled under his piercing gaze. Still there was silence. His inspection over he nodded his head. "In that case," he announced decisively, "it is time to go." Turning, he beckoned them to follow him.

He left the clearing and began to make his way through the woods in the direction of the river. Elated and expectant, the others followed him. Michael noticed Yuri's previous misgivings had vanished and he chatted animatedly with Lincoln Brown, hardly giving the black man a chance to join in the conversation.

The twins led the way, chattering gaily, their mood effervescent. Rani and Michael brought up the rear. Rani took his hand as she had done before and they walked together like brother and sister. Michael realised he was going to miss her.

The procession soon reached the river. To Michael's eyes, the wildflower meadows had never looked more beautiful and he felt a pang of regret at the thought of leaving such a peaceful place. Their leader turned and began to walk along the bank in a direction opposite to that taken by Michael and Rani before the start of the third task. He seemed to be looking for something. They walked for some time and eventually a dark smudge in the distance heralded the presence of the big house.

Shortly after that the Victorian gentleman spotted what he was searching for and increased his pace. Finally, he stopped and pointed to a tiny island in the middle of the river. Apart from a covering of grass, the scrap of land was bare of vegetation. It was completely round, its diameter no more than five metres. "That is where you must go," he said.

As he spoke, a number of stepping-stones rose with a gurgle from the water, providing a means of reaching the object of his attention.

Without hesitation Yuri stepped forward to lead the way. The others followed. When they were safely across they discovered one of their number was missing. The Victorian gentleman stood on the bank. Canis was with him.

"Come on, it's easy," Paul shouted.

"I know it is, it's not that."

"Are you not coming?" Lincoln Brown asked, more perceptive than his companions.

"I have exercised the prerogative of age. I have changed my mind."

"Why, my friend? You seemed so definite before."

"Second thoughts, I suppose. You all have a purpose in going back. I have little to go back for; nothing to attract me."

"Have you no friends, no family you might have missed?"

"None. I was taken from an orphanage when I was ten years old by a couple who wanted a child."

"Were your foster parents unkind to you?"

"Very." His face twisted in pain at the memory. "My new father put me up chimneys to sweep and clean them. I do not wish to go back to that. This place has been a paradise for me."

"Won't you be lonely?"

The Victorian gentleman smiled. "With Canis who could be lonely."

The dog barked and wagged its tail.

"Did you never know your real parents?" Paul asked.

"Indeed I did. They were fine and kindly people, but they died of consumption, one within a year of the other. I had no relatives to go to, hence the orphanage."

"Why were you chosen to come here?"

"Only the wizard knows that. He must have seen something in me that would amuse him. I was clever for my age. Perhaps it was the ability I was exhibiting at the music and the mathematics my parents were teaching me before they died that attracted his attention. I was told by older people that I had a special flair for those things. If that is true it did me no good here, for I failed his tasks like most of you."

Paula stamped her foot. "Enough," she said. "If we're going, then let's go and stop wasting time."

The Victorian gentleman smiled. "Peevish to the end, I see. That temper I won't miss. "Now," he went on briskly, "you have been stimulating companions, but, as Paula implies in her inimical way, it is time to be off. Please lie down in a circle with heads pointing inwards and hold hands. Remember, no matter what happens, do not break the contact."

They did as instructed, but before Michael complied, he had one last look round him. He saw the great house in one direction, the woods and the hills in another; he heard the river gurgling past, and all about him were great stretches of wildflowers, their perfume all-pervading, their hues breathtaking Birds sang, bees and butterflies zigzagged among the myriad coloured petals. It was indeed a paradise.

"Goodbye," he called, "and thank you."

At the sound of his voice Canis bounded along the stones and for a few moments scurried amongst them licking their faces and jumping around. Then, with a final bark, she bounced back and lay down beside the Victorian gentleman. For once her tail was not wagging.

Michael looked at his companions for the last time. The twins, with their small, animated faces; Yuri with his granite features, which concealed the kindest disposition; Lincoln Brown, the freed slave, with his mighty body and great strength of character; and lastly, the gentle Rani, with her calm beauty and sadness. A bit choked, he lay down and they said their farewells to each other. Yuri was trying hard not to cry.

When they were settled, the Victorian gentleman raised his hands towards the sky and immediately it turned crimson. "I want you to repeat something after me," he informed them. "I want you to chant in unison the following formula." He paused, then, brow furrowed as if trying to recall it, he said, "$E = mc^2$." Only Michael and the twins knew the equation. Yuri and Lincoln Brown looked mystified, but like the others, they complied with the speaker's wishes.

"$E = mc^2$," they repeated.

The last syllable had hardly been uttered when the small island began to turn in the water, slowly at first and then with increasing speed. Faster and faster it whirled, sending out waves and froth and spray until the bodies lying on it were just a blur. Just when it seemed it could go no faster, the piece of ground rose sluggishly from the river with a great, sucking sound, mud and water streaming from beneath it. Suddenly there was an explosion, and instantly, the strange vehicle was thrust upward at an enormous rate, up and up at an ever-increasing speed into the firmament, vapour trailing in its wake. It remained visible for a very short time, becoming smaller and smaller until it was just a dot in the sky. Then, even the dot disappeared.

The Victorian gentleman lowered his arms.

He stood there – silent– waiting.

CHAPTER TWENTY-ONE

The Victorian gentleman stood for about an hour, Canis lying patiently beside him. After that time the sky changed colour again to a rich gold.

As it did so the chough came swooping in over the flower speckled fields and landed beside them. It too waited.

A few minutes later they all looked up. A pinhead of black had appeared high above them. It grew in size and soon could be easily recognised. The tiny island came in like a slow landing flying saucer and settled down on the spot in the river it had left a short time before.

When the river was flowing around it normally again, and it seemed as if the bit of earth had never moved, a strange thing occurred.

Canis, who had been lying prone while all this happened, stood up and began to bark, nose pointed up-river, eyes fixed on the point where Michael had emerged from the water flowing beneath the big house. A ball of mist began to form at the spot and roll towards them. It followed the river's meandering course. Closer and closer it got to the little group, becoming thicker all the time. It stopped when it reached the island, completely obscuring it from their view. Silently they watched.

The mist swirled and then there was a movement in its depths. A figure emerged and they saw it was a man. He was old, his face wrinkled and his hair white. He wore a garment like a Roman toga, fastened at the shoulder with a gold clip. He moved towards them over the stepping stones which had again appeared.

The Victorian gentleman had seen the man once before, when he had introduced himself as Proteus, the wizard. Being the first person in a new cycle, and with no one else there to explain why he had been abducted, the wizard was the only one who could tell him about the four tasks and what he must do to free himself. When he failed, Proteus had communicated with him thereafter through the sounds of nature and had given him the task of relaying his wishes to new arrivals. He had not met the wizard since then.

As Proteus stepped on to dry ground, the chough gave a caw of welcome and began to change shape. It grew rapidly and began to take on a human form. When the transformation was complete, the bird had become a young man, stocky, and smaller than the other two. He had black hair and blue eyes. The Victorian gentleman was amazed by the bird's transformation.

"So, Orwell Thomas, it comes to an end," the wizard said to the newcomer, his voice deep and a bit gravelly. "Were we too hard on them?"

"Not so," the reply came in a lilting Welsh accent. "For the most part they were taken from stressful situations and taught that life can be harder elsewhere. They learned the value of patience, never knowing when they would return to their old situations. But it was not a physical hardship for any of them and at no time were their lives in danger."

"Even the boy, Michael?"

Orwell Thomas paused. "Perhaps him, for a time, but his discomfort was only transitory."

"And you, my long server," the wizard said turning to the Victorian gentleman. "What do you think?"

The Victorian gentleman was not listening. White faced, he said, "You're not —?"

"Dead," Orwell Thomas finished, laughing.

"Or a —?"

"Ghost." The young man's amusement increased and he laughed even harder, his eyes becoming slits in his head. At last, his hilarity abated. Wiping away tears, he said, "Hardly, my Victorian friend. I am still solid flesh. Prick me and still I will bleed."

"Then the boy was wrong."

"You disbelieve him?"

"No, I'm not sure – yes, possibly."

Orwell Thomas seemed delighted by the older man's confusion. "Did he mention there were no dates on the tombstone?" he asked, grinning broadly.

"He did make that point."

"There you are then, that was your clue. You, of all people, should know that things are seldom as they seem." Then he grew sober. "But I thank you for your concern about my welfare. I know you asked the boy to look for me."

"What have you been doing all this time?"

"Practising," the young man said vaguely.

"Am I permitted to ask what you were practising"

"Oh, this and that," Orwell Thomas replied, glancing at the old man, who had been watching the exchange with amused interest.

"Enough of this," Proteus commanded. "Now, my inquisitive friend, I asked you a question. Did we place too great a burden on them?"

The Victorian gentleman hesitated before answering, having heard rumours about the wizard's foul temper and how vindictive he could be. His mind returned to the state Michael had been in on completion of the fourth task and he thought that Orwell Thomas's words were too insensitive, too uncaring. Michael had suffered a great deal, had been close to death. So, with that in mind and picking his words carefully, he said. "At times, yes, particularly the boy, Michael. I think you went too far with him. But, on the credit side, you also taught them lessons, did them no lasting harm and amused yourself at the same time. A cruel regime, perhaps, but it may be beneficial to all of them in the long run."

The wizard's eyes narrowed. "Take care, old man. An honest answer that may be, perhaps too honest for your own good, and hardly diplomatic. Do you not fear that I will take offence and return you to your horrid life as a chimney sweep?"

Taking a risk, the Victorian gentleman replied, "You value my opinion too much."

The wizard's eyes turned to flint. "Do I indeed?" he said softly, and with some menace. "Do I indeed?" He paused, lips compressed, and the Victorian gentleman held his breath, wondering if he had been too bold. Then the moment passed and the wizard continued, his tone a fraction softer. "Now," he said, face still hard, "trusting in this valued opinion of yours, what shall I do now to amuse myself?"

Relieved, the Victorian gentleman said, "I feel that to answer that would be presumptuous of me, and somewhat irrelevant, as I am sure you have already made up your mind on the matter."

Turning to the Welshman, the wizard asked curtly, "Do you think that is so, Orwell Thomas?"

"I suspect it is," came the cautious reply. The Welshman was also being careful not to attract the old man's ire.

Noting the judicious use of words, the wizard said, "You do well to be circumspect, my young friend." Then, his face relaxed and, in an abrupt change of mood, he went on, "You suspect well. I have made a decision. You have worked hard at mastering some of my arts. The time has come to teach you all I know. No longer will you be my assistant. Soon you will be a fully-fledged wizard."

"Why now?" Orwell Thomas asked, looking surprised."

"My two thousand-year life span has almost run its course. When I fade into the ether there must be someone trained to follow on. As a good Celt you have the pedigree and the aptitude. I shall make of you another Merlin."

"And me?" enquired the Victorian gentleman. "What plans have you in store for me?"

"You will take on the role Canis has assumed until now. You will be my roving ambassador, my seeker after talent in the world above."

"And what of Canis – what will she do?" he asked, patting the dog, which was lying forlornly at his feet with ears flattened to her head,

"The dog has outlived her usefulness," the wizard said callously. "I shall have to dispose of her. Fraternising with the contestants has caused her to become too attached to them. She had begun to aid them with their tasks, and that will never do. I suggest you keep that in mind now that you are taking over her role," he added ominously.

Knowing not to argue with him, the Victorian gentleman knelt and fondled the dog's ears. She whined and licked his hand, her tail tucked disconsolately between her legs. Understanding what had been said, she was a picture of misery. "The game is to continue without her, then," he asked sadly.

"The game will always continue, only, from now on, you will select the contestants, not her."

"How shall I be disguised?"

"As a dog, of course."

"And my name?"

The wizard's eyes gleamed. "What name would you like?"

The Victorian gentleman thought for a moment. "Sweep," he replied slowly. "I think it should be Sweep."

The wizard nodded. "Predictable as ever," he said.

CHAPTER TWENTY-TWO

Young boys were fishing for tench close to the overflow system. Golfers were on the ninth green close to the clubhouse. The sun hung low in the sky striating the horizon in pink and red and purple like an artist's palette. The air was still, the surface of the lake without a single ripple.

Michael rested on his oars and took it all in. The scene was so peaceful; it mirrored his mood. Gone was the anger he had felt at his dad. Gone was the inner turmoil at being disliked by his peers, the frustration at his lack of freedom. He did not understand why. All he knew was that he felt content.

He dipped the oars in the water and swung the boat round until it was pointing towards the trees. As he rowed back to the spot where he had found it, he saw the adult swans with their cygnets sailing along like little galleons. The mallards and the moorhens clustered at the jetty not far from the park gates. He could hear their squabbling as people threw them scraps of food.

There were other boats on the lake. A few came close. He recognised some classmates from school. They smiled and waved and called out to him. Their overtures were friendly. That surprised him.

As he approached the edge of the water, he drove the boat hard through the narrow channel in the reeds, partly beaching it on the shallow bank. Abandoning the oars in the bottom, he leapt out and pulled the little craft further up until it was fully out of the water. As he was doing so he felt there was something missing. He couldn't think what it was. He had the impression that at some point he hadn't been alone in the boat, but he knew that couldn't be. Yet, the feeling persisted. He stared unseeingly across the water trying to make sense of the strange sensation. Nothing surfaced and, with a shrug, he put it from his mind.

He headed for home. With a bit of luck he could scale the tree outside his bedroom and be inside before anyone realised he'd been away.

When he reached the centre of town a car he recognised drew close to him. It slowed and the two boys who had made rude gestures at him earlier in the evening peered out. A window was rolled down.

They asked him if he wanted a lift. He had declined before he realised they were only trying to be helpful. The car moved on and they shouted that they would see him at school tomorrow. They were smiling.

Puzzled by their out-of-character behaviour he went on his way. A hundred metres on, a couple of older boys crossed over to his side of the street and began to walk in his direction. He felt a small tremor of apprehension. They were two of his worst tormentors. He thought of taking flight, but knew immediately that such an action would be useless. Bigger, and older than him by two years, they would catch him easily.

He backed against the wall of the Ulster Bank getting ready to protect himself. He hunkered down covering his head with his arms and making himself as small as possible. Then something inside told him not to be a wimp – be strong – fight them – not to succumb meekly to their bullying. He felt an inner fortitude. He rose and moved out to the centre of the pavement. There, with legs apart and shoulders squared, he prepared to face them.

The objects of his attention approached. As they drew near, each of them threw him a single glance. "Hiya, Michael," they called out as they came abreast. Then they were past, still engrossed in their conversation. Momentarily he was nonplussed – no kicks, no headlocks, no punches, no dunches with a shoulder, no finger-burns on wrist or neck, not even a sarcastic remark. He straightened, wondering what was going on.

Passers-by were eyeing him curiously, some of them nudging each other and muttering something about him. He could guess what they were saying and knew it wasn't complimentary. Feeling foolish, he quickly abandoned his aggressive stance. Elation swept through him. It was amazing. He had stood up to them; he had actually stood up to them, and nothing had happened. It was as if some latent fear in him had been conquered. And as he stood gazing at their retreating forms, a conviction began to stir in him. It grew and grew until his senses were almost overwhelmed by the magnitude of it. And in that moment, when it was at its zenith, he knew he would not be cowed by them again.

With spirits high and feeling good about himself, the rest of the walk back to the lane was a pleasure. He found he could not stop smiling. His senses seemed heightened. As never before he enjoyed the warm evening air, the sight of green fields and animals grazing, the birds giving voice to their last chorus before seeking a roosting spot for the night, Midges rose in towering columns beside oak and chestnut trees, so close they were almost brushing against leaves as large as dinner plates. There wasn't the slightest movement from any of them. The earth was holding its breath and all was right with the world.

As he neared the lane leading to the house, his state of euphoria began to subside somewhat, and by the time he had stolen through the hole in the hedge and crept to the base of the tree, he was gripped by apprehension that his parents had discovered his absence.

He scaled the tree, which was now back to its original state and triggered no recollection of ever having been any different. When he climbed through the window into his bedroom, he half expected to find his dad there waiting for him. *The room was empty.*

Relieved that his temporary revolt was known only to himself, he crossed to the chest of drawers where he kept his radio. At that point he remembered it had been confiscated and would not be returned to him for a week. He was about to throw himself down on the bed in disgust when he heard a noise from below. It sounded like music. Intrigued, and wondering if his parents were listening to it, he opened the bedroom door a fraction. His ears had not deceived him. It *was* music and it was coming from the living room.

Curiosity gnawing at him, he tiptoed down the stairs and put his ear to the door. The music sounded like a piece of Mozart. He discarded the notion that they were using his radio. They wouldn't be that cruel. He wondered if his mum had bought a CD player. She had thought of doing so a few months back, but his dad had intervened and that was the last time the subject was mentioned.

He was just about to creep upstairs again with his curiosity unassuaged, when, to his horror, the door opened. His dad stood on the threshold.

Expecting a rebuke, Michael sought desperately to come up with an explanation for his presence. But before he could speak, the tall figure came towards him. An arm went round the boy's shoulders. "Come in," his father said quietly. "I've something to show you."

Michael entered the living room, a bit dazed by his dad's reaction to him being there. Such lenience was out of character. His eyes covered the room seeking the source of the music. It was not coming from a CD player, but a TV set. An orchestra was giving a recital.

The boy stared at it, unbelieving. "Is th-that ours?" he stammered.

His mother smiled at him. "Your father and I decided that as you've been working so hard of late you deserved a reward. You always said we should have one? Mind you, it's not to interfere with your studies. It's mostly BBC 2 for you and not so much of the other stations."

Michael didn't care what he would be watching. No longer would he be the odd one out in his class; no longer the freak who could never join in the discussions about programmes on the 'box.' From now on he would be just like everyone else. He didn't know what to say. The act of generosity was so unexpected that immediately he thought there must be a catch to it. But that notion was soon dispelled.

"And another thing," his dad went on. "When school's over tomorrow, you can go with your mother to Curry's or PC World and choose a computer. I think it's time you had one. No games, mind you. It's for serious pursuits."

Michael knew he must be dreaming. This couldn't be. The man who had been such a hard taskmaster was having a Pauline conversion. Everything was unreal. He reached out and touched a chair. It was still solid and the room still looked as it always had, everything familiar and in its proper place.

His dad was still speaking. "Next week we'll all go to the USPCA shelter and pick out a dog. I've spoken to them on the phone and they tell me there's a new arrival that might suit you. I know you've always talked about having one and there's plenty of space here for an animal to run around without becoming a nuisance."

"A dog?" Michael echoed mechanically, beginning to doubt his sanity.

"Yes, a dog; you do want one, don't you?"

Michael nodded dumbly. When he found his voice it sounded as if it belonged to someone else.

"What will we call it," he asked weakly.

His dad smiled. He actually smiled. "Oh, I think a Latin name might be appropriate. What do you suggest?"

Michael was beyond rational thought and shook his head in bemusement.

"How about, Canis?" his father suggested, glancing at his wife. "That has a nice ring to it."

Michael felt as if he'd been hit on the head and then administered smelling-salts. The choice of name dragged him from his stupor, clearing his senses. It seemed familiar. The very sound of it energized him. It was as if the word had slipped into a niche in his mind, filling it completely, making it whole again. The feeling of something being missing that had stayed with him since beaching the boat in the park, suddenly vanished. He wanted to shout for sheer joy, punch the air, leap around the room.

But he didn't, for, despite his dad's new-found generosity, he knew such behaviour would still be frowned upon. So, controlling himself with difficulty, he said mildly, "Canis sounds okay, dad," while under his breath he added gleefully, "it's more than okay, dad, it's brilliant, it's fantastic, it's absolutely fantabulous."

Then, unable to control his emotions any longer, his face split in a wide grin and he punched the air in a gesture of unrestrained joy. There was no word of admonition from his parents, so, still grinning, he chanced an expression that he wasn't allowed to use.

"Yes dad. That would be absolutely cool."

He waited. There was no adverse reaction. For some reason, that didn't surprise him.

AFTERMATH

Monday was the start of a half-term holiday, bringing relief from bullying and homework. For once his father had failed to leave a daily task to fill the gap and he was at a loose end. After breakfast he decided to walk the half-kilometre to Maxie's house. To his disappointment he found no one at home. Maxie was probably somewhere out in the fields helping his father, while his mother was in town shopping.

On his return home he went into the kitchen where his mother was making soup.

"Back already," she said, dropping a home-made stock into a saucepan.

"No one there," he replied disconsolately."

"Never mind: there's something for you in the living room."

The something turned out to be a small, rectangular package wrapped in brown paper. His name was on it, but no address. He thought his father might have had a change of mind and left him something to study, but, not recognising the handwriting, the notion was gladly discarded.

"Where did this come from?" he enquired, re-entering the kitchen.

"It was on the mat in the hall. Your dad picked it up on the way out – thought the postman might have left it."

"If he did, he should have demanded the cost of postage; there are no stamps on it."

She took the package from him. "That's strange," she remarked, turning it over and examining both sides. "Must be from someone who knows you, then; maybe one of your school-friends."

"Maybe," he echoed doubtfully.

"Anyway, go and see what it is and let me get on with my cooking."

He took the object upstairs to his bedroom and tore off the covering paper. He was not surprised to find he was looking at a book. It was slim, hard-backed, and had a red cover. Unusually, it had no title.

He glanced inside the sleeve hoping to find something to suggest who had sent it, but there was nothing to indicate its origin. Details of the publisher and when it was printed were also absent and there was no accompanying message to indicate why it had been directed to him.

Mystified, he turned to the first printed page. It was headed, LINCOLN BROWN. For some reason the name seemed familiar to him. Settling down on the bed, he crossed his legs and began to read. At first he was merely intrigued, but as he continued, his interest grew and he became so engrossed in the narrative that he read non-stop for over an hour.

The subject was an ex-slave, who, at a young age, had witnessed his father being hanged after a failed attempt to escape. Clever and resourceful, he fled his plantation a few days later, taking refuge in the Louisiana swamps to evade capture by the owner and his hunting dogs.

Joining the union army, he fought against the confederates, allying himself to the more able soldiers in his platoon, knowing, that, with them, he had a greater chance of survival. He made a point of studying their ways, learning what made them different, for he was certain that when the war ended he would be on his own, and the more prepared he was for that the better.

The period of post civil war in America was a chaotic and dangerous time: armed soldiers trying to make their way home, others wanting to continue the fight, deserters still hiding out, marauders living off the land, killing and looting to survive, many plantation owners unwilling to accept the fact that the days of slavery were over. It was a bad time for the emancipated black man. The promised freedom had left many of them homeless, jobless and starving. Many regretted the situation they found themselves in. Cruel, the plantation regime might have been, but, at least, it had provided food, quarters and a hardship shared. To them, it seemed that all the war had done was to replace one living hell for a greater one.

But the man featured in the book was a success story.

When the southern states surrendered, he made his way back to his old plantation. With his parents dead, his mother having died in childbirth, his father at the hands of the plantation owner, he was seeking his only relative, a younger sister, whom he had left in the charge of an older black woman. At first he could find neither, discovering the great columned house of his former master deserted and ransacked. The slave quarters had been burned, the crops in the fields left unattended.

While searching the house, he thought he heard a noise and, descending to a cellar, he discovered a dozen or so former slaves huddling in a corner. All were women. Among them was his sister. From them he learned that a troop of guerrillas had sacked the place, killing all the white folk and driving off the men slaves. The women had buried their former master and his family in a mass grave behind the house. There being sufficient food for their immediate needs and, with nowhere to go, they had moved into the house, taking shelter in the cellar when anyone came in sight.

Taking charge, he set them to clean the rooms and throw out everything that wasn't serviceable, or required. A bonfire for the discarded items was soon blazing.

With a plan forming in his mind, he left them to finish their task and set out to find the men who had fled. A week later he had managed to round up a dozen of his former companions. Some he found hiding in the swamps, fearful of being discovered by the men who had sacked the big house, others in the nearby countryside, scavenging for food and living rough. He told them of his plan and brought them back to the plantation. Simple souls, they did not question his authority or the extraordinary thing he sought to do.

He set them to work on the cotton crop, which was ready for picking, and set off to see a neighbouring landowner, who, it was rumoured, had Federal sympathies. Incredibly, this man agreed to see him and, more incredible still, agreed to buy the cotton crop when harvested.

And Obadiah Robertson, the enlightened plantation owner, was as good as his word, making an advance payment to keep Lincoln and his workers in food until final harvesting.

But before that time came, there were many occasions when Lincoln Brown's great scheme was placed in jeopardy, but ingenuity and forward-thinking saw it through. He combed the surrounding area for black men who had fought in the war and had retained their weapons. Stray horses were rounded up and a mounted militia formed to protect the property until times became more settled and the threat of marauders was over. Then they too were put to work in the fields, their payment, food and shelter and the establishment of self-respect.

Lincoln Brown's great fear was that white folk would come back to claim the property, but none did. Other white, plantation owners tried to burn him out, and he was visited on three occasions by a newly-formed band of Ku Klux Klansmen. These were seen off by his militia, and when Obadiah Roberson, a powerful force in the area, put out the word that the ex-slave was his trading partner and to attack the man was to attack him, the hooded men did not return.

With his horse soldiers, the sympathetic support of Obadiah Robertson, a huge amount of good fortune, and what seemed like remarkable prescience, his enterprise managed to survive.

Within a few years, the capital from his sales of cotton gave him a modicum of security and the opportunity to provide his workers with a wage. He drained land on nearby swamps and began to grow tobacco. He increased his workforce and found a wife. In this latter event, good fortune was again his friend.

Lilah was a nanny to Obadiah Robertson's children. Having been raised in the north, she had gained an education, and one of her duties was to teach her charges. She was much taken with the young ex-slave who did business with her employer, and Lincoln Brown with her. When they married, with Obadiah's blessing, she immediately set about inculcating his sister and him into the mysteries of reading, writing and arithmetic. She was amazed by the speed with which he mastered all three.

When this was achieved, he built a schoolhouse, and Lilah set about giving the children of his workers an education. In due course, her own children were born; four boys and three girls, and they too did their time in the schoolhouse. When they were grown, each in their turn was sent north to finish his or her education.

The plantation prospered. After ten years, Lincoln hired a lawyer to investigate if there was any person who could lay claim to what he now considered to be his property. The search proved fruitless and no title deed was unearthed. Some Power seemed to be looking out for him. Reassured that he was not about to be dispossessed, he took advantage of a *Law of Abandonment* that granted ownership of unclaimed land to anyone who could prove they had lived on and worked it for ten years. With entitlement legally in his name, only then did he abolish the old antebellum structure that had belonged to Silas Barnstaple, his former master, and begin to build a more modest structure for his family. Only then did he burn the old slave quarters and begin to replace them with proper dwellings for his workers. Only then did he destroy the stocks where, under the old regime, the slaves were chained and whipped. And only then did he fell the tree where he had witnessed his father being hanged by Silas Barnstaple.

With tenure secure, he felt free to develop his holdings further. More land was reclaimed and the new crop of sugar-cane grown on it. On the advice of Obadiah Roberson, Lincoln began a four-year rotation to maintain the fertility of the soil. No crop was grown on the same piece of land two years in a row, and every fourth year, in its turn, one was left fallow to give it time to recuperate. Livestock was grazed on this and the resulting manure put to good use.

Obadiah Robertson acted as a broker for all Lincoln could grow. When the former died, his eldest son took his place. Eventually, just after the turn of the century, when it became less unusual for a black man to be involved in business, the job of brokering his crops was taken over by one of Lincoln's son's.

Lincoln Brown lived to see the century out. By the time he died in 1914, shortly before the commencement of the 1st World War, he was well on his way to establishing a dynasty.

His descendants increased the area of his land until it became one of the largest and most prosperous holdings in the southern states. His offspring took over brokerages, transport companies and vending houses, so controlling the production, distribution and sale of his produce.

During this time a great emphasis was placed on the importance of education for every child born to his line. As a result, doctors, lawyers, academics and other members of the professions were produced, and as the new century unfolded and black men were admitted to areas were they had never been allowed before, politicians and corporate giants joined the list of successful people who could trace their ancestry back to him. A great-grandson was with Martin Luther King on the day he was assassinated, a great grand-daughter was the first black woman to be elected a senator under the Kennedy administration; another died in an accident a week before she was due to be launched into space under the Apollo programme.

Lincoln Brown, the former slave, proved to be a remarkable man and, although, long deceased, through his lineage, he is still making his mark all over the USA to this day.

The account of the unique life ended and Michael raised his head from the book to ponder on what he had read. So enthralled had he become by the chronicle that it was only then that he became aware that his mother was calling him for lunch. He placed the book carefully on the bed and went downstairs, his head filled with the images produced by the engrossing narrative. Strangely, he felt an empathy with the subject that he could not explain.

After lunch, he returned to his room and began to read once more. The next biography was about a Russian acrobat, Yuri Gorbachev.

Born into a circus family in the 1880s, he was surrounded by people steeped in the circus tradition and when still a boy, he was already skilled in a number of different acts, being as comfortable on the high wire as he was with tumbling and clown routines. By the time he was twelve, he was beginning to make a name for himself in the acclaimed world of Russian circus, when something happened that was later to change the course of his life.

Being naturally high-spirited, he drove off one day in a troika pulled by two of the circus horses. It was springtime, but winter had yet to relax its grip and he raced carriage and horses on to the frozen surface of the river Neva in St. Petersburg. He only realised this was a mistake when the ice began to complain about the weight. With a crack, it gave way and within a few seconds, the animals and he were submerged in the chillingly cold water. Throwing himself clear, he managed to swim up to the edge of the hole the troika had created, but already the deadly chill was taking effect and he could not pull his body on to the unbroken ice surrounding it.

He yelled for help and a number of people who had been walking by the river and had witnessed the accident, began to make their way carefully towards him. But he was at least eighty metres from the bank and by the time they got anywhere near, his frozen hands betrayed him and he lost his precarious hold on the ice. He went down again, only to struggle once more to the surface, but, unable to secure a hold, and with the terrible cold taking its toll, he sank beneath the ice for the third time. Again he managed to struggle back to the surface, but he knew this would be the last time he would be able to manage it. Somehow he kept his feet and hands moving in a parody of swimming and his head above water. Then, as hypothermia took hold, he began to drift into unconsciousness and slip inexorably downward.

Just as his head disappeared below the surface, a hand reached out and grabbed his hair. Two men had made the journey across the treacherous surface and were lying prone, one stretched out behind the other. The man at the rear held his companion's feet, allowing the latter to reach down into the hole with both hands. Pulling the boy up by his hair with one hand, the rescuer succeeded in grabbing the front of Yuri's clothing with the other. Held firm by the man behind, he managed to manoeuvre both arms under the boy's armpits and wrestle the, by now, limp form from the water.

Easing away from the edge, they carried the youth back to the bank, where a small crowd had gathered. Laying him on the ground they felt for signs of life. Neither pulse nor heartbeat could be found. Thinking that his lungs might be filled with water they tried to resuscitate him. Five minutes later they gave up the attempt and someone covered the upper half of his body with a coat. Yuri Gorbachev was dead, just another young Russian who had suffered the fatal consequences of his foolhardiness.

The crowd stood round him, wondering who he was and deliberating on what should be done. At last, someone who lived close by, lifted the body and carried it to a small cottage a hundred metres away. A number of men, including the two who had risked their lives to drag him from the river, accompanied him. There, the pathetic bundle was set down reverently on a mat close to a roaring fire. A priest was sent for.

Half-an-hour went by. The priest failed to arrive. In low tones, the witnesses to the tragedy continued to speculate on the dead youth's identity. It was at that point one of them thought he saw Yuri's foot twitch. He said nothing, at first thinking he must have imagined it; but a minute later it happened again, just the slightest of movements. Kneeling down, he pulled the coat from the youth's upper body. Yuri lay still, his face ashen, his lips blue. Again the man thought he was mistaken, and not wanting to make a fool of himself, he pretended he was praying, while covertly feeling for a pulse. And to his amazement, it was there, faint, but steady. With a shout of explanation, he began to pull off Yuri's wet clothes, while calling for warm blankets and a rough cloth to be fetched. These were with him in quick time and, rubbing the unresponsive body until he was sure the blood was coursing fully, he wrapped Yuri in the blankets and placed him as close to the fire as he dared.

Ten minutes later the youth came round.

By then the priest had arrived and, when told the story, he quizzed a shivering Yuri about what he had seen when he was dead. Yuri, slightly confused, and not knowing what the holy man was talking about, said that he had dreamed he was floating above the ice and had seen his rescuers pull him from the water and carry him to the bank. After that, he knew nothing until a few minutes ago when he wakened up.

The priest declared to those around him that they had witnessed a miracle and, in unison, all there dropped to their knees and made the sign of the cross.

When Yuri returned to the circus he was not greeted so reverently. Two show horses and a troika had been lost because of his irresponsibility. Incensed, the owners made no allowance for what he had gone through and dismissed him on the spot. That was their mistake.

Yuri's life changed dramatically.

His father, a renowned high wire artiste, found him a place in a small, travelling circus that was visiting the area, and with the priest relaying the story of the miracle to all who would listen to him, such were the crowds that began to flock to see the youth that the big-top could have been filled five times over. Everywhere the circus went the result was the same, and it thrived to such an extent that, as it grew in size, the owner took on more and more performers and accommodated the crowds, firstly, in two, and then three huge tents. Yuri was the star attraction and given top billing.

The owner, an ambitious man, took his company abroad and Yuri found himself performing in the major capitals of Europe. He had been to some of these before with his father, when the St. Petersburg company took to the road, but on those occasions he was only a bit player and not the centre of attraction. Over the next five years his popularity never waned, with the dichotomy of the circus and someone who had allegedly returned from the dead, producing an insatiable curiosity in people of different races and creeds.

Yuri became the show's highest paid performer, but it was when the Big Top was taken to America that his fortune was made.

The crowds flocked to see him and he was soon being urged to give talks on his out-of-body experience. At first he did this through an interpreter in the theatres and town halls of the towns and cities the circus was visiting; but, a quick learner, as he became more proficient in English, he began to deliver the soliloquy himself. He began to attract newspaper coverage, and by the time he reached California, his fame preceded him. By then he was a married man, having wed a bareback rider called, Olga Redetzski.

It was in California that a silent film producer came to see him perform. After the show he was invited to the set of the producer's current enterprise, where he witnessed the amateurish attempts of the male actors to make their stunts seem dangerous. He laughed, and when challenged to do better, drew on his skills as a tumbler to expose the clumsiness of the stars.

The producer, much impressed, offered him a job as a stuntman at a salary five times greater than the one he was receiving in the circus. After consulting with Olga, he signed a contract that shrewdly ensured his wife was given parts in productions, where her skill as a horsewoman could be used. They left the circus behind.

Yuri flourished. Such was his expertise that he soon attracted the attention of other film companies. He was hired out as an adviser and was soon on first-name terms with stars such as W.S. Hart, Tom Mix, and later Rudolf Valentino. He acted as stand-in for them and many others. But this didn't satisfy him.

Such was the demand for his and Olga's expertise that they could not cope with the calls on their time. So, he set up his own company to teach acrobatic and horse-riding skills. As the film industry expanded, so did the size of his operation. The number of schools was increased and with the profits he made, he began to buy up old theatres and derelict properties. He converted these into cinemas and hired managers to run them for him. In the first twenty years of the century, no matter how poor a film was, it always had a ready audience. Yuri's cinemas were always full. Inside five years he had more than a thousand scattered across the country.

As his wealth grew, he branched out into the agency business, acting on behalf of a growing number of film-stars. Soon he was negotiating with studio heads on behalf of his clients, arranging better pay and conditions for them and breaking the stranglehold of their long-term contracts. For every person on his books he took a 10% cut of their salary.

Olga produced two daughters and a son, and when they reached maturity, they helped to run an empire that, by then, crossed the United States from Hollywood in the east, to New York in the west. By the time the first talking picture was made in 1927, *The Jazz Singer*, starring Al Jolson, Yuri Gorbachev was one of the richest men in America.

Despite his growing wealth, he lived simply, staying fit and still doing the occasional stunt in films until well into his thirties. When he was forty-three he was demonstrating a particularly difficult fall from a galloping horse to the pupils of one of his schools, when he landed awkwardly and broke his back. The injury could not be fixed and he spent the rest of his life in a wheelchair. Despite this, he continued to take an active interest in the running of his companies and was one of the first to invest in sound equipment in his cinemas after Jolson's groundbreaking movie. Twenty years later he saw the enormous potential of television and set about securing the rights to many old films. He bought into the fledgling industry, and when it took off in the fifties, he was in a position to supply it, not only with his stock of films, but actors on his books, making use of their talents in drama, game-shows and light entertainment. Interests in advertising companies, which he was foresighted enough to acquire, meant he was profiting from almost every aspect of the business.

He lived to see the first men land on the moon and the assassination of John F. Kennedy. He did not live to see one of his distant relatives' become President of the USSR.

His children, and their children, continued his business, diversifying where necessary and changing to accommodate modern trends. The empire that he and his wife, Olga built continues to thrive until this day.

With perfect timing, the telephone in the hall rang to interrupt Michael's thoughts. He heard his mother's voice answering it and then she was calling out to him. It was Maxie on the other end wanting him to come over. He shouted to his mother that he would be out for an hour, and left the house. As he crossed the fields to his friend's place he thought about the narrative he had just finished reading. Like the one before it, it continued to consume him like nothing else he had ever read, and like the character in the previous tale, he seemed to have an affinity with the subject that seemed unnatural. The feeling was hard to understand.

When his father came home that evening, Michael showed him the book and asked if he had left it. His question was answered with a negative, followed by a mystified look. He examined the object and passed it back to the boy with the comment that maybe Maxie or one of his peers from school had dropped it in. This answer was so similar to the one given by his mother that he looked at them closely suspecting a conspiracy. But both seemed as bewildered as he was and he didn't press the matter.

He was meeting Maxie after tea to walk into town, so it was some hours later before he settled down to read the third section of the book.

This time the account was not about the life of one person, but the lives of two, and unlike Lincoln Brown and Yuri Gorbachev, the subjects were from the modern era. They were twins, a brother and sister called Paul and Paula Livingstone.

Born in England in 1963 to high achieving parents, they were recognised at an early age to be *infant savants,* and taught, first at a private academy specialising in the education of children with exceptional talents, and then at home by their mother. Such was their intellectual capacities, that they were earmarked to sit the entrance examination to Oxford University when they were ten. But this didn't take place. Headhunted by Hewlett-Packard, their father took the family to California in 1972 and became part of the electronic revolution that led to the creation of Silicon Valley. They settled in a place called Woodside, which, ultimately, became a town with one of the wealthiest populations' in America.

Their father introduced the twins to the world of computers and by the time they were twelve they had built one for themselves. With access to their father's manuals they began to write software codes and, under a pseudonym, managed to sell these to fledgling IT companies.

That same year they enrolled at Princeton, where they eventually graduated as the highest achieving students in their faculty, having completed a three year computer science course in two years. And it was then that they caused a sensation by taking an action against Bill Gates, the founder of Microsoft, and suing him for ten billion dollars. They claimed that two years earlier, when on a summer job with Hewlett-Packard, Gates had roomed at their house when they and their mother were away on holiday. Having been allocated Paul's bedroom, they alleged that the youthful Gates would have had access to all their research. They claimed that he had stolen this and used it to revolutionise the hi-tech industry. On their return from Princeton, they had intended to set up a company called Microtech, only to discover that they had been trumped by Gates and his company Microsoft.

The case caused a sensation. Before it came to court, the twins were invited on to TV talk shows and news programmes, and their obvious intelligence, self-confidence and almost arrogant articulation, gave them a public profile that ensured most of America was drawn to the impending litigation.

Microsoft employed the best lawyers in the country. Two days into the case the twins dismissed their counsel and began to conduct the action themselves. Their behaviour caused a sensation and they became headline news, daily reports of the suit appearing on TV stations coast-to-coast and spawning leading articles in the New York Times and the Washington Post. Their faces appeared on the cover of Time Magazine.

They lost the case. In fact it was proved that Microsoft had no case to answer. The result was a financial catastrophe for the twins. Their court costs ran into millions of dollars and a counter suit by Bill Gates for defamation of character was upheld, with him being awarded a further fifty million dollars. The twins were in no position to pay and were in serious danger of being taken into custody.

But then an utterly illogical thing happened. Bill Gates asked to see the siblings, and after a two hour meeting, he emerged to inform the assembled press that Microsoft would pay their court costs. He had also agreed to waive the fifty million dollar settlement. Furthermore, so impressed was he by their knowledge of the hi-tec industry, that he had hired them to carry out research for his company. Once again Paul and Paula hit the headlines.

Within two years Bill Gates' confidence in their abilities had been vindicated. They brought two unique intelligences to the Microsoft set-up, and their lateral thinking and combined innovation was such that a constant stream of new concepts and products emanated from their industry. By the time they were twenty-one, they were among the highest paid employees on the books. It was at that point they left to set up their own company.

They did not attempt to compete with Microsoft or any of the other major software firms. Instead, they hired graduates straight from university and gave them carte-blanche to come up with new ideas. Among other things, the company began to develop search engines, anti-hacking devices and security programmes for the IT boom that the twins were certain was coming. Among the first to recognise the potential of the internet, they provided a worldwide outlet for a diverse range of products, both service and industrially based – airline tickets, theatre seats, industrial components, lists of job opportunities for highfliers, being just a few of the things on offer. Always one step ahead of their opposition, they flourished.

In a few short years their names were almost as well known as that of Bill Gates. They were great self-publicists, always ready to do TV interviews, never turning down the chance to appear on chat shows or news programmes, always appearing together and displaying an intellectual arrogance that was breathtaking, often making fun of their hosts for not understanding some esoteric point one of them was making.

Studio audiences loved them, appreciating their quick-witted ripostes and the acerbic nature of their put-downs. TV producers loved them even more, each appearance by the twins adding millions of viewers to their programmes, improving their ratings and generating huge advertising fees. Soon they were bestriding the world of the social elite and able to elicit the best seats in the finest restaurants, obtain tickets for first nights' in Broadway theatres, command favours from politicians and other influential figures in the limelight.

Paul and Paula Livingstone had become celebrities.

In 1998, at the age of thirty-five, Paul married. His bride was a young, black lawyer from a well-connected family and renowned for her beauty and intelligence. Top of her class at Harvard, and knowing all the right people, she was tipped as a future Attorney General.

Descended from a former slave, who had fought in the American civil war, her ancestor had been the first African American to own his own plantation. A remarkable man, who had made education a virtue for his children, he ensured that his descendants prospered in many fields. Paul's wife had an unusual Christian name. She was called, Lilah.

Angered by Paul's action, and seeing it as the severance of their special bond, Paula formed a relationship with a wealthy impresario, twelve years her senior. A year after her brother tied the knot, she too was married.

Her husband, a distant relative of Mikhail Gorbachev, owed his wealth and position to show-business and the perspicacity of his Russian grandfather, a former circus performer who'd had the acuity to recognise the potential of a fledgling film industry and was rewarded when the cinema became the greatest medium of mass entertainment the world had seen. His family had interests in Hollywood and theatre-land, owning outlets for film and drama in most of the large cities in America, as well as a number in London, Paris and Rome. He produced, and occasionally directed, plays and musicals and was highly regarded by actors and other impresarios alike. His companies had extensive interests in television, and it was through this that Paula met him, having been introduced after taking part in one of his shows.

Neither marriage lasted.

The twins were too self-centred, too unwilling to compromise, too prone to believe that their intellectual capacities were greater than everyone else's. Paula was divorced after eighteen months. Paul's marriage lasted three years, before it also disintegrated, and a visit to Reno ensured he was free of a union he had come to view as an encumbrance.

In 2005, having made up their differences, they were travelling from Boston to Washington in a private aeroplane, owned and piloted by Paul, when the aircraft went off the radar screen. A whiteout had been forecast and planes were being grounded all along the eastern seaboard, but the twins, ignoring meteorological advice to remain put, had taken off as the first flakes of snow began to fall. Blizzard conditions ensued and their plane was found next morning on a hill no more than two miles from their intended destination. Their dead bodies were almost unrecognisable. Paul and Paula Livingstone had paid the ultimate price for believing they always knew best.

Paula had not borne a child, but Paul had fathered a boy, in whom he had little interest. His former wife, Lilah had retained custody of the child. Lilah had insisted that her son be named Lincoln.

Michael finished reading. He felt drowsy. He wanted to read on, but found he couldn't. A warm feeling of lassitude stole over him, and despite making a valiant effort to fight the sensation, it proved to be irresistible. The book fell from his hands and within seconds he was asleep.

It was late the next evening before he picked the book up again. What with homework to do, and his father insisting that the boy accompany him to Lough Neagh for a spot of bird-watching, he was unable to continue reading until then. There was one chapter remaining. It had a single-name heading – RANI.

Rani was born in 1943 into a high-caste family in India. Her mother was a schoolteacher, her father a diplomat who had helped in his country's transition to independence from British rule. He wielded great influence in political circles and was a friend of Mahatma Ghandi.

Blessed with an acute intelligence and a favoured background, she was educated privately until accepted shortly after her sixteenth birthday by the University of Bombay to study medicine. An exceptional student, she graduated at the age of twenty, taking two years less than the normal student to complete such a course.

Five years attached to a teaching hospital in Madras, saw her specialise in tropical diseases, a decision influenced by the fact that a younger sister had died from malaria. After a further two years enhancing her practical skills, she moved to Calcutta. Here, with financial assistance from her parents, she set up a health clinic in a poor area of a city whose slums where among the worst in Asia. Compassionate and caring, she saw all who came to her, taking no stance on their lowly status or their poverty, making no charge for their treatments. She built up and trained a small team of nurses and aides, and in time managed to persuade a stream of newly qualified doctors to spend a year helping her for only their food and board. Under this arrangement, she received valuable assistance, and they got invaluable experience in the treatment of a wide range of illnesses.

Eventually, with the help of government grants secured by her father, she opened two more clinics in different parts of the city. By advertising in medical journals, she managed to recruit staff to run them. The scheme of assistance from the young doctors keen to broaden their experience was widened. Thousands of people were treated each year; many lives were saved.

Her efforts did not go unnoticed, and thanks to friends of her father, a pact was made with the Office of Health in Delhi, that trainee doctors would spend a year in one of her clinics as part of their university course. This allowed her empire to expand further, and over the course of the next ten years, taking time off only to marry a fellow doctor and bear him a son and a daughter, she established seventeen more clinics in five other cities – Delhi, Madras, Bombay, (now Mumbai), Bangalore, and Kanpur. She was indefatigable. She regularly worked sixteen hour days' and never thought of taking a holiday. Her family and her clinics were her life.

When her father died, she took over the role of intermediary with the Government and politicians. She cajoled, bullied and charmed those in a position to help secure the funding she needed. In a country where the plight of the poor was a secondary consideration of those with influence, and where political handouts to deprived areas were almost unknown, she managed to succeed where no one else had done so. Amazingly, no one seemed able to resist her.

By the time she was in her mid-forties, her clinics, and the work done there, had become renowned throughout India and beyond. She adopted an open-house policy and welcomed interested observers from other countries keen to set up establishments modelled on her own.

Astonishingly, despite the enormous toll on her time, she managed to carry out research in her specialised field of tropical diseases. She published books and pamphlets, using medical journals to disseminate her findings. As a result, her work became well known outside India.

She was invited to lecture both in the USA and Europe, but did so only occasionally, feeling that she could not spare the time away from her projects. The large fees she earned, especially in America, were used in the furtherance of her work.

By the time she was fifty, the network of clinics she had established was spread right across the sub-continent, their number almost matching her age. Government aid now came annually and was placed on a formal basis. Arm-twisting of politicians and public servants was no longer required. Her fame was now international.

In 1997 she flew to Stockholm to accept a special Nobel prize for humanitarian endeavour. The King of Sweden stated that the £500,000 cheque which accompanied the award was hardly proper recompense for her efforts.

A year later her son joined her in her work, followed two years later by her daughter.

She did not have long to enjoy the experience. Three months after the latter event, she contracted a rare disease, always a hazard in her work, and despite the attention of some of the world's finest consultants, she died six weeks later.

Her funeral was one of the largest seen in India, and such was the international flavour of those present, that it was described by one of the large body of the world's press attending, as more akin to the funeral of a Head of State than the burial of a humble physician. Another dubbed her the Mother Theresa of the medical world.

A year after her death, a well-known American film producer came to India. Visiting Rani's family, he sought permission to make a documentary on her life. At first this was refused, for her widower husband and her children felt that this might glorify her and that was the last thing she would have wanted. But the man was persistent. He stayed for a time and got to know them, establishing a rapport. Then he left. Six months later he tried again. Again he was refused. As on the previous occasion, he extended his visit, making friends with Rani's son and daughter. He waited a further year and returned once more. Intrigued by his persistence, and with the pain of their mother's death now eased, this time they agreed to consider his request. Given his chance, the producer was persuasive, and when he convinced them that the documentary would be sympathetic and non-invasive, they agreed to speak to their father on his behalf. Their intercession was successful. On the condition that the final product would be vetted by him before it went on public release, the producer would be allowed to proceed. The producer's name was Gorbachev.

The film was a huge success. It won the Palme-D'or prize at the Cannes film festival and was shown in forty-seven different countries. A record of Rani's achievements was captured for posterity.

Michael's eyes had grown tired from reading. He closed them for a few minutes, trying to analyse the effect the biography had had on him. At first, the account of Rani's life had excited him, but when her death was recorded, this had engendered in him such a feeling of melancholy that tears came to his eyes. And he didn't know why. He sighed. The contents of the book and its author were a mystery to him and the mixed emotions he was now experiencing was just another puzzle to add to the others he was unable to solve.

His mood remained sombre, the fate of Rani still continuing to move him. Outside, the late evening sun was on the point of disappearing below the horizon. The resident doves in the orchard were making themselves heard, their coo-cooing carrying clearly to his room in the still air. Rooks circled in a great cluster, blacking out the sky, their aerodynamics a final robust fling before they settled for the night in a nearby copse of trees. On the road at the bottom of the lane, a lorry droned up a steep hill. He heard none of this, his mind filled with what he had read.

As with the other accounts, he felt he should know the last subject, yet he had not met her, and, like the others, had never heard of her before. It was most bewildering. He was fascinated by their stories, which surprised him, biographies not being his favourite sort of reading, given the number of these his father insisted he tackle. But, perhaps, it was just his old curiosity streak kicking in again. That might or might not be the case, he didn't know, but there was one thing he *was* certain about. As he had been reading the various histories, the feeling had grown inexorably that someday he would travel the world and, at some point, his journeys would take him to America and India. And somewhere in those vast countries, his path would cross those of the living descendants of the old slave, Lincoln Brown and the circus performer, Yuri Gorbachev; he would meet the only son of Paul Livingstone, and the children of Rani, the woman dubbed by the press as the Mother Theresa of the medical world. Of that he was certain.

He was about to put the book aside and go to bed when, for some reason his eyes were drawn to some writing enclosed in an oblong design at the bottom of the final page. The script was so small he was unable to read it. Crossing to his dressing table, he rummaged around in a drawer until he found his magnifying glass. Holding it above the tiny writing, he moved it about until the print swam into view. Now it was legible. It read, *Wizard Publications.* He put the magnifying glass away and closed the book. Something stirred faintly in his brain, nothing of understanding, just an impression that at any second something amazing was about to be revealed. He wrestled with it for a while, trying to turn it into something comprehensible, but his effort was in vain. No matter how hard he tried to bring meaning to the sensation, nothing materialised. It was like trying to view a dead cell in your eye. Every time you focussed on it, it moved away.

He sighed and gave up the attempt.

Later, as he was on the verge of sleep, the oblong design containing the writing entered his consciousness again. *Wizard Publications*, he mused inwardly. As the words formed in his head, an instantaneous contentment enveloped him. And, in that moment, he knew that something previously unfinished had come to completion. He mouthed the phrase once more, hoping to find greater meaning in it. *Wizard Publications*.

Nothing came.

As he slipped into sleep, the feeling grew in him that no matter how often he contemplated the words, he would never fathom the mysteries they contained. But deep inside, he was convinced that the amazing success of the people he had read about was no accident.

And more; he felt it was fitting that a little bit of magic had touched all of their lives.